SHADOW RUIN

AUDREY GREY

D1598947

STARFALL PRESS

For my dad, the best father a girl could ask for

ONE

The steel sword flashes as it arcs toward my neck. It's meant to cleave my head from my shoulders, but a million reconstructed synapses fire down my nerves and I duck low on instinct, away from the sharpened edge that promises a quick death. A branch from the closest tree scrapes my cheek, but I hardly feel it.

The blade whistles just above in a short viper's hiss.

Ssss.

The sound sends a tingle of adrenaline coursing over my flesh, followed by a wave of burning nausea. I fall back against the thick trunk of a cypress tree. Summer-spent leaves shiver from above as Bramble chirps in alarm.

Gripping the pommel of my sword, I lunge to strike my opponent. A grunt slips from my parched lips. Sweat dribbles into my eyes, turning the forest into a blurry wall of brown and green.

I blink and my sword bites empty air. *Fienian hell.*

I barely stop the sword before it thwacks into the mottled trunk of an oak. Bramble, clinging to a spindly branch just above, screeches as he scuttles away from my wild swings.

When he reaches the upper branch, away from my reach, his antennae twist around his sleek body, probing the air. Searching for her.

Where is she?

Shadows play across the maze of moss-bound trunks around me as I scour the forest, my breath heaving out in dense wheezes. Leaves dance around us like falling stars.

There. A figure leaps from the shadows—a wraith in an emerald cape. She couldn't be more commanding if she were a giant stag with nine-point horns, a fanged beast meant to kill me.

My heart dances sideways against my ribs.

"If this were real you'd be dead by now."

My mother grins at me, her smile sharper than any weapon. A crimson flush settles across her high cheekbones, her hair, the same color as the tree trunks, wrangled into a now-loose bun. A few frizzled tendrils form a corona over her head.

Against my will, I search her eyes for warmth, her face for pride. But her expression is cold, her lips curled downward at the corners.

She's barren of any emotion save disdain.

"You're leaving your left flank exposed," she adds. "And you still telegraph your movements when you tire."

Just like I've been taught, I pull in steady, even breaths from my nose while my mother regards me cruelly. It doesn't help that she's right. All I have to do is look down at my tunic where her sword split the fabric to confirm her words.

She angles her head. "I thought you were reconstructed with advanced swordplay techniques?"

"I *was.*"

"Hmm."

I hate the disappointment in her voice, the mocking tone. "Are we done?"

She gives a curt nod. "For now."

How long have we been practicing? A minute? An hour? It feels like ten hours. A day. A lifetime—a lifetime we don't have.

Sensing the fight is over, Bramble scrambles halfway down the tree's thick trunk and lunges onto my shoulder. Although he's roughly the size of a box turtle, he's lighter than he looks, and the impact feels like being hit by a pinecone.

As he nestles into my neck, his spindly legs twist in my braid, and I tug the rope of hair onto my other shoulder.

He chirps once and settles down, his familiar presence calming me.

"You have that thing trained well," my mother says, glancing curiously at Bramble.

"He's not a thing," I amend, trying and failing to hide my annoyance. "And I didn't train him."

"Indeed."

Sunlight dapples the oval sweat stain darkening her back as she turns around and grabs a tan waterskin. She tosses it to me without a word. After I've drank just enough to satisfy my thirst—but not enough to weigh me down and make me sluggish—I toss it back. Even though I want to drink until I empty it.

"Why don't you like the council idea?" I ask, wiping my mouth on my shirt sleeve to cover the painful tug of my lips.

"Does my opinion mean that much to you?" She lifts a graceful eyebrow the color of old honey. "I don't remember it mattering before."

You mean when I was six? I want to say.

Instead, I shrug, feeling the sting of her disapproval. Most of the Sleepers who made up the ten-thousand-man army occupying the surrounding hillside came from the nearest towns.

The first thing I did after leaving the Fienian stronghold and breaking away from Nicolai was set up a council filled with elected representatives from each town.

"Do you really want to set this precedent?" Her lips twitch at the corners as if she's biting back a smile. "Once you give away power, it's water through a sieve and you will never reclaim it."

"Maybe I don't want power, but if you'd been around you'd know that about me."

"Everyone wants power," she says, ignoring my barb at the end. "In our world, power equals survival."

I try to swallow but my dry tongue settles in the back of my throat. "Well, I didn't give it up. I still have a high seat in the council."

"One of three."

Riser, Caspian, and I form a triumvirate of sorts. It's still a roughshod idea, and, according to my mother, a bad one. "I want the masses to feel included, to want to fight."

"Don't be naïve. No one wants to fight."

"You know what I mean." I cringe at how petulant my voice sounds. How utterly incompetent. "Besides, I don't feel confident making all the decisions when there are more experienced leaders at hand twice my age."

"Experience doesn't make a leader great."

A sigh tumbles from my lips. "Then what does?"

"The ability to make hard decisions and never question oneself, for one. But more importantly, a great leader accepts the belief that they, and they alone, are the only one who can lead."

"Well that basically discounts me then."

"Whether you like it or not, Maia, you are the face of this war." My mother pushes an errant strand of hair behind her ear and clears the impatient look from her eyes.

Ever since we've been together, I've caught her *trying.*

Trying to be more understanding. Trying to be warmer. Trying to listen instead of ordering. To be affectionate when she would normally be curt.

To be more *motherly*.

I'm trying too. And yet we can hardly look at each other without arguing over every tiny little thing.

"If you're so keen on opinions," she begins carefully. "Then you should know your plan has some flaws."

"What plan?"

"To stay at camp another day."

I draw a figure eight in the air with my sword, watching the warm rays of sunlight trickle down the beveled blade. "All plans have flaws."

"We cannot afford to wait to attack the castle. Already, the Rebels move closer. Scouts were caught near the western edge of the forest."

"Yes, and the information from those scouts points to Nicolai waiting two more days to attack."

"They're lying." Her voice is flat, but her hazel eyes shimmer with the fire of certainty I lack, the kind that comes from experience. "Nicolai wanted them to get taken in to plant false information."

I sheathe my blade in the leather holster positioned against the base of the tree and roll out my shoulders, careful not to disturb Bramble. Lately, he's sensitive to my moods and gestures and even sighing too loud makes him worry.

A light breeze whispers through the air, carrying the eye-watering tang of burnt forest. Smoke chars the landscape above, darkening the skies prematurely, even though there's still at least half an hour until dusk, and Shadow Fall was over two hours ago.

As if suddenly the four horsemen of the apocalypse were loosed, the world has erupted into chaos in the last two days. Wild bouts of weather ravage the lands. Storms appear out of nowhere, tornadoes developing seemingly from thin air and consuming giant swaths of woodland. The oceans have risen, swallowing entire towns whole. The animals have fled, leaving our starved camp without even the luxury of hunting small game for dinner.

"I understand you're trying to feed and clothe these people before we strike, and that's admirable, Maia." My name tumbles awkwardly from her lips, as if she can't remember exactly how to say it. "But we can't feed ourselves, much less the army. The castle will have food stores, if we're lucky."

I flex my hands at my sides and refocus on my mother. She's wiping down her sword with a graceful meticulousness I'll never possess. The same as her confidence and poise.

All traits that skipped my genetics and obviously didn't take during my reconstruction.

"Most of the men in our camp came from the mines and the mills," I say. "They need training before we send them to fight against the Emperor's Centurions. And the ones who can't fight have a full day's march to the shelters beneath the mountains. Without another day . . . most won't make it."

Our army is just a ruse, something to distract the Emperor while we sneak inside the castle and find the Mercurian. But they still need to stand a chance.

"True." She pauses, but I can feel her argument gathering life on the tip of her tongue. "And yet, we don't have a day. Nicolai will strike soon, and if he captures the Mercurian then all of these people will certainly die."

"Riser has his best Rebels positioned at various points around their camp. The moment they mobilize, we'll know."

I force my face to appear more confident than I feel. Perhaps she's right. I should give the order to wage battle tonight against the Emperor. If Nicolai gets there first he might accidentally blow up the Mercurian during the assault —or not so accidentally, knowing Nicolai.

An image of the gaunt, pale faces of my army comes to mind. Most have been in cryosleep inside their pods for months and now they can hardly walk two feet without resting. They need food and water and time to strengthen their muscles.

All things we're in short supply of.

"Just one more day," I insist. "Let them build up their strength enough to hold a weapon, at least." I don my sword belt and turn to go, hating how it feels like I'm asking for permission. "We'll attack at dusk tomorrow. I'll inform Prince Laevus and Prince Thornbrook."

At the mention of the princes, a glimmer of amusement crinkles the corners of her eyes, and her gaze flicks over the forest. "Prince Thornbrook? I'm not sure the title suits him."

I follow her gaze, expecting to see Riser pop up from the dense layer of dusky shadows that have suddenly draped the trees and settled in the space around us. He's out there watching me. Protecting me.

He's never said as much, but I can feel him. "I disagree. Not all princes wear fine clothes and know how to bow."

"That's not what I mean. There's a darkness in him, Maia. Something only living inside that wretched prison could create—and that kind of thing, you can't remove it, can't reconstruct it out of him."

My braid flops against my shoulder blades as I shake my head. "I'm not worried."

"You should be." A tight smile lifts her cheeks. "The people follow you because you're familiar. They were inside your head, they know you'll protect them, in your own way. But he was there too. Remember that. They know what he is. They saw his savagery, and they will never follow an Empress married to such a person."

"Married? We haven't even—"

"Everyone but you, apparently, knows exactly how much that boy loves you. We watched your love story unfold, against all odds."

Her words stir my anger. "So you were watching?" I can tell by the way her face stills that it's true. "What was that like? Being a spectator as the daughter you abandoned struggled? Watching me be abused, tortured, nearly murdered? It must kill you that someone like Riser did more for me than you ever did."

Her eyes narrow, the thin skin at the corners bunching. "What are your intentions for Prince Thornbrook?"

I blink at her, unable to hide my surprise at the new direction in conversation. "Intentions?"

She blinks back at me, managing to make the gesture appear less idiotic and more regal. "Once we have the Mercurian and have taken control of the land, you'll need an alliance with Prince Caspian. Otherwise, the Royalists will never follow you—even if you do stop Pandora."

"Alliance? Why can't you say it? You need me to marry Caspian so you can keep a stranglehold on your power. But what if I don't love him?"

"Love?" She spits the word. "Love is a fleeting cascade of hormones. A trick of the mind."

"Oh, really?" I clench and unclench my hands. "Is that why you married dad? A trick?"

A muscle ticks in her temple. "You are matched to Caspian, Maia. That is not a trick. Love will fade, but compatibility at that level ensures a strong, happy partnership."

My lips part, but I can't think of a single thing to say.

"Watch," she continues. "This . . . this wild boy who follows you around like a feral puppy will only cause you heartache and pain. He has nothing to offer you but misery."

"Except loyalty," I quip, feeling a deep sense of satisfaction as she practically flinches at the word. If I were to finish my thought, I'd say: *You know, the one thing you have so much trouble with.*

But I'm tired of fighting with my mother, even if I'm right.

"Loyalty will not win you this war." Her voice carries a rare gentleness that scares me, and the knotted rope that's been coiled in my belly since my mother arrived suddenly jerks taut.

I turn to leave. "I think I'll be the judge of that."

"Maia." The vulnerable edge in her tone makes me halt. "Tell Max . . . tell Max I would like to see him."

A curt nod is my only reply.

Just like the last five times I've asked on her behalf, he's likely to ignore me.

I'm forced to deal with my mother for logistical and strategic reasons. He isn't. And if it was hard for him to forgive *me* for leaving him, then forgiving the woman he's grown up thinking a traitor who abandoned us and murdered our father is near impossible.

"Wait," my mother says, her voice strangely breathless. "Shields up, daggers out, head high."

I fight the urge to roll my eyes. My mother and I had a silly game when I was younger. Anytime one of us had to leave, instead of goodbye, we both repeated that phrase.

But I'm too old to play games anymore.

Ignoring her, I break into a jog through the faded path toward camp, my boots rustling against pine needles and dried leaves littering the ground. A giant lump is lodged in my throat.

Being around my mother for longer than five minutes always leaves me on edge. As if the very air around her permeates with a toxic chemical my body can't handle.

I'm not sure what I expected on that rainy night when she

approached the Rebel stronghold. Part of me was sure I'd kill her. But the other part hoped for . . . what?

Reconciliation? A return to, if not love, then the begrudging relationship we had before?

Not evening sword fights where she picks me apart physically and mentally, or meetings where she practically rolls her eyes at everything I say. Just like when I was six, I feel her judging everything I do. Every decision. Every move or word I make. Even her silence seems weighted with derision.

It's exhausting.

I miss Brogue. I miss him so much that my chest hurts when I think about him, which is all the time. Especially when I train.

As I crest the ridge and the valley opens up below, I release a tense breath. Gray smoke drifts from smoldering campfires. A quilt of makeshift tents, patched together with rib-boned corsets and mounds of cheerful skirts, overflows the valley and spills up the mountainside.

My stomach churns as the tinny smell of horsemeat hits my nose, mixing with the fishy tang of a nearby river. Bramble seems to pick up the scent on his sensors too because he shifts nervously on my shoulder, his metal legs like pinpoints needling my shoulder.

When my mother escaped the castle, she stole over thirty horses. Thirty beautiful, noble specimens bred for centuries by Golds to be the fastest, most regal steeds ever created.

Now they're feeding our army. A mixture of gratefulness and loss fills me at the thought of all those gorgeous creatures being slaughtered to feed us.

Ironically, that was one decision my mother and I both agreed on, and I imagine it pained her more than me. Horses are her passion, and yet she willingly gave up her own beloved mare, Lightstead, to be slaughtered.

Then again, she willingly gave me up too. And now she's

willing to offer me up to Caspian on a silver platter without a second thought. As if I'm a bargaining chip to leverage, not her daughter.

Twisting sideways, I scramble down the side of the mountain. If I'm to believe my mother, she didn't actually give me up. It was all in my parents' plan. Keep Max and me away from the Emperor until she could get me on the Island under a false identity.

Except, after my father's death, Brogue was supposed to grab us before we escaped and take us somewhere safe. My bodyguard, my friend and protector failed, and he spent the rest of his life trying to find us.

So my parents' plan took longer than they ever meant for it to.

A tight grin finds my jaw. *See, even she isn't perfect.*

A noise calls my attention to the dense wall of gray birch trees on my right. The birdcall pierces the air. Once. Twice. Similar to a morning dove's mournful coo.

A trill of excitement zips through me and before I know it I'm jogging back the other direction, the day's exhaustion slipping away.

Pit Boy.

TWO

Twilight hits as soon as I spot Riser, as if the two are connected somehow. He's perched on the lowest limb of a tree in a casual stance that *almost* masks his predatory nature, hunched over his knees, his mother's diary open and held gingerly inside his hands.

This isn't the first time I've caught him lost in his mother's words, and I wonder what they say. Does she talk about his father, the Emperor? Or his uncle, the infamous, long-dead Rebel leader, Ezra Croft?

Or maybe she simply talks about falling in love with a prince far out of her reach, and eventually becoming pregnant with his baby.

Slowly, Riser looks up from the pages. There's no surprise in his gaze as he drinks me in the same way I do him.

I shiver as the intensity sends a wave of goose bumps crashing over my flesh.

Just before I reach him, I pause, hesitation surely written across my face.

Most of the time I can tamp down the unease his wildness

conjures, the instinctive, knee-jerk fear that occasionally hits me around him. Knowing what he can do . . .

He would never hurt me. I know this deep down in my soul. Yet sometimes his predatory litheness, the potential for violence oozing from his body like radiation, overrides my brain and I hesitate.

In that split second of time, I wonder if my mother is right. If there's a savageness in him that I can never tame. That will leave me hurt and broken . . .

He pockets the diary and drops to the ground like a fleet-footed cat, hardly making a sound. Bramble chirps hello before scampering down my arm and launching himself at Riser's feet. He does an odd little dance that I've come to recognize as a greeting, then edges into the forest to inspect the flora for edibles.

Riser's unreadable gaze slides from Bramble back to me. "Come here."

His words are soft, nearly lost to the sigh of the forest. But the command is clear as day.

I comply with a step. Another. When I'm close enough to feel the warmth leaching from his dark tunic and leather vest, he reaches for me.

Slowly. Protectively. As if he senses my jumpiness.

The second his arms slide around my waist, my worries melt away. He smells of leather and pine and something else wholly unique to him.

I meet his eyes. One bruised-blue and shadowy in this light. The other a bright shade of green that matches the pine needles speckling his too-black hair. He's cut it short on the sides and just long enough on the top to form a messy peak. The hairstyle somehow makes him look both roguish and young.

I'm still getting used to it.

"You okay?" His breath warms my lips, the smell of

chicory and honey. I nod, but my mother's words about an *alliance* with Caspian echo inside my mind, tinging my cheeks with guilt.

If he knew she suggested his half-brother, the one person he seemed to hate more than all the rest . . .

His arms tighten around my waist, his sharp gaze seeming to whittle through my careful expression and into my thoughts. "Maia?"

"Fine." I catch my lower lip between my teeth, worrying it—

He brings his hand up to my mouth, the calloused pad of his thumb gently tugging on my trapped lip until it slips from my teeth. "You sure?"

He knows how much my mother gets to me, but I'm not ready to discuss it. I roll my eyes. "Can't you let me internalize my emotions like a normal person?"

A chuckle slips from his lips, a sultry sound that reminds me I have no idea who Riser really is. Sometimes Pit Boy. Sometimes Prince Thornbrook. And sometimes something else entirely . . . like a shadow shifting and fluttering so you can never tell the shape of it.

"I will if you want me to." I freeze as he pulls me into him. His mouth brushes over mine, nipping the bottom lip I bit earlier. "Still, I can't help but think if you'd trusted me a week ago enough to tell me who you were, that they'd erased you from my mind, you would have never had to suffer the way you did in the Blood Courts."

I stiffen as the hurt from his forgetting me comes rushing back. I thought he'd chosen to have me erased . . . "Let's not talk about it."

He pulls back slightly. "Or, you can trust me enough to tell me what's wrong."

My arms slip behind his neck, raining bits of bark onto his

shoulders. For a moment, I lose myself in his warmth. His protection. Overcome by how good this feels.

"Let me guess," he breathes. "Your mother thinks you're making bad decisions."

Story of my life. My palms break out in a sweat, my heart hammering so hard I think he'll hear it. "Wow, it's like you know her."

A laugh. "I see the way she rides you. The way she second guesses every decision you make." His breath blows back wisps of my hair as he exhales. "I also see the way she looks at me."

Of course he does. Riser misses nothing. But I don't want to talk about this, not now, and I catch his bottom lip between my teeth.

A growl slips from his throat. When I release his lip, he pulls away from my kiss. "She only wants what's best for you."

I release a bitter laugh, remembering the derisive way she talked about him. She doesn't deserve his respect. "I rarely see you," I murmur, trying to change the subject. "Do you really want to spend the two seconds I do talking?"

This time his chuckle rumbles low in his chest. I can tell by the way his breath tumbles out in ragged pants, the way the muscles of his neck and back go rigid, that he feels the same way.

"No talking. Got it."

His hands slip lower to cup the small of my back, pressing me into him. Heat spills over my neck as he drops his head and trails his lips over the tender apex of my collarbone, his hair tickling my jaw.

His fingers tuck under the back of my shirt and then the rough, warm pads of his fingers are skipping along my spine, like he's counting each bone. Carving out little circles of pleasure over my back. My shoulder blades. My hips.

Like a blind man trying to shape me in his mind, he maps out my flesh as his hands slide around to my stomach and press flat. Then his mouth comes down on mine, harder this time, and I match his intensity as a cord of fire goes taut low in my belly.

I want to burn away any thoughts of my mother. Of all the responsibilities that wait for me down below. I want to lose myself to the one person in the world I trust.

A moan tumbles from my lips as his hands skim lower, below my waistband. The sound makes his fingers halt. They hover over my flesh for a long moment, and then he sighs, his breath stirring the hairs around my face, and removes his hands to rest on both sides of my face.

The kisses become gentler after that, more controlled. As if there's a line he doesn't yet want to cross.

I'm disappointed, but I settle into him, enjoying the softness of his touch.

We spend the next few minutes like this. And when I resurface back into reality, I notice that darkness has fallen, the air already a few degrees cooler.

The fact that I could lose myself so completely in one person . . .

"We should get back to camp," I say, my voice thick and hoarse. "Plus . . . it's dark."

Great observation, Maia.

But now that I'm back to reality, my mind is being pulled in a hundred different directions. I have countless things to do before tomorrow. Supplies have to be checked. I need to meet with Lash to discuss the illness infecting the outer rim of the camp, and Teagan will be waiting to go over our strategy after we enter Laevus Castle.

Plus, Max has to be prepared for the possibility of an earlier strike, since he's literally the map to the Mercurian.

Then there's the uncomfortable fact that people have gone

into the woods after nightfall for the usual things. Gathering firewood. Collecting water. Relieving themselves. And more than a few have never returned.

Nicolai made good on his promise to treat us as the enemy, and Rebels are picking us off.

Riser, who's quietly watching me, arches a black eyebrow. "Maia, do you really think you're not safe right now? With me?"

My gaze falls on the array of knives glinting from various body parts; a double-edged dagger stashed in his boot; a hunting knife for cutting wood and skinning game bared in a calf-leather sheath at his waist; a short sword peeking from its spot behind his shoulder blades.

"Is that why you keep following me whenever I'm in the woods? To keep me safe?"

A little shock of surprise ripples across his face. He didn't know I'd noticed.

"I've found bodies scattered in these woods," he admits. "All members of our army."

"Who's killing them?"

He lifts a shoulder. "Rebels. Royalist drones. The Archduchess. Scavengers. The point is, the woods aren't safe for anyone."

"Except you?"

A grin splashes across his face, arrogant and boyish at the same time. "Except me. And you, Maia. You're safe. For as long as I'm alive, that's my promise to you."

The breath catches in my throat, all the words I could say in response trapped just beneath my sternum. Is this what love feels like? An unbearable mixture of joy and passion and something else, not quite fear . . . but close.

I remember what my mother said about love. It's hormones. A trick.

Yet this feels more real than anything I've ever experienced . . .

I flinch, suddenly sure the sky will open up and swallow Riser. That the darkness that's basically taken away everything good in my life will suddenly take notice and claim this too.

Don't think about it.

But I can't help it. The rules I've lived by for so long—don't care. Don't hope. Don't love—are impossible now. Riser is asking me to break them all and it terrifies me.

"Maia." His voice draws me back. My thoughts must show on my face because he releases his hold on me, allowing another few inches between us. "I have more intel from the Rebels."

I raise my eyebrows. "Already?"

"Surprised?" Amusement tinges his voice.

"Maybe," I tease. Except I'm not. In this short time since we left Ezra Croft's derelict estate, Riser has managed to set up an intricate network of lookouts and spies loyal to him. It's actually really impressive, not that I'll tell him that. "And worried," I continue. "You need to be careful."

"Always."

He seems about to say more but the ferns to our left rustle and Bramble appears, the delicate silvery moonlight gliding off his convex back. He rushes up my leg, emitting a series of high-pitched chirps that mean he's collected something good.

"Gloat much," I whisper, stroking his back as he takes his place on my shoulder, the metal of his body cool and packed with loamy-smelling earth.

More proud chirps follow, and I pat his head, cooing about what a good boy he is until he nestles into my neck.

Rivet added a cache compartment for him recently—along with some other neat tricks—and the little green light at the base of his neck glows, meaning the compartment is full.

Pushing off the tree, Riser slips his fingers through mine,

drumming them against the back of my hand, a frenetic energy pulsing off his flesh. "We should get back to camp. As much as I'd like to do this forever, I have to check the comms from my spies at basecamp. I'll tell you what I learned on the way."

I nod, hiding my disappointment. With Bramble lighting the path with one of his sensors, we wind down the mountainside and Riser unloads what he's discovered. A flurry of activity inside rebel walls. The training has intensified. The food has improved. Carts with supplies for a siege are being prepared.

Most damning of all, according to one of Riser's sources, he heard Nicolai's trusted general telling his girlfriend he was about to leave.

"So," I say, trying to keep my voice steady. "They're mobilizing."

Riser's eyes are cautious as he nods. "There's a possibility we still have a few days, but there's a possibility they could march tonight."

"If they left tonight, how long until they would reach the castle walls?"

"Daybreak."

I pinch the bridge of my nose. Darkness has fallen, and the campfires in the valley below look like stars of fire winking in a shadowy sky. "We can't go tonight. The people aren't ready. They need another night of food and sleep. Another day of preparation."

Riser again nods, slowly. Whatever his thoughts are on the matter, he's not outright saying them.

"You think it's a bad idea?" Normally I wouldn't need Riser's approval, or question my decisions, but my mother's getting under my skin. Dismantling my confidence the way one might chop down a tree: methodically, with hard, measured strokes delivered over and over.

"Not a bad idea, Maia." Even in the light of a half-moon, I can see the tight skin around his eyes soften, his dark smudge of eyebrows relaxing. "You're thinking of the people. That's exactly why they trust you. Why they follow you around and gaze at you with hope."

Fire rushes over my cheeks as I hip check him. "No they don't."

Bramble beeps his agreement with Riser in my ear, but I ignore him.

"They do." His eyes sharpen. "But this is war. People are going to die."

My shoulders tense. "So, you're saying you think I'm making the wrong decision?"

"No. In this situation there is no right decision. I just want you to brace for what's about to come. You can't save them all, and no matter what option you decide, a large number of the people in camp are going to die."

"I know that. I just . . . I want to give them a chance. I can't send them to battle without a basic knowledge of the weapons they wield or the food to fight. They'll be slaughtered before they get to the castle."

"Our weapon supplies are low," he points out, not unkindly. "Most won't even carry a sword."

I dislodge a rock the size of my fist and watch it sputter down the winding path. Crickets chirp around us, causing Bramble to imitate the sound in a soft, beautiful song. The forest has fallen away to a rocky landscape blanketed with tall grass, the sheen of moonlight coloring the foliage blue.

"We'll take a vote." My voice comes off harder than I intend, making Bramble stop belting out the song of his people. "Assemble the first meeting tonight. We'll inform the council what you learned and decide whether to attack tonight or tomorrow night."

"There's something else." He scratches his neck and

glances at the sky, his sharp jawline trapping shadows along the edge. "My sources say Nicolai has been training a few of the Rebels to fly starcrafts."

I blink, sure I've misheard. "You mean cloudcrafts? Do they have any of those left?"

I don't remember seeing cloudcrafts at Bloodwyn Castle, but they could be hidden somewhere, ready to use during the assault.

"*Starcrafts.*" He scrapes a hand through his hair, disheveling the inky mass even more than usual and sending a pine needle tumbling down to catch in the black ribbon lacing his vest. "They're using simulators, not actual crafts."

Starcrafts have the ability to fly above our atmosphere all the way to Hyperion, the city in the sky. "Why would they do that?"

His shoulders lift in a careful shrug. "A lot of reasons, although none that make any sense."

"Bloodwyn Castle will have hundreds of starcrafts. Assuming at least half will be damaged in the battle, and more will be used for escape, odds are likely there won't be enough crafts to take even a tenth of the Rebels to Hyperion. And the starcrafts aren't equipped with guns, at least, that I know of. So they wouldn't use them to hunt the fleeing Royalists from the sky."

"Nor would they be able to use the crafts to breach Hyperion and take it over. Not with that small number." Riser's face is unreadable, but he must have already thought the same thing through. "That's why it's troubling. It doesn't make sense."

"Not to us," I clarify.

My hands curl into themselves until they're hard as rocks. *Who knows what makes sense to a madman like Nicolai?*

Obviously sensing my frustration, Riser halts and draws me to him. For a moment, a breath, I let myself sink into his chest again. Bramble purrs between us like a hairless metal cat with klepto tendencies.

"In a few days, this will all be over," Riser murmurs. "And there's no one else in this gods' forsaken world I trust to get us there than you, Digger Girl."

But the breeze has increased, stirring up dust and handfuls of dead grass that roll across the boulders and crags. My hair lifts to lash across my eyes. Through the stripes of crimson, I chance a look up at Pandora.

I've made it a point not to notice the fiery pit. Not to let Her intimidate me. But Pandora's size makes me gasp. She's swollen. Bigger than ever. Writhing with shadows and flame. A corona of fire encircles the black center like a cruel crown, a promise of our impending destruction.

It's a reminder. Whatever we humans do down here, whatever little battles we rage against one another, none of it matters. She's intent on our total destruction.

And I'm the only one who can stop Her.

THREE

From high up on the mountain, the camp looks orderly and clean. But from up close, it's the opposite. Bodies sit or lay wherever they can. Some draped over one another. Some curled up in the muddy earth, sodden from the storm earlier and wracked with chills. The lucky ones are healthy enough to have erected makeshift shelters.

The breeze surges through the camp, causing the fabric tents to flicker and dance in the wind and the teepees of corrugated metal to groan.

A thick, dank fog clings to the muddy earth, swirling around my boots as I walk.

Riser ducks into the command center, a four-post tent Riser put together from willow branches and a stolen bedspread. Inside are the radios he uses to communicate with his spies.

Deeper into camp, the stench of waste hits me. The people are terrified of going into the woods now, which means they relieve themselves inside camp borders. Not exactly hygienic. I make a mental note to address that later.

I don't get very far before Lash finds me. A threadbare

cape cascades over his lanky body, unable to mask the sharp bones beneath. I can tell it's him before the moonlight falls on his face by his dragging limp.

His mouth is pulled into a grim line. "Love, we're in trouble."

"What kind of trouble?" I hardly slow as I wind through a circle of people gathered around a fire. They stare as I pass, and I cringe at their hopeful expressions when they recognize me.

"There's shit everywhere."

"I know." I wrinkle my nose. "Very aware, I promise."

"They can't keep doing that. It's polluting the river and spreading disease. There's only one of me, and more are coming down sick daily."

"What about the healers from the other districts?"

"Either too weak or sick to help." He rubs the back of his neck as we talk, his right shoulder dipping low as he struggles to catch up.

Because he has a lame leg, Maia. How could you forget? Embarrassed at my callousness, I finally slow to a leisurely pace. "I'll make an announcement. Good enough?"

He draws in a breath and exhales forcefully. Dark purple shadows pool below his eyes, the hollows beneath his cheeks deep craters that speak of long nights and hardly any food. Russet stubble shades the lower half of his jaw. "I've seen entire camps perish from dysentery and worse. Fix it, okay?"

"I will." My voice sounds more confident than I feel.

How can I control a force this large? A callous part of me knows that after the march, it will be more manageable, but I shove that idea aside.

A shape stalks between two wooden lean-tos and approaches. Tall and graceful, Teagan could pass for a general with her stern lips and fierce gaze. The tail end of a crimson cape nips at her heels.

Max and Rivet trail her. They could be twins with their soldier's attire: crimson-dyed leather breastplates, shoulder harness heavy with daggers and short swords, waist sheaths carrying matching broad swords. Both wear too-long red capes grimed with mud at the end, a stark contrast to Teagan's pristine one.

I give Max a tired smile before turning to Teagan.

Unlike Lash, who seems frazzled and near the end of his rope, she's a study of composure. "Don't you look beaten down, darling?"

I give a weak laugh. "Thanks. I'm just . . . tired. Who knew being responsible for an army of people was this hard?"

"Or . . . unhygienic." Her nose curls slightly upward.

Max and Rivet chuckle. For a moment I'm jealous of their closeness, the bond they share. Then I shake it off. At least he has someone he can talk to.

"Exactly," Lash says, punching Teagan's shoulder. They both ignore Max and Rivet. "Maia is falling down on the job."

"Last I checked," I snap, hating myself as soon as I do. "I wasn't in control of where people relieve themselves."

He and Teagan exchange glances, and then Teagan pulls something out of her shirt pocket. Moonlight glimmers off the sleek silver flask in her hand. "Would you like some, darling?"

"Please." I don't notice the rebel emblem until she tosses it to me, the scorpion wrapped around a dying phoenix raised beneath my thumb.

I tip back the drink without even asking what's inside. Teagan doesn't disappoint; brandy singes a trail down my throat and into my belly.

I cough and then pull another long dreg, the pain burning off the day's stress. "That's . . . nice."

Lash holds out his hand. "What am I, a Dandy bastard? C'mon, ladies. Hand it over."

Waving the flask out of Lash's reach, I toss it to Teagan.

"Really?" Lash groans. "That's just plain cruel, Graystone."

Rolling her eyes, Teagan slaps the flask against Lash's chest, hard. "A sip. Got it? If I get it back half empty you'll pay with those tiny stones you call man goods."

Lash makes a face as I hold in my laugh. "So stingy. The two of you."

After a generous drink, he goes to hand it back. Max and Rivet both vie for the flask. Lash makes to hand it over and then, apparently remembering Max isn't even sixteen yet, looks to me.

"No, Lash!" Teagan and I both order.

"Not fair," Max mumbles. "You're the only ones in camp who won't let me drink."

"Mom wants to speak to you, and if you have alcohol on your breath when you do, gods help us all."

"Not gonna happen. Ever. Problem solved."

I raise an eyebrow and switch tactics. "Aren't you supposed to be on duty, Max? You too, Rivet."

Rivet nods, elbowing Max hard. "You're right. We are." She pushes into a jog to catch up with me so we're shoulder to shoulder and runs a proud glance over Bramble. "So you like what I did to your bot?"

"Yeah. The extra storage comes in handy."

She beams, and I catch Max shaking his head in my periphery. "What about the lasers? Or the electric shock capabilities? He use those yet?"

I chuckle, wondering if I should be worried that I have a weapon on my shoulder. "No, Rivet. Not yet." She frowns and I add, "But that will come in handy very soon, I'm sure."

The brandy has blown through my empty stomach and into my body, and my arms feel hot and loose, my chest light. Another sip and I'll be buzzed, so I decline Teagan's gesture for more, grinning as Lash shoots her a hurt look for not offering him the same.

The lighthearted moment passes, and Teagan puts the flask away. We spend the next few minutes going over the plan to get inside the castle. With the Emperor distracted by the first wave of battle, a small crew including Rivet, Teagan, Caspian, Riser, Max, and myself will infiltrate the castle via the tunnel.

The hope is that, once inside, the map device inside Max will activate and lead us from there.

Maybe it's the liquor, but right now that hope feels flimsy at best.

FOUR

Only my mother makes a meeting this dramatic. A long table stretches across the bottom of the gorge, filled with platters of nuts, berries, and stale soda bread—only the gods know where my mother found an actual dining table in the woods. Torches planted in a large circle around us crackle guttering flames that send golden splashes of light over the rocky steel-gray walls of the canyon.

Soldiers line the rock face, mostly Rebels like Max and Rivet, but also a few of the healthier Sleepers. Firelight dances across the heads of the spears they hold.

They all glance over the pittance of food on the table, and I find myself doing the same as I slide into the head seat, a rickety splinter-trap with a broken leg. Caspian already sits to my left. Lank golden hair, weighed down with sweat and days in the forest, falls over his forehead. His eyes are the color of cognac in this light, and they watch me with unabashed curiosity as the rest take their seats.

"Lady Graystone," he says, the whisper of a smile crinkling his eyes.

"Prince Caspian. Hope the forest is treating you well."

My joke coaxes out the rest of his smile, showing off his white teeth. Something flutters under my rib cage. An invisible butterfly of emotion I'd rather not name.

The feeling is gentle, predictable, safe. Basically the opposite of how I feel with Riser.

From my periphery, I see Riser frowning at the interaction with his half-brother, but he refuses to sit before doing a quick recon of the gorge, sweeping through the shadows and checking the soldiers, sending a few out farther into the woods to widen the perimeter.

When he finally joins me on my right, he flicks a quick, savage look across Caspian. The muscles of Riser's jaw, hidden beneath a thin layer of stubble, feather, and he slowly tears his gaze away, a smirk catching his lips.

I cringe. The anger rising up between them feels like a living, breathing thing. A beast I'm constantly trying to slay.

Before we left the Rebels' camp, I thought there might be a chance Riser and Caspian could grow to, if not *like*, then tolerate each other.

But something about this camp, or maybe the looming battle, has brought out the bitter hatred simmering between them. Now I'm constantly on edge, trying to prevent one from provoking the other.

Usually I fail, and now is no exception. Raw fury smolders beneath Caspian's cheeks, ruddy with too much sun and not enough sleep.

The Royalist prince leans back into his chair with his hands threaded behind his golden head, and I silently curse as his lips curl into a cruel smile. "Paranoid, Thornbrook?"

Riser doesn't even look at Caspian as he responds. "I'll do whatever it takes to keep Maia safe. Can you say the same?"

"Safe, from what?" Caspian taunts, swiveling his head to do a sweep over the cliffs, the long stretch of rocky, uneven ground leading to the woods. "Shadows?"

"From what lurks inside the shadows, Prince." Riser sweeps his hand out toward the darkness, layered with silver mist and trees. "But if you don't believe me, feel free to relieve your large retinue of guards when we travel through the woods later."

Shit. Because both Princes are well known—and because many of the Rebels would be just as happy watching Caspian hang—I ordered guards for them. Riser, of course, refused. But behind Caspian sit four sleepy-eyed guards, looking bored and not overly excited about their charge.

All I need is Caspian sending his guards away so I can worry about yet another thing.

Thankfully Caspian ignores Riser's barb and goes back to glaring at him. Bramble circles nervously on my shoulder, his little legs tickling my skin as he assesses the situation. Maybe it's Rivet's new modifications, but he's become incredibly sensitive to picking up tension between humans.

"It's okay, buddy," I coo, his sleek body cool against my cheek as I nuzzle him.

From behind my chair, a muffled laugh reaches me. I don't have to turn around to know Flame, head of the Rebel guards, is laughing at the exchange between half-brothers. Stoking their feud like the flame she's nicknamed after.

A headache nips at my temples. Turning to face the shadows at my back, I throw her a pleading look. *Just let us get through this.*

She's standing just beyond the sweep of guttering fire-light, arms crossed, head canted slightly. One side of her head is shaved, the other dyed scarlet and sculpted into an intricate pattern of braids. Tall leather boots hug her legs, and twin scorpion earrings follow the curves of her dainty ears.

Even in the dim light I make out the tug of her lips as she lifts her bird-boned shoulders into a shrug before mouthing back, *fine.*

Silence falls heavy. Night sounds stir the air—crickets, a lone owl somewhere in the distance, the torches crackling. Perhaps there's some life left in these woods after all. A part of me is happy the owl hasn't been found by the hunters and killed just yet, as sentimental as the emotion is.

My mother claims the other side of the table, her face steeped in half-shadows. Bramble gives a distraught chirp at her presence and tucks behind my hair. She jerks her chin at me, a quick, subtle gesture, making him flinch even more.

Oh—*oh*.

They're waiting for me to speak.

I shove to a stand. Bramble squeaks his surprise and drops to the table, scaring more than a few council members as he begins efficiently gathering the berries from the first tray into his cache.

Tamping down my smile, I sweep a steady gaze over the table.

Normally my throat begins to close up when I have to speak publicly like this, but I'm too hungry and tired right now to care. "Prince Thornbrook has discovered new information on the Rebels' movements. In light of this, we need to vote. Stay one more night so the Sleepers in camp can rest and attack tomorrow at dusk, or mobilize tonight and march on Laevus Palace at dawn."

There. Short, sweet, and to the point.

I nod to Riser as I sit, aware of the complete silence following my announcement. The appointed council members from the various districts have gone from gawking at Bramble to rapt attention, and they exchange nervous glances. Half are from Bronze districts, the other half Silver districts who fared much better when they were woken up.

The Silver Sleepers had resources nearby—food and clean water and supplies.

Which means there's a chance they'll vote for leaving tonight.

Riser presses his hands flat on the table, and I blush, remembering how they pressed much the same way on my flesh earlier. Bramble scampers to him and rubs his body over Riser's arms like a cat.

"The Rebels are mobilizing," Riser says, his voice cutting through the silence and echoing off the rock face. "As we speak, they gather supplies and Swifters, even horses."

"So they're attacking tonight?" a woman from the northern lake district asks, her voice breathless with nerves.

"They could be. Or they could leave tomorrow night. Nicolai will attack at daybreak, before the castle has time to wake up, of that, I'm sure. But we don't know which night."

"And your scouts?" my mother asks, slipping her hood back to reveal the upper portion of her face. "The ones posted around the Rebels. Have they seen any movement, Prince?"

I cringe at the way she says prince, the undercurrent of derision. Or maybe that's all in my head.

Riser doesn't seem to notice as he says, "We lost contact with them thirty minutes ago."

I suck in a breath. "Why didn't you tell me that?"

"I just discovered the lost connection after we parted." His voice is flat, his expression unreadable.

I exhale, trying to fit this new information into what we already know. "Cressia," I say, addressing the Bronze council member who spoke earlier. "If we need to march tonight, will your people be ready?"

She clasps her hands together over the nuts and berries on her plate. Her fingers are stained purple from surreptitiously shoving them into her mouth earlier, when she thought no one noticed. Now they fidget. When she looks at me, her mouth presses into a painfully tight line.

As if she's warring with the right words to say.

Finally she shakes her head and drops her gaze to the table. "No, I'm sorry. We are weak, many of us starving. If we march tonight, most of us . . . we won't make the mountainous trek to the castle."

"And another night of food and rest?" I ask, quietly. "Would that make a difference?"

"Another night, my Empress"—I cringe at the title the Sleepers gave me—"and my people will be ready."

Her eyes implore me for mercy until I have to tear my gaze away. An invisible fist of dread knuckles my diaphragm, making me strain for breath. Leaving tonight most likely means the death of her district. I might as well line them up and execute them right now.

"It's time," my mother says. I can feel her gaze all the way over here. Watching to see what I do. If I'm worthy.

The vote starts with the council members from the Sleeper districts. Each vote from the lower council members counts as one point. As expected, the Silver council members vote to leave tonight, while the Bronze members vote to stay. The Silvers sway the vote seven points to the Bronze's five.

My mother goes next. As a high-ranking Gold, her vote counts as two.

"Leave tonight," she says, holding up her palm face forward.

So now there's nine votes for leaving tonight.

My teeth grind, but I wipe any emotion from my face. The Bronze council woman watches us with a desperate, almost feral intensity. We are, after all, deciding her district's fate.

Caspian holds up his palm and looks at me. "Stay."

My shoulders relax a little, and I go next. "Stay."

That's it. We have the vote. I look to Riser as I mentally tally the numbers. Each vote from the triumvirates count as three. Right now the numbers sit at nine for leaving tonight, and eleven for staying. With Riser's vote to stay, we'll have fourteen.

Riser glances at me, his face a mask of apathy. Why is he hesitating? For a breath, his face softens as he holds my stare. His expression is clear. *Forgive me.*

No—

"Leave." He never breaks my gaze, nor does his voice sound repentant.

It takes a few seconds to realize he didn't make a mistake. He meant to go against me. I open my mouth to question him but then fall silent. Bramble, picking up on the tension, leaves Riser to come to me, pausing halfway across the table, a kid torn between parents.

The betrayal lodges deep in my core, my chest tightening until I have to scrape in each breath—but I can't let the other members of the council see how I feel. So I crack my neck and pretend to take it in stride.

Caspian shakes his head, obviously disapproving of Riser's vote.

Riser glares at him, that horrible fury rising between them again, threatening to spill over into the meeting.

"Then it's settled." I expected my mother to sound triumphant, but there's a business-like briskness to her voice that makes this even harder to take. The Bronze council members slowly stand. Their shoulders stoop, their faces slacken with shock.

They look stricken. I can't imagine what it must be like to have to tell a group of emaciated families barely clinging to life that they have to march countless miles over steep terrain to war.

All at once, I catch Riser go rigid in my periphery. That's when I notice what he must have picked up. The forest is still. Absolutely silent.

The scrape of Riser's short sword pierces the air, causing

other members to cry out. The soldiers around us all reach for their weapons, looking around in confusion. Silver blurs across the table as Bramble launches himself at me, taking refuge on my shoulder.

A whining hiss reverberates through the gorge. A second later, a bright streak arcs over the sky and grows larger, larger—

I don't see Riser move, but his hands connect with my arm and he's shoving me out of the way. Warmth kisses my cheek as I fall, Bramble squeaking in alarm. Fire slashes across my vision and blinds me. Then there's a dull *thunk*.

The moment the dewy grass meets my fingers, I pop back up, sword in hand. Riser and Caspian form lethal bookends on my either side, both holding steel. Flame leaps onto the table, her boots knocking over the food platters with a clatter, her scarlet cape whipping out behind her.

She stomps at something, but before she crushes it with her steel-toed boot, I see what rushed past me—a single flaming arrow sticks straight up on the wooden table. Pinned beneath its steel arrowhead is a patch of pale orange fabric. Faded and stained and frayed.

The color rouses a memory deep in the recesses of my brain, calling forth a flood of raw emotion. And I know without even asking whose arrow it is.

The Puppet Master.

FIVE

I f Nicolai's intention was to kill me, that arrow wouldn't have missed. That's what I tell myself, at least, as I grab the patch of fabric—a piece of my old jumpsuit from the pit—and break free from Riser and Caspian's tight formation.

I circle the gorge, calling out his name. "Nicolai!" My voice is unrecognizable as it echoes off the canyon walls.

Rocks tumble down the cliff, drawing my attention above. In the silvery darkness, it takes a moment to make out the Rebels that stand behind our retinue of soldiers above. Large knives glitter at their throats.

Flame grunts and swivels her crossbow at the Rebel in the middle, the one holding a thin blonde girl from behind.

I hold out my hand. "Wait, Flame."

With a growl, she lowers the weapon—if only a few inches. "Why?"

"Because Nicolai wants to talk." I raise my voice. "Don't you, Puppet Master!"

His laughter floats through the trees like a ghost song, bending and twisting with the breeze, echoing off the high canyon walls. The eerie sound lifts the hairs of my arms and neck one by one.

A flash of red near the edge of the wood. I pivot to face the threat—red cape, red metallic mask, scorpion cane.

Twenty Rebels escort Nicolai, a halo of steel that reflects fireflies of light all around the leader of the Fienians. He walks slowly, every movement hinting at the pain and discomfort he must feel. Somewhere close by will be the vehicle that transported him—no way in Fienian hell did he march on foot with his army.

"I thought the castle was that way," I call, jerking my arm to my left.

"Do I look like I am lost?" Beneath the robotic qualities of Nicolai's Electro-larynx, his voice has the slippery quality I remember, except now it's brittle with pain. Any other human being I might feel pity for, but not Nicolai. No—even his pain could be a ruse meant to distract.

What is he up to?

When they get within twenty feet, my mother steps forward. For some stupid reason, I'm surprised to see her sword held low and ready at her side. Reflecting firelight down its beautiful polished steel edge.

"That's far enough, Nicolai," she informs him. Her slender hand turns ever so slightly back and forth in excitement, making the fire's reflection trapped in the blade seem to twist and dance.

He throws an impatient glance at my mother before locking his eyes on her steel. "I require a word with your daughter, Baroness."

"The hell you do," she replies, her voice so casual I almost miss the warning. The implied violence seething beneath the surface.

But Nicolai doesn't miss it. With an aggrieved sigh, he waves off his guards and approaches alone. Every step seems an effort, the steel-tipped end of his lacquered cane sinking deep into the muddy ground. His breath coming out in rapid, gurgled spurts that I can hear from here.

Tension thickens the air until it feels combustible, ready to erupt into violence any second. Our guards' gazes bounce around with wild, egg-white eyes, and I hold up a hand to steady them. The last thing we need is a nervous soldier drawing their sword.

When Nicolai is a man's length away, I align my sword tip with his heart. "Far enough, Puppet Master."

Bramble backs up my threat with a staccato of warning shrieks that nearly shred my eardrums.

Nicolai regards Bramble for a long moment, then flicks a derisive look at the soldiers against the wall. "You should train them better. A few public whippings and the occasional execution usually does the trick."

"You came all the way here to give me advice?"

Nicolai's long cloak rustles as he holds out a gloved hand, his nubby fingers nearly hidden by the darkness. "Come, let us talk."

"Tell your Fienians to release my soldiers and I'll consider it."

"There's the Maia I know." His silver gaze falls to the tip of my sword. "All bluster and no bite. Unfortunately, you don't have much to bargain with. Come with me or I raise my arm, lift two mangled fingers, and my guards slit the throats of the soldiers above."

Sweat slicks my grip over my sword pommel. I can feel the collective stare of the council prickling my skin. Waiting to see what I'll do.

Breathe in, out. Now hold your ground, Maia.

"Go ahead." I smile. "Then my friends and I will race to see who kills you first. My bet is Riser, then again Flame does have the drop on you from behind, and I hate you the most, so really, it's a toss-up on who gets the pleasure of ramming a blade through your heart."

Nicolai lobs a curious look at Caspian and then Riser, his focus settling on the latter. Assessing his willingness. Perhaps Nicolai assumed the Rebels who left him would be tired of scraping by with little food or supplies.

Perhaps they are, and I'm about to have a rebellion on my hands.

I freeze as Nicolai lifts his hand, watching his fingers . . .

He closes his fist, and the Rebels above all retreat on command, disappearing from the cliff-line and releasing our soldiers.

"Now," Nicolai says. "I've played nice. Your turn. I have a proposition for you."

I'm not stupid enough to walk alone with him through the forest. Instead I clear a spot for Nicolai at the table. The guards stay, and Riser and Caspian both claim guard positions at my back, while Rivet and Max take the positions on the other side.

Flame and my mother stay near the soldiers, but close enough to be handy if Nicolai tries something, each refusing to put down their weapon. In this position, Nicolai would be suicidal to try anything—but that does nothing to dissuade my unease.

How do you predict the actions of a madman?

I wait until Nicolai lowers himself, slowly, into the chair, before sitting across from him. His breath comes out in rattling pants, and he takes a puff from an inhaler type device before speaking.

"I had . . . a speech ready," he wheezes. "But that was . . . was before I had to walk these woods." Firelight flickers across the smooth planes of the mask covering his face, making it seem to float against the surrounding darkness. "Did they tell you these woods are haunted?"

I crack my neck, dizzy with hunger and fatigue. At this point even talking is a chore that requires energy I don't have, so I simply level Nicolai with an impatient stare.

"Whole regiments of Fienians murdered here. They really didn't tell . . . you?" His pale eyes shimmer bright and feverish. "This soil was watered in blood—"

"You have two seconds to get to the point, or we're done."

Mangled lips press into a frown. "My army moves on Laevus Castle on the first sliver of light."

"I've gathered as much." I manage to keep my disappointment hidden.

"I cannot promise the thing you are looking for will stay . . . intact. Or not fall into my grasp—and I'm not feeling particularly generous at the moment."

My throat spasms in a dry swallow that becomes a stilted cough. My mother sends a soldier over to pour me a cup of water from the plastic pitcher in the center of the table, but I wave him away without breaking Nicolai's gaze. "What are you offering?"

"In a few short hours, Castle Laevus will either litter the ground in pieces, or—if you play nice—I will hold off on destroying the castle until after you find this device."

The flesh between my shoulder blades tingles, and I straighten. "At what price?"

Nicolai flicks a glance at his hands, as if he wasn't wearing gloves and still had fingernails to examine. "March with me. Your untrained army of Sleepers to fill the ranks of my Rebels."

His words stun me into silence. In my periphery I see my mother go rigid, her spine ramrod straight. The council members mutter their obvious suspicions under their breath. They were inside my head during the Blood Trials. They saw what Nicolai did to me.

Flame shakes her head, a gesture so subtle it could mean

anything, before pursing her lips and lifting her middle finger in a gesture that's perfectly clear.

Playing it cool, I examine my fingernails. "Combine our forces? Say we're successful. Then what?"

"Then," he says, "we split the jewel of the Royalist regime in half."

"Just like that?"

"Just like that."

Liar. The word clangs through my skull. "We would choose the boundaries."

He shrugs as if such a suggestion is unimportant, causing more alarm bells to trill inside my head.

What are you up to, Puppet Master?

From the corner of my eye I see Riser peel from the shadows and approach, his stalking strides silent and ghost-like. Somehow even the leaves seem not to crunch beneath his feet.

"Nicolai, I don't know what you're playing at," Riser says, his quiet voice cutting through the moan of the wind through the trees. "But the answer is no."

What the Fienian hell?

His declaration hits me like a slap in the face, and it takes all my focus not to react as a sliver of hurt pierces my chest. He should know that speaking *for* me makes me look weak—something I can't afford right now.

An oily grin forms beneath the delicate edge of Nicolai's mask. "Do you have a representative who speaks for you now, Maia? I thought Pit Boy was only good at betraying his masters and taking what doesn't belong to him, but apparently his list of accomplishments includes diplomacy too."

Nicolai's reference to the Hot Weapons Riser filched before we left isn't a surprise—he was bound to find out sooner or later. But the hurt in his voice is.

Why would Nicolai take Riser's leaving personally?

Surely he has a slew of murderous soldiers to take his place, if the Blood Courts were any indication.

Caspian chuckles and throws his half-brother a taunting grin. "Forget your place, Thornbrook? Why don't you slither back to the shadows and let the adults handle this?"

Riser slowly cuts his mismatched eyes at Caspian, as if the Gold prince is hardly worth his breath. "I doubt you'd say that to me without your guards present, little brother."

I shrink from the lethal quiet of his words. Bramble chirps quietly in alarm. This is the very worst time their feud could erupt . . .

"And I doubt Maia will keep you around much longer, now that the world is beginning to see what a savage you are."

"Because I'm not nodding and agreeing with everything she says like you, that makes me an animal?"

"No." Caspian's eyes go cold. "You're an animal because you walk around here like you're a heartbeat away from slitting everyone's throat. Because you ooze violence." Caspian rakes a hand through his hair. "How she finds you attractive is beyond me."

My heart stutters into my throat. The council members exchange tight-lipped glances while Nicolai just grins and grins.

Don't take the bait, Riser . . .

"Right," Riser snarls. "That's what this is about. Just because you have more money than the gods, and some computer said you're matched, you think she's going to fall into your arms?"

"Maybe not. But there will come a day when she realizes what you are, and I'll be here, Thornbrook. Waiting."

I can hardly move. Hardly suck in air. How has this so quickly spun out of control?

"Sorry, Laevus." Riser's taunting tone makes my gut clench. "Pretty boy princes just aren't her type."

"Like you are?" Caspian spits, his polished tone dissolving into hatred. "A one-eyed whore's bastard?"

Nonono—

"Your family left my mother to die like an animal in prison." Riser's words are sharp-edged whispers, each one a dagger. "Dare utter another breath staining her memory and it will be the last breath you take."

"Maybe," Caspian seethes, "my father left her to rot like an animal . . . because she was one."

I know before Riser even reacts that Caspian has gone too far. Gotten too personal. I can feel the mood in the air shift as something dark and deadly flickers inside Riser's eyes—the shadow of a beast awakened.

Riser reaches for his blade—

SIX

"Enough!" I order, strangely breathless. Part of me is terrified Riser won't listen. That the frenzied violence he learned in the pit will come roaring back. "That's—that's enough."

A collective gasp rises from the table. A few of the council members have shrunken away from Riser, eyes wide and panicked in the delicate firelight.

Riser goes still, his fingers clenched around the dagger handle protruding from his waistband. For a moment he does nothing. One by one, his fingers unwrap from his weapon. As if removing each one is painful.

His fingers curl into a white-knuckled fist and he drops his hand at his side.

Finally, he inhales two breaths and slowly, *slowly* the promise of violence dissipates from his visage.

Enough, at least, that I can breathe again.

When Riser meets my gaze his face is flat, emotionless, the loyal, mindless soldier—and then he turns to stare blankly at a beaming Nicolai.

Heat stains my cheeks as I tear my gaze from him to his half-brother.

Caspian doesn't even dare look at me, his eyes downcast and shoulders rolled forward. At least he has the sense to realize the predicament he's put me in. Or perhaps he remembers their last fight where both of them nearly died and understands how close he was to death just now.

"That was . . . entertaining." My mother's gaze, sharp as the blade Riser reached for, hovers over me. She looks me up and down, the hint of a frown worrying her lips and highlighting the spider-thin wrinkles lining her mouth.

She's waiting for me to do something. To punish them for losing their cool and making us appear weak in front of an enemy.

I blow out a breath to keep my teeth from grinding and address Caspian. "Prince Laevus, please refrain from any more comments. I think we've heard quite enough."

A muscle clenches and feathers beneath Caspian's jaw.

I cast a glance at Riser, masking the hurt over his actions with a tight smile that surely makes my mother proud. "Prince Thornbrook, I think it's time you assessed the perimeter again to ensure there are no more *surprises*."

My words feel wrong on every level. I'm basically dismissing him and blaming him for Nicolai sneaking around our defenses. While deep in my heart I know there's no one I'm safer with than Riser. No one who I trust more.

And yet . . . *yet*, he nearly unraveled the future of our world just now.

One second later and Riser would have killed Caspian.

One second later and any future alliance with the Royalists would have been forever tainted. I would have had to punish him—probably execute him.

How could he not see that?

As is, he's single-handedly dismantled the hard-earned

respect I've built up over the last two days with the Sleepers while making me look weak to Nicolai.

I hate the smug look my mother wears, the one that reminds me of her warning from earlier. Almost as much as I hate the flicker of betrayal that passes over Riser's face. Our eyes lock, and I brace myself for an argument.

But whatever Riser's feeling, he buries it beneath a hard mask that even I can't penetrate.

A breath, a heartbeat, and he slips away into the shadows to do his job. Protect me. As soon as he's gone, the tension in the air lessens until I can breathe again without struggling.

Nicolai clicks his tongue and rests his unyielding stare on me, his eyes dancing with cruel amusement. He's been here less than five minutes and he's already finding fissures of dissent in our ranks. Exposing cracks and fatal flaws I'd rather keep hidden.

"As I mentioned earlier," Nicolai says, his electronic voice somehow managing to come off smooth and taunting. "Hang a few unruly soldiers from a tree and the rest become obedient as hounds. Although sometimes I find"—his gaze slides to where Riser stood moments before—"some can't be tamed and need to be put down."

I refocus on Nicolai, my stomach in knots, and force myself to forget Riser and Caspian. Find a shred of composure. Enough that I can pretend two princes didn't nearly fight to the death over me.

"Why this sudden offer?" My voice wobbles, but I forge ahead, imbuing each word with more confidence than the last. "You have an army. A well trained one."

"The gods have turned on us." A heartbeat ticks by as he hesitates. "The day you left, we were hit with a virus brought by the Sleepers. The day after, a lightning strike sparked a fire that killed hundreds more, even as a flash flood took out a group of Rebels foraging for supplies thirty miles east."

It's hard to feel pity for Nicolai, but my heart hurts for the Fienians. Even if most never trusted me, it's hard not to feel a comradery with them after my time there.

"I can't imagine that decimated your forces," I point out, keeping any sympathy out of my voice.

A low, raspy chuckle. "Fienians believe in the old gods. And three unlucky incidents in two days speak of the gods' wrath, the loss of their favor. Not exactly fortuitous right before battle."

Understanding dawns. "They're deserting?"

The only reply I get is a blink, which I take to mean yes.

"How many?"

"Enough to require your ragged band of Sleepers. They may not be trained, but we need bodies on the field."

"Most of my Sleepers are starving. They can barely hold weapons, and the ones that can have no idea what to do with them."

"Still." He runs his index finger around a knobby hole in the table.

"You don't want the Emperor to know your soldiers are deserting, do you?" I laugh, feeling a little closer to figuring out Nicolai's game. "He would have a rough idea of your numbers, and if you show up with half that . . ."

The Emperor would spot his weakness.

"What happened to your speech about whippings and executions?" I ask. If the Rebels are truly deserting in such numbers, they must really want to leave.

His mangled lips tug into a crooked smile. "Oh, the ones we could find paid the blood price, along with Lord Thornbrook's spies . . . after we were done feeding them information."

I release a breath, trying to steady my mind. Could Nicolai really need my help? Or is this a trick? Riser's spies never mentioned the fire or desertions, but if what Nicolai is saying is true, their information was carefully controlled anyway and unreliable.

If Nicolai *is* lying, I can't see his angle. Even if we march together, my soldiers will still fall under my command.

Riser's lithe form solidifies near the trees to my left. Done with the task, he leans quietly against a large slab of rock, his head canted to the side. Watching me.

I shiver, running my hands down the ridged gooseflesh of my arms.

"I need an hour to decide," I say, ignoring the shocked looks from basically everyone but Nicolai. Even Riser seems to straighten at this. "And . . . if I take the deal, we march tomorrow night and you feed my army meat and grain from your stores."

He hardly hesitates before countering, "You have half an hour to decide."

My gaze locks on Riser's. Pushing away the emotions his face elicits, I shift my attention back to Nicolai. "Prince Thornbrook will deliver our answer soon."

My voice leaves no room for argument. Riser's lips pull into a frown, but he nods once, a lock of dark hair falling over his moss-green eye. In this light, and from this distance, his blue eye looks black as the slate veining the boulders at the base of the cliffs.

Nicolai groans to a stand, two Rebels rushing to assist him. As he taps his cane into the rocky earth, my brain whirs with this new development, questions floating to the surface of my mind like corpses.

What are Nicolai's true motivations?

How does this benefit him?

But all I can think about is how this plan benefits us the most—which, knowing Nicolai, means this is one-hundred-percent a trap.

SEVEN

Half an hour isn't enough time to make such a big decision.

"How can you even think about trusting that Rebel?" Caspian asks, although his usual princely tone is frayed with guilt over his actions earlier. He's taken his place again at the table, his arms crossed and resting in front of him. Acorns scatter around his elbows.

The crowned prince, reduced to eating nuts and berries.

I would laugh out loud if not for the circumstances.

One glance around the table tells me everyone shares his sentiment. My mother, Flame, Max, Rivet, and Caspian. The council members, who sit bleary-eyed, wearing frowns carved deep into their jaws.

The only one not sitting is Riser, who stands a few feet away, his face turned toward the slumbering forest. A prickle of unease grows at not being able to catch his eye.

"I don't trust him," I answer, refocusing on Caspian. "Only a fool would. But I'm not sure we have a choice. He has food and supplies, and if we ally with him we can monitor and control his movements."

Flame, who's spent the last five minutes grinding an acorn to dust with the butt of her gold-handled dagger, cuts her eyes at me beneath lowered brows. "That's exactly what a fool would say."

I glare at her. "Okay, Flame. What would you do?"

She shrugs. "Send the Prince over there to carve out his eyes. Then his heart. Finally, his ball—"

"Okay," I interrupt. "We get it."

Max chuckles under his breath, and I lift my eyebrows at him. *Don't make me sorry I let you join us,* my look says.

"Why would Nicolai trust Caspian?" I add.

"Not that *prince,*" she snaps, the word prince this time edged with derision. "Our prince."

Oh—she means Riser. Sometimes I forget. "Then Prince Thornbrook would die."

"Maybe. Maybe not." She beams at Riser, who doesn't seem the least bit offended she's offering his life. In fact, his face is a mask of apathy.

"That's not happening. And that wouldn't solve our current problem." I look around the table, clearing my mind as I slowly rest on a decision. "I think we should work with Nicolai, but assume he plans to betray us on the battlefield."

Silence descends. My mother's lips tug to the side, and I hate how closely I watch her. How my breath hitches as I wait to see if she agrees.

Caspian leans back in his chair and exhales. "How would we do that?"

I spend the next five minutes laying out the plan. Because it was so quickly put together, we'll have to rework parts of it tomorrow, but when I'm done explaining my thoughts, I catch my mother's frown relax, the edges of her lips lifting slightly. A surge of hope expands inside my chest.

The only one who doesn't show any reaction at all is Riser. After we call the meeting and everyone drags themselves out of their chairs on the way to camp, I find Riser and pull him to the side. Most of the torches have extinguished, but a single flame gutters near us, and I find myself inching closer to the kiss of warmth it provides.

Normally Riser would have noticed me shivering and wrapped me in his arms. But now—now he simply stares beyond me at something in the distance.

"Tell Nicolai we accept. I'll send soldiers for the promised food and supplies before noon tomorrow, and by nightfall we'll be ready to march." Perhaps it's my fatigue, or the lingering hurt over earlier, but my words come out short and defensive. "And . . . report back to me when you're done."

So I know you're safe, I almost say . . . but the words lodge firmly in my throat.

I swallow, fidgeting with the collar of my shirt. Talking with Riser has never been this hard. My mouth parts as I urge words forward, something—anything to break this cold barrier between us.

But before I can get out a breath he makes a mock salute and slips away.

EIGHT

B ack at camp, I sleepwalk into the slumping tent Riser
helped me put together two days ago and fall into a
nightmarish sleep full of death. After a few hours suffering
through my bad dreams—my friends dying in horrible ways
while I watch—I drag myself from my scratchy blankets and
yank my hair into a ratty braid. Since I slept in my clothes last
night, I don't even bother changing.

There's just too much to do.

Impending dawn lightens the seams of my tent, and by
the time I duck under the doorway and down the hill to
camp, a tangerine-gold sunrise sweeps over the valley. A
crisp breeze ruffles the corners of the tents lined in messy
rows and stirs trash around.

Bramble pops from the tent and follows me, stretching
and grumbling his protest.

I check Riser's tent first. His is just down the hill from
mine, hidden by a copse of alder trees near a thin river.

Empty. The bed—a collection of folded blankets—is neat,
unslept on.

Blowing out a tired breath, I skirt through a line of

women snagging their clothes from the clotheslines that zag from tent to tent. Most people in camp only have two pairs of clothes—their day attire and whatever they wear to sleep—and they wash their day clothes every night.

The infirmary is a collection of tents cobbled together in a meadow two hundred yards out from camp. The edge of the mountains form a protective wall at their back, shading the dilapidated camp from the morning sun.

I find Lash in the last tent, tending to a sick girl no older than seven. A fever-sweat pastes her pale hair around her skull, and a blue tint shadows her lips. Even after Lash fixes his glassy gaze on me, it takes a moment for recognition to spark inside his tired eyes.

"Hello, love," he rasps, his voice nearly gone from the constant discussions with his patients and their families.

"You didn't sleep at all, did you?" I ask, brushing back a flyaway piece of hair.

"Sleep is overrated." He forces a lopsided smile that doesn't reach his eyes. "Until they make more of me, darling, I don't really have a choice."

"I don't think the world could handle more of you."

He winks. "Damn right, Graystone."

Dropping a hand on his shoulder, I guide him out into the fresh air. The bones beneath his flesh feel sharper than normal and I pull away too quickly. Smoke drifts from the east. Bramble finds a moss-slick rock and settles atop it, taking the moment to sun himself.

"Have you eaten?" I try to keep the worry from my face.

"Acorn stew. A delicatessen meant for emperors, I assure you."

"When?" I persist, my own stomach rumbling.

He scratches the hollow of his cheek. A line of dirt rims his fingernails to match the dark circles beneath his eyes. In this light his hair is the vibrant red of the sunrise, pulled back at his nape. Sweat darkens his temples to rust.

"Okay, I'm taking you to eat."

He glances back at the sick bay. "But—"

"Nope. You need to eat and *bathe*."

"That an offer to help me wash?" But his voice lacks its usual charm, and my concern grows. "Because if it is, we need to discuss your amount of princely suitors."

"You heard about last night?"

"Love, the entire camp heard about last night. Now, I don't mind sharing, but the others . . ."

I roll my eyes and drag him toward the pale smoke darkening the sky on the other side of camp. When we near the cooking fires, lines of people appear, swaying and half-asleep. I discover why a moment later when I spy Teagan flitting over the fires, directing attendants and helping ladle thick stew into bowls.

A nest of dark hair sits atop her head, which hangs low on her long neck, and her body bends and sways with the breeze. Seems like Lash isn't the only one who was up all night.

Nicolai's first batch of supplies must have been delivered because the dark sludge simmering inside the cast iron pots smells delicious, a greasy-rich promise of real food thickening the air.

Most people in line barely have the energy to stand. Otherwise, Teagan would have already been overrun, despite the three soldiers there to guard her.

Teagan shoves two bowls of stew our way, wipes her hands on the towel apron around her waist, and continues. Before we leave, I grab her by the shoulders and make her promise me she'll eat soon.

She gives a tired nod, the best I'm going to get, and then

Lash and I find a flat patch of ground to settle on near the river.

With no spoons in sight, we both tip our bowls until they're empty. I hardly notice how hot the food is until afterward, when my tongue finds a raw blister on the roof of my mouth.

The food makes me sleepy, but I force myself to stand. There are a million things to do, the most important of which is to find Riser.

I run a sleeve over my mouth. "Have you seen Riser this morning?"

The food must have made Lash sleepy too because he barely has the energy to shake his head. "No. But I've been at the infirmary all morning. Why? Did you misplace the Dark Prince?"

I raise an eyebrow. "Dark Prince?"

He picks at something in his teeth. "What they're calling him. He's the Dark Prince and the other one is the Gold Prince."

"That's original." And fitting, though I don't say that.

He lifts a shoulder in a tired shrug. "Well, the question you should be asking is, where's all the meat?"

"The what?"

"That stew was supposed to have meat. I heard patients saying they saw Nicolai's people bringing in barrel loads of meat for the camp, but what we just ate was all potatoes and turnips."

He's right. I did specify meat to Nicolai, and he wouldn't jeopardize our alliance over something like that when he has meat to spare. With a grateful nod, I make my way back to the cooking fires. The crowd has grown, and I have to shove my way through a five-person deep circle to find Teagan hovering over a bowl.

"What happened to the meat?"

She hardly looks up from the pot she's stirring. "Darling, I recommend you not say that too loud or we'll have some very angry people in a few moments."

I draw in closer, heat from the fire below warming my arm and pulling sweat along my shoulder blades. "Nicolai brought it, though, right?"

"He did." Her eyes trail behind me to the forest. "Then I dumped it."

"Why?"

"Riser's orders. A shame, too. We could have really used it."

At least he made it back to camp. I wipe a hand across my forehead, gathering more sweat. "Did he give you a reason?"

She pauses mid-ladling and cuts her eyes at me. "No. He asked me to trust him, and I did. The only thing he said was for me to trash the meat in secret and add in whatever horse-meat we have left."

"Why would he do that? Why wouldn't he tell me?"

She gives a final, tired shrug. "You'll have to ask him when you find him."

Right. Except it's pretty clear Riser doesn't want to be found.

Especially by me.

And it's becoming harder and harder to make excuses as to why.

NINE

As confusing as Teagan's revelation was, it renews my resolve to find Riser. My search takes me through the camp, now teeming with life. Kids lug water in buckets from the river and boil them over open fires. On the far side of camp, Flame leads a group of healthier Sleepers up the hillside to train in the flat terrain above, their swords sparkling in the morning sun.

The weakest members are rolling up their tents and packing their meager belongings for the long march to the shelters beneath the mountains.

The Silvers who can afford them pack their things onto the backs of rusty Swifters sad versions of the ones in the Rebel stronghold. A few old cloudcrafts rest on the other side of camp, beneath an outcropping of rocks. Those will be used to transport the most important supplies.

Above, the air shimmers and twitches. Just slightly. Enough that a human would notice if they were looking, but to the drones above, the camp below appears to be another unoccupied valley full of rocks and knee-high grass.

The maligner shields my mother stole from the Royalists are doing their job, at least.

I press deeper into the crush of people. After nearly thirty minutes searching with no luck, I force Riser from my thoughts and begin preparations for tonight. Checking that the weapons are cleaned and sharpened, ensuring we have enough food and water for the journey, even making sure everyone who is going to fight has proper shoes that fit.

Not everyone will fight. Over half of our camp is made up of the sick, elderly, and children. As soon as we embark toward the Island, they will travel northwest to the shelters beneath the mountains. Hopefully, if everything goes right, they can emerge in a few days.

But if not . . .

I bury myself in my work. After a few hours, my shoulders ache and a layer of sweat-streaked grime covers my face. I fill my canteen at the water station near a patch of yellow black-eyed Susans and then trek through boulder-marred hillsides to the training area.

A nice breeze whips my hair back and cools my cheeks as I top the hill. Hundreds of people spread across the meadow, shaded by the snow-capped mountain at their backs. Their red vests and capes swirl and eddy as they spar. Flickers of light dance off their steel, the sound of metal on metal filling the valley.

Dread swells just below my sternum, a tiny spark of ice that spreads into my veins, my bones.

I've gotten used to the idea that I'll never be able to hear the sounds of war again without reliving the Rebel attack on the Island, and even now, the mere sound of swords clanging is enough to set me off.

My mouth goes dry, a roar growing louder in my head as I gasp for breath. Flashes of the bombing invade my mind. I see Centurions running civilians through with swords already coated red. See the injured and dead strewn across a field. See Ophelia's bone-white face and vacant stare . . .

Closing my eyes, I clear the ghosts from my head and refocus on the training soldiers spread out in orderly rows. *Focus, Maia. They need you.*

When I'm certain I have my anxiety under control, I pick my way down the hill, thankful for the light breeze that dries the sweat coating my skin.

When it came to appointing commanders for the regiments in our army, we somehow had enough Sleepers with experience to fill the roles. My mother was the obvious choice for general—one of her degrees is in military science, and there's no one more cunning or ruthless when it comes to warfare.

Flame was also easy to nominate for trainer, and I almost feel sorry for the recruits under her command.

As if on cue, I spot her holding court beneath the shade of an oak tree. Hips wide. Wielding a metal bow nearly as big as she is as five new recruits watch her nock the arrow. She draws the bowstring back, squints one eye, looses a breath, and puts the arrow into the center of a target drawn into the trunk of a tree eighty yards away.

"Showing off?" I call as I approach. Bramble tops the hill behind me and rushes off toward the training soldiers, his antennae flashing.

She shades her eyes, her lips tugging into a reluctant grin. "Being better than everyone else isn't showing off." She holds out the bow. "Want to demonstrate?"

My muscles twitch. It seems like years ago that I was reconstructed to use a bow and arrow, but I know I could still easily hit the mark with my eyes closed. That some lessons imprinted on my brain—like taking a life or shooting an arrow through a target the size of a man's eye—will never fade.

"Another time." I gaze past her to a storm brewing in the distance, steel-gray clouds shrouding the mountaintop like an ominous shadow.

"Max is down there." She jerks her head near the far side of the recruits. "Toying with some poor girl."

"Thanks, but . . . have you seen Riser anywhere?"

She raises an eyebrow, but it's impossible to tell if she's shocked or just taunting me. "He lost?"

"Not exactly. But I haven't seen him since . . . last night."

A knowing look washes over her face. "Ah. You mean you're fighting and he doesn't want to talk to you."

"No." *Surely Riser isn't mad at me?* Even if my actions hurt him, he wouldn't just ignore me, especially today. I suck in my bottom lip. "I don't know. Look, just tell him I need to talk to him, okay?"

She salutes before putting another arrow into the target. I watch it split the first arrow shaft straight down the middle, wood splinters flying, before wandering through the ranks.

Max is easy to find. He's the one dancing and twirling around his opponent, a reedy brunette my age, every move made to show off his skills. As I watch, he disarms the girl with a stop thrust attack, flinging her sword high into the air before catching it in his left hand.

I snort and swoop in, plucking the weapon from his hand. "Too much flourish. You're wasting energy."

He whips around. "Wow, you sound just like *her*."

Ouch. Max knows comparing me to our mother is an easy way to wound me, but I brush his comment off and hand the girl her sword back, trying not to cringe as she slinks away, defeated.

I return my focus to Max. "Real tough guy. That girl literally just woke up from cryosleep like three days ago. She's probably never held a sword before."

"That's not why I beat her."

Somehow I manage to suppress my scoff. "I know, I know. Just . . . maybe don't go so hard on the new recruits? We're here to train them, not humiliate them into never touching a weapon again."

A lopsided smile brightens his face. "Hey, I can't help it if I'm that good."

I smack his arm. "Don't get cocky or I'll have to put you on your ass in front of your friends."

"Want to test that? I have an extra sword." He taps the sword pommel jutting from the belt at his waist.

"Nope, no time."

A flash of silver draws our attention to Bramble. He's scurrying across the grass toward me, proudly holding the arrows he's collected in the air.

"I think your bot is becoming a klepto," Max remarks.

"I think you're right." I frown at Bramble as he waves his prize at my feet, hoping the other soldiers don't notice their stolen arrows. "I blame your girlfriend."

"She's not my girlfriend." But the red splotching his face says otherwise.

I pause, a million tasks calling me back to camp. "Max, I just . . . I want to say that I'm—you . . ." I clear my throat, searching for the words. "I'm proud of you."

He fidgets with his sword, twisting on his feet. "Yeah, whatever. Thanks."

"Sure." Heat stains my cheeks, and I clear my throat again like an idiot. I want to say a million more things but I don't know how. "Your stuff packed and ready to go?"

He snorts. "Yes, *Mother*."

I barely keep from flinching this time. "Speaking of Mom," I begin, cautiously feeling out his reaction. "You need to talk to her before we leave."

"No." His eyes harden to slits, and I can almost feel the wall he puts up as he shifts his attention to his blade, twisting his sword side to side. "Never going to happen. Okay? So stop asking."

I crack my neck, countless retorts weighing down my tongue. But I know how he's feeling, and I can't make him see her. Can't erase the thousand traumas she inflicted, or the years of abandonment and anguish that followed.

"Look . . . just—you may not have another chance after this. Anything could happen tonight. I get that you don't want to talk to her, gods know I don't either, but . . . this could be your only chance."

His eyes never leave the edge of his sword as he says, "I can't, okay?" My heart aches at the pain in his voice. "And there's nothing she can say to change the fact that she left us. Just abandoned us like we were . . ." His voice breaks, and he slams his sword into his shoulder belt sheath. "Look, I don't want to talk about it, okay?"

"Okay."

I want to touch his shoulder. Wrap him in a hug. Somehow soften the anger and hurt clenching his face into a grimace of pain. Tell him I love him. But he's beyond reaching, his walls too strong after years of reinforcement.

Or perhaps I'm simply too much of a coward to try.

So I walk away and give him space, knowing to push him now on the subject, right before our big mission, isn't fair.

Later, I tell myself. *There's always later.*

TEN

I'm the first to arrive at my mother's tent. Unlike the rest of the camp's hodge-podge contraptions, it's a real tent, with windows, a cordoned off sleeping area, small kitchenette, and even a few hanging lanterns cobbled together near the center like a chandelier.

Bramble shadows me, scampering near my feet and making cooing noises at the tent's grandeur.

As soon as I see her perched in her red velvet baroque chair—procured from gods know where—a cup of tea held loosely in one hand and papers in the other, I want to turn around and escape. She wears an ivory cloak similar to the one from the Island, only black rabbit fur lines this one. A high collared blouse and dark leather pants end in polished mid-calf riding boots.

In comparison I feel like a pauper, a pretender.

She raises an eyebrow at my hesitation—or maybe at Bramble circling my legs like a loyal puppy.

I lift my head high and approach, sliding into the seat next to hers as Bramble settles on the high cushioned back. "Nice furniture, very comfy and practical."

A chuckle. She glances back down at her papers before folding them on the side table. "If you don't act the part, how will others believe you can lead them?"

"Who knew being a leader meant your ass has to be comfortable?"

She clicks her tongue. "Did prison teach you such crass talk?"

"Oh, you mean the prison where you left me to rot?"

Her face sours, her lips crumpling at the corners . . .

Thank the gods Caspian enters before she can respond, taking our attention off each other. She immediately stands to offer him tea, which he refuses.

As soon as his focus drifts to me, he plunges his hands into his pants pockets and frowns. "Lady Graystone."

"Prince Laevus."

Silence follows. Thirty seconds tick by, a minute.

Well this isn't awkward.

My mother mentions something about a map, and before I can protest, she leaves us alone. *Great one, Mom.* As if leaving Caspian and me alone together will make us fall into each other's arms.

Besides, I can't look at Caspian without remembering last night. Part of me is royally pissed that he acted that way under my command. But the other part squirms just thinking about how they were fighting over *me*.

Heat warms my cheeks, and I cross and uncross my legs, unsure where to look. Where to put my hands without appearing fidgety and embarrassed.

"Look—"

"Caspian—"

We both speak at the same time, and Caspian nods his head toward me, ever the gentleman. "You first."

"No, I . . . go ahead."

"Okay." He strides toward me until he's a few feet away,

close enough to make out the phoenix cufflinks in his sleeves, the vibrant champagne hue of his eyes. I hardly hear the muffled chirp behind me.

"I'm sorry, Maia. I should have never let him goad me into saying those things about you, and I know we embarrassed you in front of the others. I just, I want you to know that's not who I am. I'm not like *him*."

I push to my feet, mainly because with Caspian's height, it feels odd sitting. But there's also a small part of me that wants to comfort him. That can't stand to see him hurting, despite my anger over his actions. "Thank you. Apology accepted." I hesitate before adding, "You haven't seen him today, have you?"

His eyes tighten at the corners. "No—probably a good thing, considering."

"Right. I just . . . he never reported back after taking my message to Nicolai."

He seems to hesitate, fiddling with one of his cufflinks. "Maia—I don't think you should trust Riser. Someone like him, they don't have a code, an ethos. At the end of the day, you have no idea where he stands."

"He's loyal to me," I say, my tone edged with caution. "And there's no one I trust more."

"To trust someone, you have to understand them. What they want. What drives them. Who they are inside. If you can't answer those questions about Riser, then you can't trust him. Not fully."

Anger prickles my cheeks, even as part of me searches for the answers to those questions.

What does Riser want? What drives him? Revenge? Anger? Does he even know?

Perhaps sensing my hesitation, Caspian takes a step forward. "We're the same, Maia."

Before I can react, his fingers glide over mine, curling until their tips press into the palm of my hand. Bramble's feet patter on the back of the chair as he begins to pace, making strange beeping noises.

I'm too shocked to pull away as he adds, "The same thing propels us forward. We want to create a world where our people can live free of death and violence. We want peace. Can you say the same of Riser?"

I feel him before I hear him. A sensation like daggers prickling my skin. I glance over in time to see the shadows of the tent stir, and then a casual male voice says, "If you're interested in my motivations, Prince, why not just ask *me*?"

Oh, no.

At the sound of Riser's voice, Caspian's entire body goes rigid. His fingers clamp around mine, hard, and I gasp in surprise.

Riser's gaze flicks to our hands. Entwined. Intimate.

He blinks. Once.

Then he tears his eyes away to me. Whatever he feels, it's hidden behind a stone wall I can't penetrate. Not even as I rip my hand free of Caspian's and step back. Nor when I search his face with my eyes, willing him to show a shred of warmth. To explain where he's been. Why he's acting this way now.

"Sneaking into tents and skulking around shadows?" Caspian taunts. "Why am I not surprised?"

"I didn't sneak anywhere." Quiet anger barbs his voice. "You were too caught up in your *discussion* to notice me walk in. No bodyguards today, Prince?"

I don't like the way the conversation is turning, and my heart leaps wildly as I remember how quickly everything escalated last night.

"They're outside," Caspian replies, his taunting tone doing nothing to help my racing pulse. "Not that I need them to deal with you."

Before I can say a word, Lash ducks under the tent flap and wanders inside. His limp is more pronounced than usual, and his body sways side to side as he joins us, oblivious to the tension. "Is that tea?" he groans, flopping into my mother's chair. "Gods and all things holy, say it is."

For a too-long second, we all stare silently at Lash, who still has no clue what he interrupted.

Seizing the opportunity, I rush past Caspian to find the teapot on the table in the middle of the tent. My hand shakes as I pour the tea, jostling the teacup loud enough I know Riser notices. Probably Caspian too. But Riser ignores me entirely, his gaze glued to the wall where a map of the Royalist-held Northern territories hangs.

Caspian just watches me, the hand that grasped mine held slightly aloft and open.

Teagan and Flame enter next, just as I'm handing Lash his cup of tea, the porcelain cup rimmed in gold and bearing my mother's seal, two doves. Steel drips from their bodies, covered in various hues of red leather. Both wear scorpion cuffs on their ears and their hair spiked in the Rebel style, the vibrant streaks of crimson and blue making it hard to look away.

They're deep in conversation, only glancing over at us as Lash takes a sip of his tea and moans with pleasure.

Teagan winks at me, her long eyelashes fluttering over the scorpion painted around her left eye. "Darling, I'll have whatever he's having."

Flame grunts something that I think means she will too, before busying herself cataloguing her weapons.

Max and Rivet are last inside. They swagger in singing some Rebel song I don't know but sounds familiar, holding hands and acting almost drunk. Except no way they would have touched liquor right before our mission.

War drunk, my mother once called it. The high that comes

before battle, usually for those who've never actually been in a real one. My mouth falls open at the hastily wrought scorpion tattoo that darkens his chest, just above the overlarge breastplate he wears.

Mom's going to love that, I mouth.

He grins, a beaming smile I can't quite manage. Not with our mission so close. *Good,* he mouths in reply.

As soon as Max and Rivet grab cups of tea and settle down, their wild energy fading into something more somber, the air in the tent seems to grow heavy. The shadow of what lies ahead in a few short hours darkens the mood, despite the late afternoon sun lapping beneath the canvas walls and surging in through the two windows.

Flame and Teagan each take my offer of tea. After I fill their cups to the brim, they stand quietly around the table with the maps and the papers, waiting for my mother to return. Steam curls in the streams of sunlight seeping inside, and I find myself growing sleepy while watching the eddies churn the air.

After a few swigs of tea, Lash draws into himself, his red-rimmed gaze on something I can't see.

None of us can escape the ominous feeling suddenly strangling the room.

As if sensing the other's attitudes, Max and Rivet follow Flame's example, checking over their weapons. If not for my nerves, I'd laugh at the giant switchblade Max pulls out, plunking it on the table and checking the opening mechanism. Watching him now, his ease with the weapon, it's hard to remember he's only fifteen.

Fifteen. Way too young to be so proficient with a blade—or comfortable. And definitely too young for war.

I steal a breath and scan the tent. Caspian and Riser have managed to claim opposite sides of the room, and I catch them eyeing the other every few seconds like enemies forced inside the same prison cell.

For the first time ever, I'm actually glad to see my mother enter a room. She strides in, cloak whirling behind her, eyes steely with confidence. A leather-bound scroll gripped inside her hand. Without a word, she opens the case, pulls out the rolled map, and spreads it out across the table.

Her gaze snags on Max, who's suddenly found an interest in his fingernails. For a long moment, she simply stares at him. She seems about to say something, lips parted, but then she inhales deeply and turns her attention to the map.

Something about her mannerisms, her confidence, chases away the shadows weighing down the air. But then she speaks . . .

"This is the most recent map I have." There's something in her voice. Not reverence, not exactly. But close—mixed with fear. "I would have gotten it sooner, but the Emperor had it under lock and key and I just received it this morning from one of my spies."

"Map of where, exactly?" Lash asks. He's risen from the chair and limps over slowly to the table, almost as if he's afraid of the map.

"The Island."

Hot, sour bile rises in the back of my throat.

For the first time since escaping the Rebel stronghold and planning the mission, a jolt of panic bubbles beneath my ribs as I'm forced to remember the hellish place where I nearly died. Where I was made to play deadly games to amuse the Golds. Where my friend perished and I was stranded, not knowing if Riser was okay. If any of my friends survived.

Where I was drugged and interrogated and tortured until I would have gladly accepted death.

And now, against all reason, we're going back to the place that haunts my nightmares.

ELEVEN

The problem with marching to an island is, well . . . marching to an island. Because islands are surrounded by water.

My mother traces a finger over the cobalt blue lake around Emerald Island.

"Here," she says, tapping a point just north of the wall. "The drought this year means the lake is shallow enough to wade through. Just barely." She frowns at the water, the terrain, then slides the tip of her manicured finger up to circle the castle. "We should be mostly protected from sight until shore. I'll send a team ahead to take care of any lookouts, and activate our drone killers once we're in range."

"How many are marching on the castle?" Lash asks.

"Just over three thousand, plus Nicolai's two thousand." She glances at me, then lets her gaze slide to Riser. "You were right, Maia. Nicolai plans to betray us."

"How do you know?"

"Lord Thornbrook, care to elaborate?"

Riser glides forward and the others part, allowing him

access to the map. Our eyes meet, briefly, but I can't glean anything from them at all.

"When I took the message to Nicolai last night, he offered me a proposition." Again his eyes flick to me. "And I accepted."

My mouth hangs open. "Why would he believe you'd betray us?"

His lips twitch into a grin. "Because I'm obviously unhappy and underappreciated, and don't forget, a violent psychopath who can't be trusted."

"What the Fienian hell are you playing at?" Caspian growls.

Riser's grin widens, and my heart aches at how handsome he is. "Thanks to you, little brother, Nicolai believed I would turn. That because of our feud and Maia's dismissal, I was ready to betray all of you."

I tangle my arms across my chest. "Your actions—everything you said. It was a trick?"

He scrapes his hand through his hair, fisting the ends. "As soon as Nicolai appeared, I knew he'd offer you an alliance, and that it would be a trap. So I played a part. That's all."

Despite knowing he did what he had to, his actions still sting. I remember he and Caspian's fight, the way the council members stared at me with disappointment.

"You should have told me," I say, wishing immediately I'd said nothing at all. A flush warms my cheeks. This is almost worse.

Now I just look incompetent, like I was one step behind. A pawn in his plan.

"I couldn't." His hands press flat on the table, a sable-black strand of hair slipping down his forehead. "He has spies in our camp, and if I went straight to you, if I was even seen talking to you . . ."

"Enough apologies," my mother snaps. "Tell us what you learned."

Riser nods, his face growing solemn as he returns his attention back to the map. "Once our forces get here"—He circles the spot in the water just before the shoreline —"Nicolai will attack."

"How?" my mother demands.

"His plan rests on this." He pulls a handkerchief from his pocket and slowly unwraps it. A grayish-red piece of what looks like beef sits in the middle. Setting the napkin on the table, he takes a slim, wand-like device from his other pocket and runs it over the meat.

"What are we looking for?" Teagan asks, but Riser gestures with his hand to be quiet.

A sound like swarming insects cuts through the stillness. My focus settles on movement around the meat. Drawing closer, I see tiny metallic spiders emerging from the meat— thousands of them.

"Fienian hell," Flame breathes, taking a step back. "We nearly ate *that*?"

"Nanites," Riser explains. "All the meat is infected with them. They're dormant now, but the plan was to awaken them while our army was in the water. Many would die immediately as the nanites invade their organs, and the ones who didn't perish right away would—"

"Drown," I finish, a chill racing down my spine. The nanites would render our entire army unconscious. "But why?" I look to Flame, who knows Nicolai better than any of us.

All the blood has drained from her face, her eyes ringed in white. "I can't believe—can't believe he would go that far."

"He's a madman," my mother snaps. "Of course he would."

Caspian's face has darkened, and he raps his knuckles on

the table, a frown marring his lips. "And how do we know Riser can be trusted?"

"Funny," Riser says. "I was thinking the same thing about you. Will you suddenly change sides when we enter Royalist territory?"

"Well, technically this is part of Royalist territory, and yet here I am. Loyal to Maia. Can you say the same? In fact, how do we know this isn't some ruse to split our forces and weaken us?"

The tent goes quiet. Riser matches Caspian's sour expression with a deadly stare of his own.

I look at Riser until he catches my gaze. "I trust Riser and the information he gives us. I may not like the . . . method in which he tricked Nicolai into believing he would betray us, but if not for him, we would have eaten the meat and been powerless to fight back."

My mother clears her throat. "Enough discussion on the subject. Maia, it's time you go over your plan once more."

Taking a deep breath, I wave an arm over the map. "Nicolai thinks we'll drop as soon as he activates the nanites, but he has no idea how many people actually comprise our army, nor would his spies know since we haven't listed how many are staying to fight. So half our army will meet with his just past the wall, like he expects. But the other half will skirt around the mountains and, once given the signal, swoop down from the other side."

"Trapping his forces between ours," Flame says, her voice begrudgingly impressed.

"Exactly."

My mother gives me a pleased look.

"The Rebels will be outflanked and outnumbered," I add. "They'll fold quickly and be given a choice: fight against the real enemy, the Royalists, or die."

"And while the Emperor is distracted protecting the

Island," Max says, "we'll be inside." There's a hint of disappointment in his voice. "Unless you can spare me to fight with the army?"

I scoff. "Not a chance. You're with us, Max, until whatever Dad put inside you tells us where the Mercurian is."

"Then I call first dibs on the Emperor." Max gives a confident grin well beyond his years.

"Not if I get to him first," Rivet counters.

These two. I don't know whether to laugh or roll my eyes.

Caspian's gaze collapses to the floor, and I remember that we're talking about his father, even if he is a murdering tyrant. This must be incredibly hard for him. If not for my intervention, there's a possibility he'd already be on Hyperion, enjoying whatever finery that palace in the skies offers.

"If Emperor Laevus is even there," my mother says, waving her hand distractedly. "The Royalists have gone dark, all public broadcasts ceased. My sources say their mass exodus to Hyperion is imminent. Although they will send their court in waves, depending on rank."

"Then we should go now," Flame snarls, her hand tapping the dagger across her shoulder belt. "We can't win this war without his death."

My mother smiles as she glances at Flame, but I know the look is anything but sweet. "Patience, soldier. We don't require his death to win."

"I do. He killed my friend."

Cage. I shiver, remembering the beautiful, elegant soul hidden beneath his painted mask—and the man at the end. A broken, desperate soul.

"He might still be alive," I add, but the words feel stupid and naïve the second they leave my lips.

"Really?" She gives me a Flame-smile that more resembles a cat baring its fangs. "What is it, exactly, about Emperor

Laevus that gives you the idea he would keep prisoners alive?"

"We can't give up hope."

"Hope? The only hope I have left is capturing the Emperor and making him pay for his sins. Unless you want to give me the prodigal son over there instead?"

I flash her a warning look, but her blood's up and she stares down poor Caspian, who looks like a hen trapped in a cage with foxes.

"All in due time, soldier." I cringe at the patronizing tone in my mother's voice. She's misreading Flame as an angry soldier who can be placated with meaningless words.

Flame sneers at my mother. "You wouldn't be saying that because you're one of them, would you? I've seen the pictures of you and the Emperor together. One happy little Royalist family."

Crap. I expect my mother to bite back, to put Flame in her place, but she barely affords Flame an annoyed once over, like a pesky fly she's contemplating smashing or not.

"Once the asteroid is destroyed and we have control of the Royalists territories," she explains, "the Emperor and his court of Golds won't have a home to come back to. They'll be forgotten rulers stuck on a ship without a future, destined to float in space for eternity. That almost seems more fitting than death, wouldn't you agree . . . Flame?"

Flame opens her mouth to argue, but then seems to think better about it, muttering expletives under her breath.

Caspian's jaw sets, and he says, "If my father is gone, he'll have left Victoria in charge. If anyone needs to pay for the actions of my court, it's her."

The Archduchess. The way my mother stills at the name, she fears her almost as much as I do.

"Once inside," my mother says, "everyone must protect Maia and Max. Without them, the Mercurian is lost. Caspian and Flame, you'll guard Maia. Riser and Rivet, you're on Maximus."

Teagan frowns, but my mother adds, "Teagan and Lash, your only task is to find the castle gates and open them." Her finger hovers over the castle on the map until it nears the east end, then she circles a tiny spot. "Here is the gate. Open that and the battle will be lost for the Royalists before it can even begin."

We all stare at the map, and I can almost hear everyone's hearts hammering beneath their leathers and armor as the time approaches to leave. I focus on the dark blue waters vignetting the inner edge of the map, and then farther in. Studying the castle. Trying to commit everything to memory.

My focus snags on a large shaded rectangle that runs along the center of the castle all the way to the outer edges of the Island. "What's that?"

My mother flicks a glance to where I'm pointing and frowns, obviously as clueless as I am to its identity.

Caspian's eyes narrow on the shaded icon, and he seems to hesitate before adding, "My father—the Emperor has an underground shelter in place, in case there was ever an emergency or Pandora's effects hit earlier than projected and we were trapped there."

I make a mental note to find it and search it for food and supplies, after we've taken the castle.

"Would you like to say anything else before we go, Maia?" my mother asks. "A rallying speech, perhaps?"

A speech? I swallow. I can almost hear the speech my mother would give, full of hope and confidence. But the idea makes me queasy for some reason. *Who am I to speak?*

"Okay." It's impossible to miss the disappointment in my mother's voice. She taps her fingers on the table, hard enough that we all go quiet. "One more thing."

My heart skips a beat as I read her tense expression, the lines deepening on her forehead.

"While I don't have the location of the Mercurian, I do know it has a timeline for when it's safe to use. By my calculations, we have just under four days to activate it and destroy Pandora."

"Bloody Fienian hell," Lash mutters.

I exhale, trying to hide my shock. "When were you going to tell me that?"

"When it became relevant."

"Okay, now that it's relevant, what happens if we go past the deadline?" Part of me doesn't want to know, even as I lean forward to hear her answer.

"Once that time passes, the Mercurian will need to use a higher power to completely destroy Pandora."

I raise an eyebrow.

"That power will kill whoever operates the device, as well as destroy the surrounding land for hundreds of miles."

A collective gasp erupts in the room.

Awesome. I shove the looming deadline deep down into the place where I store all the what-ifs and move on. Once we're in the castle with Max, his map should activate, leading us to the Mercurian immediately.

Simple and easy. No need for waiting and deadlines.

On that note, we all leave to finish last minute preparations. Both Riser and Caspian angle in my direction, but my mother waves them away and pulls me to the side.

In this light, the lines etched into her pale skin seem deep as cuts. "I'm trusting you with Max. Keep him safe."

"What about me?" I ask, trying to keep the hurt from my voice. "My blood bleeds just as easily as his."

"You've . . . seen things. Done things. *Things* your brother has not. He's not ready for what's coming."

"Things? You mean like murder?" Merida's face flashes in

my mind. "Don't worry, I'll keep him safe and his hands clean."

My throat aches with emotion, but I leave before she can see the tears inexplicably stinging my eyes. She might as well have said I'm broken. That, while Max can still be saved, there's no hope for me.

I think I hear her call out for me, but I don't look back.

As soon as the sun hits my face, Lash grabs my arm. I quickly brush away any tears that escaped.

His cheeks sag, eyes shiny with fatigue, and he blinks against the setting sun. "You know, before I met her, I didn't understand why you never mentioned your mom."

I chuckle, the sound frayed from holding back tears. "And now?"

"Now—let's just say I get why you didn't talk about her." He glances around. "She's . . ."

"Intense?"

"Terrifying." He grimaces as if just the thought of my mother makes him uncomfortable, his copper eyebrows lowering. "Why are all high-ranking Golds so intimidating? Her demeanor, the way she talks, as if she takes for granted that everyone will listen the moment she speaks."

"Because they usually freaking do."

"She reminds me of the Gold who had me whipped, love. And that's not a compliment."

"I don't think she's as bad as that, although when I was six I would have argued the opposite." But Lash is staring off into space. "Hey, you never said who he was, the man who did . . . *that* to you."

"I refuse to say the bastard's name. Or his daughter's. But if I see them inside . . . " A rush of air escapes his chest, and he clears his throat. "Enough talk. I'll go grab my things and meet you in ten."

"See you." I watch him go, hobbling on his stiff leg as he weaves through the tents, his face a tight grimace of pain.

I can't help but think how every person in camp has a story like Lash's. Like Flame, Riser, Teagan. A loved one lost, an injustice done, a humility cruelly suffered.

And every single person here has a reason to wish the Emperor punished and the Royalists destroyed.

"Please," I whisper to any gods who might be listening. "Let us finally have our revenge."

TWELVE

The silver-blue veil of night has fallen by the time we make it to the Swifters that will take us to the tunnel. All are marred with age, their emerald colors sun-bleached and rusted, nothing like the shiny toys Nicolai keeps.

But they purr to life on the first try, their engines like angry hornets swarming from their nest. I hesitate when I notice there are only four—the rest being used for the army's supplies.

I glance at Max, but he's already hopped on the back of the matted silver machine Rivet claimed. Teagan and Lash share a Swifter that must have once been red but now more resembles the color of rust. Both Caspian and Riser have already chosen the two Swifters on opposite ends, and they watch me quietly.

Waiting for my choice.

Flame grins, muttering, "I know which Prince I'm pick-ing," before she hops on the back of Riser's vehicle.

Thank the gods I don't have to publicly choose between them. Caspian holds out a hand for me. As I take it, his flesh smooth and warm, I feel Riser watching us. Bramble stirs from his perch on my back.

Caspian's midnight-black Swifter still has most of its paint, and the shiny lacquer coating remains, for the most part. It doesn't take long for its impressive engine to heat up, warming the flesh of my thighs.

He hands me a tiny earpiece radio. "To communicate," he adds. Apparently we each have a channel. He doesn't need to explain why.

If one of us is caught, the Royalists could use a shared channel to spy on us.

Bramble settles on the seat behind me. He moves around, trying to find a comfortable position in the tiny space before chirping his displeasure. I pat my shoulder and he scurries back up my arm.

"You're so spoiled," I whisper.

Last second before we take off down the hillside, Caspian reaches his arms back, finds my hands, and slides them around his waist.

"For your safety," he murmurs, his voice sending my heart clattering against its bony cage.

My grip is light until, without warning, the Swifter lurches forward and screams down the hill. Jerked backward, I tangle my arms around his body and press my chest into his back. It would be easier to rest my head on his shoulder, but that feels wrong. Too intimate.

Even if I'm actively resisting the physical urge to melt into him. His strange, alluring familiarity.

Stupid matched feelings.

We don't use our lights, and even with the moonlight, the landscape is a shadowy blur. Caspian slips on a pair of night goggles, the dark band wrapping around his golden hair. Then he hands me a pair.

As soon as I don them, my world transforms into hues of

green ranging from emerald to near-black. Trees appear as we cut through the forest. The path is thin so we line up with Riser in the lead. Other than the lulling growl of the Swifters, the night is quiet.

"Comfortable?" a sultry voice teases through the earpiece.

Riser. I automatically loosen my grip on Caspian. "Maybe."

A little growl. "Can I talk to you in the tunnel?"

"You're talking to me now."

Caspian tilts his head back. "What?"

"Nothing," I say, cutting my eyes at Riser ahead as he veers to the right, taking a curve hard. From this angle, I can't make out his expression, only the side of his face. The corner of his mouth is tilted up.

"I'd like to speak in private," Riser says. "Without your arms wrapped around my brother."

"I'll just pretend he's you," I whisper, my joke falling flat.

"Don't pretend too hard." A pause. "So? Meet me inside?"

"Yes."

It feels like a day passes before we make it to the tunnel entrance, although I know enough about adrenaline to understand how it warps time. Makes it either go by in a blink or stretched out like taffy.

The hole where I emerged after escaping the Island the last time, when I had enough sense to flee the place, shows up as a pitch-black semi-circle in my goggles.

We park the Swifters inside, hauling each heavy machine through the hole one at a time. When we're done, sweat wets my forehead and chest, and I'm breathing hard.

"Just think," Lash says, grunting as he helps drop the last Swifter to the tunnel floor. "In a few short hours, the war will be over, Pandora will be gone, and I can take a proper bath with hot water that doesn't stink like the river."

Teagan prods his ribs with her elbow. "Believe me, Lash, we'll all be overjoyed by the prospect."

Flame and Riser check over the cache of Hot Weapons Riser stole from Nicolai—it's all still here. We fill our packs with a variety of devices, each one able to kill us in gruesome and unique ways if accidentally set off.

Riser finishes stuffing my pack, carefully, then meets my stare. "Watch out with those."

"Yep." I give a rueful smile. "You know how much I love them."

My hint at my fiasco with Hot Weapons in the Blood Court isn't lost, and Riser's lips twist sideways. He hesitates, then slips his night vision goggles up his forehead until his hair sticks up in wild angles. A lumen lifts from his palm and fills the air with buttery-gold light.

"Can we talk?" he asks. All the bluster gone from his voice.

I glance over at the others, who are doing an expert job of pretending they aren't watching us. "Sure. But we have to hurry."

The lumen bobs just above Riser's head. It follows us, casting our shadows over the walls as we find a spot near the right of the entrance, away from the others. A tiny river cuts through the rocks and across the floor, filling the chamber with the tinkling of running water.

"I'm sorry," Riser begins. "I know I took a risk when I fought with Caspian in front of the council. If there was a way to tell you, I would have."

"I know." I fiddle with the side zipper of my backpack. "I'm not angry about that."

"I don't believe you." He leans in close, sending my heart fluttering sideways in my chest.

"Okay, sure. I don't enjoy you using our relationship as a distraction, or publicly making use of Caspian and my . . .

former match. Even if it advanced our cause, it was still wrong."

"You're right."

"And the way things escalated," I say, cringing at the memory of Riser and Caspian's argument. "Not all of that was a façade."

"Oh, you mean the part where my half-brother called my mother a whore?" Riser's eyes glimmer with barely bridled anger. "Or the part where he said I don't deserve you?"

I twist on my toes, unsure how to respond.

"Is that it, then?" Riser persists. "Or is there another reason you have trouble looking at me now?"

"Why did you disagree with me?" I stop messing with my zipper and move on to the hem of my shirt. "When we voted."

"Because it was the right move." Caution lines his voice. "Look, I'll never be the guy who agrees with everything you say and blindly takes your orders. If you want that, my brother's right there."

"Stop." Bramble fidgets on my shoulder, and I lower my voice. "I don't want you to feel like you have to agree with me, and I don't want *him*."

His voice frays as he says, "Are you sure about that? You're matched, your DNA perfectly complementary or some Royalist propaganda bull-crap."

"I don't care about that."

"Then what, Maia?" His hands come up, find my jaw. The warmth is wonderful, delicious, and I want to melt into it. One of his thumbs strokes my jaw.

"I . . ."

He arches a jet-black eyebrow, his eyes soft. "Whatever it is, you can tell me."

"I—I don't know." I shake my head. Everything is coming out wrong. "When I'm with you, you're so strong and you know exactly what to say. What to do. You never hesitate. But I don't have that. It's not . . . I just need to figure out where I stand. Without my mother or—or anyone else."

His hands drop. His face could be a statue for all the emotion he's showing. "Anyone else? You mean me?"

"C'mon, lovebirds," Flame growls, her voice echoing off the tight walls. "Get your asses back here!"

The others are waiting for us. This is basically the worst time ever to have this conversation. *You're a genius, Maia.* I wish I could unload my brain into his, wish I could explain things the right way.

"Maia, I understand you're going through a lot, but I'm not giving up on you. On us." Riser's hand is outstretched. Waiting for mine. A declaration that we're okay.

I hesitate. "I can't—I need . . . time. To stand on my own. To prove to myself that I can."

His hand falls.

I feel like puking as four more lumens fill the air, chasing away our shadows and exposing the hurt written all over his face. The air seems to thin as I set off deep into the tunnel toward the castle. Riser stays behind, creating distance between us. Our footfalls merging into the cadence of my racing heartbeat.

When we near the first wall the Royalists erected to keep people like us out, Riser's voice crackles in my frequency. "I'll give you all the time you need, Maia. You should figure out who you are, and if that means without me, so be it. Just remember, time's the one thing in this world none of us are guaranteed."

I open my mouth to respond, but the correspondence ends with a crackle.

THIRTEEN

The walls crumple in on themselves, bucking and pitting before disappearing. Each time Flame throws the Hot Weapon, the world goes noiseless for a few ticks of my heart. And then there's a rumble and the tunnel clears.

Once again, I'm reminded how much I despise Hot Weapons.

With the paths cleared, we make good time. By Teagan's pocket watch—a present from her father—it's not even midnight when we clear the final wall and find the door Caspian and I came through just over a week ago. Except then we'd been enemies and I was fleeing the Island, not running toward it.

I blow out a breath as we flatten against the walls on either side of the door leading into the famed Red Tunnel. Memories of me stumbling through its dank corridors, in between some maniacal torture session, twists my gut.

Lash draws near, careful not to touch the lichen and sludge darkening the stone.

"Trying to look pretty for someone?" I tease.

"Hey, you never know when you need to look your best,"

Lash replies, totally serious. His gaze slides from Riser to me. "You okay, love?"

"Dandy. You?"

"Gods, I can't stop daydreaming about that bath." He winks, his stare shifting to Riser. "By the sound of things, you may be free to help bathe me after all."

I snort. "Glad even breaking into the Emperor's castle can't dampen your humor."

"It's a gift . . ." But he can't hide the fear tightening the corners of his lips.

Max slides against the wall between us. "Stop hitting on my sister, Lash. It's gross."

Grinning, I capture Max in a hug before he can get away. He squirms in my arms, his breath hot on my cheek.

"Let go," he growls.

"I'm trying to say I love you, dummy." I squeeze him until he stills. "Don't do anything stupid, okay?"

He finally wins the battle and escapes, fixing his hair and readjusting the weapons that adorn his body. He's nearly bigger than me, his limbs in that gangly too-long stage teetering between adolescence and adulthood.

When did he grow up?

"Why do you have to be so annoying?" he mutters in that half-boy half-man tone.

I need to let him go. I know that, yet I can't. Not yet.

"Because," I say, voice raw with emotion, "I'm your big sister. That's my job."

Rolling his eyes, he takes his place near Rivet. The two of them immediately trade punches before falling into conversation.

He'll be fine, Maia. He might be an idiot when it comes to girls and other stuff, but he's ready for this.

I rest against the stone as Flame works on the door standing between us and the tunnel. This time she uses something that eats a cavernous hole through the three-inch-thick metal door.

When it's done, the door is partially melted, molten bits of iron dripping down the sides.

"Well, that's one way to open a door," Teagan remarks as we slip through, each one of us dropping our packs through first to fit.

At this point, we're all quiet. Contemplating the task at hand.

The tunnel is just like I remember it, right down to the moldy floors, guttering torches, and mildew stench. As soon as all of us are inside, we look expectantly at Max.

Rivet peers into his face, examining him.

He shoves her away. "I'm not a freak show, Rivet."

"Sorry." She cuts her eyes at me. "What are we looking for?"

"We need to be inside the castle for it to work," I say, hoping it's true. Saying the truth—we have no idea how to activate his map . . . or even if it's still accessible—isn't exactly confidence inspiring.

Max beams. "So you're saying I'm integral to this mission's success?"

I swat his arm. "Get over yourself. We all are."

"The door to the first floor is up here!" Caspian calls. He's jogged ahead and perches on a steep set of stairs, half his body in shadow. I faintly recall climbing up the same stairs back when I thought I was going to die.

Not that I'm so sure now anything is different.

Lash clicks his tongue, his boots squelching against the wet stone. "What are we waiting for? A signal?"

"No, just—" A muffled thud cuts me off, followed by reverberations that shake the walls and rain dust over us. "*That.* We were waiting for that."

Another explosion rattles the air, softened by the layer of

dirt and stone around us. A mental image of my mother leading the charge of our army comes to mind. They must have made it past the water and are now on shore.

"What I wouldn't give to see the Puppet Master's face when he tried to activate the nanites," Flame says.

We all laugh, but it dies quickly, leaving only a sense of nervous excitement that feels too big to fit inside my chest. *You can do this, Maia.*

"Go time," Riser orders.

My heart thuds wildly and my mouth goes paper-dry as we rush up the stairs. Caspian shoulders open the door with a creak. Past him, a wide hallway appears, the candles burnt down and shadows thick.

For a terrifying moment, I think Caspian betrayed us and someone will be waiting on the other side. But there's no one. Just an empty stretch of corridor lined with a frayed carpet runner and a few dusty gold drapes.

From the other end of the hallway, worried voices call out.

"What if they come this way?" Flame snarls. A Hot Weapon shaped like a pyramid glints in her palm, ready to throw.

"Put that away." Caspian closes her fingers over the device. "In events such as this, civilians who can't fight are trained to take refuge in the underground shelters. You know, women and children?"

She reluctantly pockets the weapon and we pad down the stone corridors. Something begins to glow, not a torch . . . the light's too blue for firelight.

I glance around, searching for the source . . .

And freeze. Everyone else has too. All of us focused on Max and the stream of light pouring from his eyes. Bramble coos, once, in awe.

"What's happening?" Max whispers. Gone is the bravado, the soldier's confidence. He's scared.

I grab his hand and squeeze, my gaze riveted to the light emanating around his head. "It's okay, Max. It's just the map. This is what we needed."

Memories of the day our father implanted the map inside Max flood me. It was just before dinner. We'd been playing a game . . .

"Max, what game was Dad's favorite?" His hand has begun to shake, and I grip it tighter, clenching until it stops quivering. "Remember? With that light?"

"No," Max breathes, the shadow of memory darkening his face. "It was an orb. He used to hide things and we'd have to unravel puzzles to find them. The orb's light would change colors the closer we got to the hidden object."

"What color did it turn when we were headed in the right direction?" I ask, unable to take my eyes off the beautiful blue light flickering just above him.

"Blue, like the ocean. He said it was the color of my eyes." His lips press together and his eyes seem to look through the stone walls into something beyond. "I think . . . I think we have to go right."

The walls shudder around us, the windowpanes rattling. "Let's go!" I order. "The blue means we're going in the right direction."

My body thrums with excitement as we race through the hallways. Max jogs in a daze, his eyes unfocused as he follows some map only he can see. His arms held out and fingers splayed, like a blind man trying to find his way.

The blue light confirms we're going the right way. Every time Max hesitates or second guesses the direction and takes a wrong turn, the blue fades into a bright warning yellow.

Once, when we veer totally off course and turn back the other way, the light changes into an angry red.

As we weave deeper and deeper into the castle, the walls

rumbling and shaking, screams shredding the night, hope takes over. The Mercurian is here. It's *close*.

Once it's activated . . .

I can't imagine a world without Pandora's ominous shadow darkening it. Without the promise of death hanging over us all. Can't let myself dare dream of what it would be like.

We hit a fork in the hallway, and Lash and Teagan branch off toward where Caspian says a courtyard awaits. Beyond that are the doors inside the outer wall that will let in our army. I squeeze both their shoulders before they depart, trying to express in a touch what I should say in words.

Be careful. I can't fight this war without you.

We press on. Fleeing courtiers pass us on their way down the stairs, but they hardly even spare us a glance. The few times they do, Caspian flashes a steady, determined look that convinces them we're okay.

They want to believe it—so much so that they force themselves to ignore the light emanating from Max's eyes and splashing across the walls.

Then again, it's hard to see much when you're terrified. Each time, I have to look away from the fear plastered on their faces. Most probably thought they would be on a flight to Hyperion soon. This is the last thing they expected.

The corridors open up and Max leads us to a part of the castle I recognize from our hazing. We pause near the door that leads to the great hall, and a wave of emotion from that day threatens to crash over me.

Max blinks and turns a half circle—

My comm crackles in my ear, making me jump.

"We're in trouble!" Teagan's breathless voice struggles to stay composed as the reception goes in and out, giving me tidbits. "Centurions . . . too many . . . hurt."

"Who's hurt?" I demand. The others must be able to hear too because they all go rigid, breath drawn.

"Lash."

I think of all the reasons I should keep on course, but even as I do, I know there's no way in Fienian hell I'm leaving Lash to die. Bramble must be thinking the same thing because he leaps to the floor, beeping frantically.

"I'm coming," I say into the comm. "Caspian, you're with me." Riser puts a hand out but I shake my head. "Get Max to the Mercurian. Once you have the location, let me know."

He gives me a searching look, as if evaluating my resolve. Whatever he sees, he decides it's best not to argue. "Be careful."

I try to think of a smart retort. But nothing comes, and all I can do is draw my sword and force a grim smile as I take off in a sprint toward the courtyard.

FOURTEEN

I find Teagan and Lash halfway across the outer courtyard, pinned down by six Centurions. The Centurions carry pistols, the muzzles flashing as they shoot at my friends going off in erratic spurts that match my heartbeat.

Each pop of orange, each following thud as the bullets ricochet off stone pillars, knocks the oxygen from my lungs. Across the wall, screams shred the air, the occasional cannon or gunshot far enough away it sounds like fireworks. I crouch near a hedge maze, the sounds of war and death bringing back unwanted memories of the bombing.

You're okay, Maia.

Caspian grabs my collar and tugs me to my feet. *When did I kneel?*

We're partially hidden by neatly trimmed hedges that lead out to a gazebo. Pale purple blossoms of wisteria, lavender, and clematis thread through the wooden slats of the gazebo and scent the air.

They can't mask the tang of smoke and blood.

Caspian's breath wheezes out hard and fast beside me,

bent over his knees as he tries to catch his breath. "We have to . . . sneak up on them."

I nod. Of course he's right. They have guns while we have swords. And Hot Weapons, but I don't even consider the horrible little devices practically burning a hole in my backpack.

Not yet.

Bent low, we wind through the garden toward the Centurions. Teagan and Lash are twenty feet away from the soldiers, shielded by the bowl of a fountain. Horses rise in the middle, their sharp marble hooves clawing the sky.

I catch sight of Teagan's dark hair swaying as she first peers around the fountain . . . then leaps out to run. Her backpack lies fallen in the courtyard halfway between her and the Centurions.

One of the soldiers yells. They all take aim at the same time and shoot. My entire body goes still, each bullet that strafes the gravel at her feet seemingly in slow motion. One hits a stone paver and bounces off with a tiny *thunk*.

A second later, she grabs her arm and cries out. My brain takes a moment to process that the dark stain spreading across her shirt is blood. That she's hurt, maybe badly.

I realize I'm yelling just as Caspian slams a hand over my mouth. My upper lip scrapes my teeth; coppery blood prickles my taste buds.

He holds up a finger to his mouth and removes his hand. I nod, relief flooding me as Teagan scrambles across the stones back to where Lash must be sitting and disappears.

I tune my frequency to hers. "Teagan, how badly are you hurt?"

A long moment of silence stretches out. "A flesh wound, darling. Where are you?"

Her voice doesn't convince me, not nearly. "We're here,

fifty meters two o'clock. Stay put and wait till we give the signal."

"Yes, ma'am." Her voice sounds tired. "Shouldn't you be with Max?"

"I'm right where I should be." A burst of lightheadedness spins my vision. I let my head fall back as I exhale, trying to work some calm into my body. "How's Lash?"

"Whining and complaining." Lash's voice barks in the background, something like "how would she like to be shot in the ass?"

I stifle a laugh. "Tell Lash we're coming . . . just give us a minute. I'm sending over a friendly face."

"Careful, darling."

Pressing my hand to my chest, I feel the racing boom of my heart. Then I concentrate on slowing the thud-thud-thud until it stops rattling my sternum and my vision stops dancing.

"Bramble," I whisper.

Bramble pops up from underfoot and watches me expectantly.

"You need to provide a distraction while we move closer. Can you go to Teagan and Lash? Once you get there you protect them until I collect you."

His antennae flash green for yes.

"Good. Be careful . . ." I remember Rivet's new upgrades to Bramble. He hasn't tried out his lasers yet . . . but I can't stomach him being a weapon when he feels more like my kid. "And no hurting the soldiers."

Red flashes. *No.*

"Okay, no hurting them unless it's in self-defense protecting Lash and Teagan."

Without agreeing, he scuttles off across the stones toward the fountain.

I crack my neck and motion to Caspian. "Let's go!"

On our hands and knees, we slide along the ground sideways. It doesn't take the soldiers long to spot Bramble's silver body as he makes his way to them, ten feet out. The little sensor actually stops and sends a barrage of angry, taunting chirps at them.

One of the Centurions lifts his revolver and shoots.

My heart slams into my throat. *Bramble!*

But he dodges the bullet, and a spray of gravel bursts a few feet away.

Bramble turns his back to the Centurions, waves his rump in defiance, and then rushes to the fountain.

That's my boy.

Relief propels me the last few feet to a moss-veiled mausoleum that partially hides us from view. A stagnant, musty scent drenches the air. Stretching out from the building's doors is a rectangular pool flickering with koi, their orange and white bodies nearly hidden by lily pads. Lights glow beneath the water.

Caspian nods to the pond, and I don't even hesitate before slipping in. Lily pads bump against my elbows, the koi darting away from my legs. The water laps at my waist, surprisingly cold. Cattails rise up on the other side, masking our approach from the Centurions.

Near the end, I set my backpack on the side of the pool and drop low. Crouched, my sword scraping the scummy bottom of the pond, I push through the fronds and thick cattails. Caspian's breath whooshes in my ear as he follows, breathing too hard for my comfort.

"You okay?" I whisper.

He hardly glances in my direction. "Yeah."

The Centurions are on the other side, not ten feet away. I can hear them, their voices tinny with excitement as they decide who will finish off my friends.

"The Rebels are hurt," the biggest one says, clapping a

younger Centurion on the shoulder. "Just walk up there and put a bullet in their skulls."

"You saw that thing that joined them," the younger one says. "You do it."

He has brown hair that scrapes his chin and young, wide eyes, his lips surprisingly full. He would be handsome, if not for his silver uniform with the phoenix insignia.

I turn to Caspian, but he's frozen. Long golden lashes flutter as he blinks at the soldiers. "I think I—I might know him. He trained with me once."

Shit. "Okay, Caspian. Listen to me. We need a diversion so they can get away and open the doors."

It's like he doesn't hear me. His focus stuck on the soldiers. The handsome one has stopped arguing and begins checking his pistol for bullets. He closes the chamber with a casual flick of his wrist that hints he's been in numerous situations just like this one.

A tiny voice inside my head whispers, *he needs to be the first to die.*

We have to do something. My mind goes blank. I can't think. We don't have enough time. "Caspian, we need to—"

He shifts as if startled, his elbow knocking against a cat-sized rock. The rock dislodges and falls into the water with a loud *plop.*

Great.

"What was that?" the bigger Centurion growls. He swings around, his beady eyes narrowed as he scans the water. His gaze snags on us. Slowly, recognition flashes across his face.

Followed by rage.

He comes at us in a full sprint, his pistol pointed at my head. My body freezes for a half-second, then I duck on instinct. At the same moment, a bang discharges. It's so loud it rattles my skull, my chest.

I think my eardrums explode.

The concrete side of the pool behind my head erupts. Shrapnel hits me, drawing blood. But adrenaline masks the pain so I only feel a strange numbness. My ears ring and ring.

The Centurion is raising his pistol again. In shock, I focus on the pale gray smoke drifting from the muzzle. The spittle wetting the man's lips.

Caspian shoves me to the side as the Centurion shoots again. This time, I feel the bullet whiz past my cheek.

Get your shit together, Maia.

Fear breaks the trance, and I yank my sword up. Water flies off its blade and forms beautiful patterns in the air as I perform a series of strikes that just miss the Centurion's legs. Face red and twisted with rage, he levels his gun point blank at my face.

I can smell the tinny smoke, the gunpowder.

There's a clack as the hammer pulls back. *Ohnono—*

Click. Nothing happens.

Misfire.

I slam the sword down on his arm, but he catches it by the blade inside his giant hand. Blood drips down the edge, but he holds firm. A howl of pain rips from his throat. I try to jerk my sword back but he's too strong.

In one hard twist, he yanks my sword from my hand and sends it flying. Murder glints inside his eyes.

"Caspian," I breathe.

But he's frozen, looking from me to the guards. His mouth parted like a stupid fish and his breathing ragged and gods, *gods* I could kill him right now.

The youngest Centurion takes a step toward Caspian. "Prince?"

The others stop looking at me and glance at him. I can see from their shocked expressions they recognize him.

"Prince Caspian," the biggest Centurion says. "Are you being held captive?"

"Caspian," I whisper. Pleading with him. "Caspian!"

He doesn't look at me. He refuses.

Max is still waiting for me. Riser and the others are all counting on me to show up and activate the Mercurian.

Rage opens up inside me—a well of deep, limitless rage.

I will not die today.

Using their focus on the Prince, I inch backward until the backpack is within reach. My heart slams into my throat, my entire body numb. This has to work. It *has* to.

I lunge.

At the same time, a blur of silver streaks for the biggest Centurion. Bramble! He claws around the Centurion's head, poking and scraping with his legs as the Centurion screams.

In one smooth motion I have the zipper yanked open and a Hot Weapon in my hand. One of the Centurions yells. I stare at the innocuous looking device in my palm. An ender, same as the ones Flame used to take out the walls.

The Centurions raise their weapons, but they're weak, and they hesitate, afraid to hit Caspian.

I don't. The second I throw the weapon, fear appears in their eyes. I call Bramble to me and lunge for Caspian, grabbing hold of his sleeve and jerking him backward. As I feel Bramble wrap around my neck, I use Caspian like a shield to keep them from shooting.

He lets me, going almost limp as all three of us sink into the cold water.

For a drawn-out second, the rush of air bubbles is the only sound. I half expect the Centurions to unload their weapons and shoot us anyway—but thank the gods, they still think the Prince is with them.

Maybe he is.

Above the water, there's a whoosh. Pressure builds around us. Invisible hands of death pulling, trying to draw us forward. The koi's slick bodies dance across my cheeks and arms as they try to get away from the surface. Four get too close and are sucked into the air. Gone in a second.

Bramble chirps in alarm, his branchlike legs digging into my flesh. I flail against the walls, skinning my knuckles and bruising my knees, pulling Caspian and Bramble deeper toward the bottom. A burst of light blinds me . . .

Then silence.

An ache fills my lungs. I'm going to swallow water if we don't surface. Shoving Caspian, I lurch up, coughing and gasping and dry heaving. Caspian pulls himself to the side and flops on his back. When wet, his hair is wheat-colored, and it's plastered in all directions, his legs resting half-in and half-out of the water. One arm drapes across his chest.

His hand is a trembling, white-knuckled fist over his heart.

I glance at where the Centurions stood, searching for any remaining threat. But they're gone. Just *gone*.

"I'm sorry," Caspian mutters, hacking up water. "I couldn't."

I stare at him for a second, trying to catch my breath as Teagan and Lash hobble over. Trying to sift through my emotions enough to know how to deal with what just happened.

Still clutching my neck, Bramble shivers violently. His lights flash red in a wild rhythm, pulsing in my periphery.

"You okay?" Teagan demands. She's purposefully looking away from the flattened grass where the Centurions once stood.

I nod, fiddling with my ear comm. But the water must have fried it.

I yank the device out. "Teagan, is yours working?"

Teagan tries hers, waiting a moment before shaking her head. After a pointed look at Lash, who's holding his butt and making a big deal of limping more than usual, he checks his and says the same.

"Crap. They should be answering." I glance over to the castle, not sure what I'm looking for. "Lash, give me yours. I'll circle back to where I left them. Maybe it's a distance thing."

"Maybe." But the edge in Teagan's voice gets under my skin.

A rapid succession of gunshots pepper the air outside the wall. A horse whinnies. Screams erupt and then die.

Teagan finishes wrapping a strip of her cape around her wounded arm and picks up her sword. "You should go, Maia. If they've found the Mercurian, they'll need you."

"Did you have to vaporize them?" Lash groans, toeing the flattened grass. "We needed their pistols."

"You're welcome," I mutter.

"Sorry, love." Lash looks me over from head to toe. "You hurt?"

"No."

"What about him?" Lash nods to Bramble.

Bramble answers with a few weak *cheeps*.

"He's tough," I add, translating for the sensor. "He'll be okay."

"Good."

All of us glance down at the Prince, who's now sitting up with his head propped in his hands. His mouth gapes wide, his chest heaving, as if he can't get enough air.

I offer him my hand. "Caspian, you have to get up. I need you to help them open the doors to the wall."

He glances up at me. A heartbeat ticks by while I wait for him to acknowledge he heard my command. Finally, he nods and I tug him to a stand.

I lean in and whisper into his ear, "I trust you."

He stares at something just beyond me. "Maybe you shouldn't."

"I don't have a choice." On impulse, I brush my lips across his cheek. Maybe if he feels our connection—maybe if he thinks I feel the same way about him, he won't freeze next time. Won't forget who's side he's on now. "You can do this."

Something flares to life inside his eyes, and he pins me with a determined stare. "I'll keep them safe."

As I pivot to go, Teagan grabs my arm. "Darling, be careful. Without you . . . we have no future."

"Got it." I force a grin. "No pressure, right?"

Then I sprint to the castle, serenaded by explosions and my thundering heart.

FIFTEEN

By the time I reach the door of the great hall where I left them earlier, I know something is wrong.

The castle is silent, empty. The only sound the occasional muffled roar from the battle outside and the squeak of my wet boots against the stone floor. I tune the comm to each of the Rebel frequencies as I slink down the corridor, passing antechambers and storage rooms.

A large hall I don't remember opens up, and I peek around the door frame.

The moment my gaze snags on the body curled on the floor, I go cold. A wave of alarm washing over me. The Centurion's eyes stare blankly at the ceiling. Half-dried blood congeals in a puddle around him.

Another Centurion slumps over on his knees. His hands still clawed over his cheeks, where several enormous red lumps appear. Bramble hits the floor with a light tap and approaches, his antennae pointed at the body.

Freezing, he emits a single, loud beep, reaches his arm out, and snags something by the dead Centurion. The broken body of a scorpion . . . just like the ones used on us in the Blood Court.

My friends were here. I scan the floor for other clues, but other than a few dried spots of blood, there's nothing in this room that can tell me what happened or where they went.

"Bramble," I whisper, "they have to be okay."

For the first time, he doesn't have a sassy reply. And I swear I can make out sadness and worry in his features.

Please let them be okay. Please.

I can't breathe. Can't think. Terror floods my veins, filling me with horrible scenarios. I scramble from the room and keep searching, clenching my stomach to keep from puking.

A crackle startles me. The comm. Words, jumbled and frantic, tumble in my ear. I can't make them out. Can't hear them properly.

Then, like the lid of a jar being removed, they suddenly come across crystal clear. "Maia, are you there?"

"Riser?" *Oh, gods. He's okay.* "Riser, where are you?"

"Trap. Don't come." Roaring, high-pitched shrieks muffle his words.

What? "Riser, tell me where you are!"

"Taken." His voice is raspy and frayed with pain, and I begin to run—even though I have no idea where to go. "Stay . . . away."

"Riser, please!" I have no idea where to go, how to help him. I feel helpless. Powerless. I fall against a wall, sliding halfway down before catching myself. "Max? Tell me he's okay."

Silence. Then a garbled word comes across the comm that rips the air from my lungs. "Archduchess."

My body reacts to the word, flooding my brain with memories of my torture. I see a hammer coming down on my knee. My elbow. My stomach. I see myself being pieced back together again. Being drugged, starved. Ridiculed.

I hear the Archduchess's cruel laugh, and nausea punches the back of my throat as I groan and slide the rest of the way down the wall. I'm the helpless girl from the pit. The girl she captured and tortured. I want to hide.

No one can hurt me if I hide.

Bramble crawls up my legs and chirps frantically, but I barely hear him. My brain struggles to come to terms with this new, horrifying reality. The Archduchess—the Archduchess has Max. My friends.

My friends are in *trouble*.

I lurch to my feet. Riser said not to come.

To Fienian hell with that.

"Where are they, Bramble?"

I focus on the noises I heard, the whining roar of . . . an engine. Countless machines—crafts. And only one place I know has that many.

The roof.

My boots slam against the stone as I sprint upstairs and through hallways, slamming open doors. A set of steep stairs opens up before me.

Have to find them have to find them have to—

A body lays on the stairs. I glance down—and my heart sinks. I recognize the mahogany hair immediately. "Oh, no." I whisper. "Rivet."

No response. She's facedown, arm outstretched, and I'm terrified to touch her—to know if she's injured or dead. "Rivet."

Braving my fear, I squeeze her shoulder. Her body is warm. I recoil before exhaling with relief. "Bramble," I order. "Stay with her and don't let anyone touch her."

He chirps in alarm, flashing his red sensor, *no,* over and over. But I pry him from my shoulder and set him down on the step above her head. "This is important. Protect her. Use force if you have to."

Chittering, he scampers onto her shoulder and looks proudly at me.

"Good. I'll be back, I promise."

The door to the roof is heavy, reinforced iron. On the other side is a gravel roof thick with the stench of tar and burning oil. A dark cloud snakes between the silver teardrop-shaped starcrafts spread out in rows of five. The smoky tendrils reach to the night sky like angry dragons marching across the stars.

Most of the crafts are charred and blackened beyond repair.

A few are missing.

Shouts drift across the roof from the other side. Breathing hard, I follow the sounds, my heart pounding against my skull. Sweat drips in my eyes and blurs my vision. I wipe the sweat away and pause as the breeze shifts, clearing a section of smoke.

It's like a wet cloth wiped away a grimy window to a hellish world of death.

I see Max first. His hair blows gently in the wind, his eyes all-white with panic. I've never seen him so still—frozen with fear. The Archduchess has a pistol rammed against his temple. Dead Centurions scatter the roof around them.

My friends fought hard.

I search for the others, my gaze snagging on a lithe body folded over a twisted piece of metal that was once part of a craft.

Riser.

No. I gasp at all the blood, my only comfort the subtle rise of his chest that hints he's still alive. Part of me goes numb with terror at the position of his body, the hurt etched into his face. The pain is a living thing splitting me open, carving a hollow beneath my ribs.

If I don't compartmentalize my emotions, I'll shatter, so I bury my feelings deep and assess my surroundings.

I spot Flame next, positioned on her belly, using the debris Riser drapes over as cover.

"I can't do anything," she yells to me. "Not without hurting Max."

I force myself to look at my brother. Our eyes lock. Gone is the soldier, the boy who isn't afraid. He tries to say something but I'm too far away and I can't read his lips. Slinging my backpack off, I tear open the pockets, desperately searching for the Hot Weapons.

Useless. They're useless. I can't use them against the Archduchess without hurting him too.

There's nothing I can do.

I mouth, *I love you.* Over and over and over until it's one continuous, never-ending phrase.

A grin slowly spreads over the Archduchess's face as she spots me, and something passes between us—hatred that could destroy worlds.

With a smirk, she drags him up the ramp into the belly of the starcraft. The ramp door slams closed, and my mouth splits open in a silent scream as the craft darts into the sky.

It all happens in the blink of an eye.

For a blessed moment, I'm numb to the pressure building inside my chest. A black hole of grief collapsing inward. My thoughts tumble together.

I wasn't here. Now he's scared. Hurt. Alone.

I did it again. I failed him. Again.

You let the monster take him.

"No," I whisper. "Please, just . . . no."

I know he's gone. Know he's not coming back. *Ever.* Oh, gods. The pain.

But I can't move, can't stop staring up at the craft holding my brother captive, as if I can see through the mass of metal to his terrified form. As if I can somehow save him if I don't blink. Don't look away.

Only after the craft blends in with the thousands of stars winking from the haze of smoke and destruction, and I finally pry my eyes away, do I finally react.

A strangled, half-choked wail of anguish rips from my throat. And I scream and scream until I can't scream anymore.

SIXTEEN

I don't speak as the Rebels swarm onto the roof, let in by Teagan and Lash. I don't say a word as two soldiers create a makeshift stretcher out of a banner and help me carry Riser down the stairs. On the way, we find Rivet. Bramble huddles on her chest, occasionally touching her face as if trying to wake her. I assign three Rebels to carry her just like I was once carried after the Blood Courts.

I thought Max was injured then, maybe dead. I remember writhing and screaming and raging against the agony that pierced my soul. Now I hardly talk, hardly move beyond the smallest of actions. Because this time there's no hope he'll make it.

This time . . . he's really gone.

One step. Then another. Now lift the stretcher. Don't jostle Riser. Now step over an overturned chair. Now down more stairs. My body shivers with a strange, feverish heat, anguish pouring through every cell, every molecule of my body.

How will I tell my mother?

It won't be real until then. I can pretend this is a dream, no, a nightmare for now. But once I have to look my mother in the eye and tell her I lost my baby brother, that I left him again . . .

A moan rips me from my bubble of shock. I drag in a breath and focus on Riser. A deep gash slices from his shoulder, down his chest, over his hip bone.

He's hurt—he's dying. Rivet too. The need to save them breaks through my grief. *Get it together, Maia. Save the others and mourn later.*

"He needs a Reconstructor," I say, finally finding my voice.

The Rebels, unfamiliar with the Island, glance around helplessly. I spy Caspian and flag him over.

As soon as he sees Riser's injury, the color leeches from his face.

"Reconstructor," I bark. "We need one now. Can you show them the way?"

After a brief hesitation, Caspian nods. I watch them disappear around a corner and then search the halls until I find Rivet being carried down the stairs. Flame has her feet, while another Rebel holds up her waist and another her torso. Bramble still crouches protectively over her chest, looking ready to kill anyone he deems a threat.

"What happened?" I hiss to Flame, taking a leg as we carry Rivet to the infirmary.

Her nostrils are flared, face pale. In one word, she looks gutted. "Drones. There were so many of them. They were activated somehow, by our faces or voices, I don't know. They chased us to the roof. If I had known they were herding us to an ambush—"

"Slow down," I sooth, trying to calm her with my voice. "Take your time."

She swipes a hand over her eyes as if trying to erase what comes next. "The Archduchess was waiting for us. We were trapped between the drones and her soldiers. It all happened so fast. So fucking fast."

I release a shallow breath, afraid of her the next question. "And . . . the Mercurian? Did you get any closer to finding it?"

Her eyes mist over as she shakes her head. "The drones attacked us as soon as you left." The vulnerability in her expression gives way to cold anger. "The bitch knew we were coming. Someone betrayed us."

Nicolai. Rage heats my chest. *I'll kill him.*

Flame's haunted gaze settles on Rivet. "Once the Arch-duchess took Max, the girl fought like a lioness."

Rivet. I remember how she got her name. The horrible things she's already had to endure in her too-short life. And yet, she was always smiling. Always making Max laugh. Always pushing forward, fighting without complaint for a better world.

And now . . . I force myself to take in her condition. A swollen gash mars her forehead, purple unfurling from the bruised flesh. Her eyes are closed, her face the color of fresh-fallen snow. Blood crusts her leather breastplate, and even more darkens her pants.

We see where it's coming from after we place her on a bed in the infirmary and, after assuring Bramble she's okay, Flame cuts off her armor and shirt. Blood bubbles from a sucking wound just above her heart.

Fienian hell. Even I know that's bad.

Lash appears. The pain in his eyes from his injury transforms to alarm at the sight of Rivet's condition. Hobbling over, he finds a penlight from a drawer and lifts her right eyelid. The pupil is a pinpoint and doesn't react to the light. Neither does the left one.

He clicks off the light. "She's . . . it's not good."

I brush back the hair from her face. "She can't die, she's a .

. . a baby. And we have Reconstructors. And when Max returns, I can't tell him she—I can't, Lash. Fix her."

Lash seems about to argue—about Max returning or Rivet surviving, I haven't a clue—but then he runs a hand through his hair and gives a tired sigh. "I'll do what I can."

I brush a kiss over his cheek. "Thank you."

The infirmary is a ten-bed room separated by curtains. The Reconstructors are in the back. Shiny long capsules, the caskets drag memories of being Reconstructed to the surface. The terror of not knowing. My panic as the lid closed and I knew everything would change.

Riser was in the casket next to me and he nearly died . . .

A Rebel girl is closing the lid of one, and I glimpse a flash of jet-black hair and pale, high cheekbones before it shuts. *Riser.* Bramble perches on the lid, scrambling back and forth.

I grab the girl's arm; she recoils. I can't imagine what I look like, the desperation in my eyes. "Do you know what you're doing?"

Her lips tremble as she nods. "I worked on one at a clinic in a nearby Diamond City."

Only one? I glance around, but there's no one else. "Okay. Just . . . come get me when he's done."

I don't say what I feel. That if I lose Riser too I'll never recover. I allow myself one last look at Riser, drinking him in. Every part of me wants to stay with him until he wakes up. But there's too much to do.

More than anything, I need to clear my head and find a way to get Max back.

So, with Bramble on my shoulder, I plow ahead, numbing myself in directing the injured. A long line of the wounded who can still walk filter into the castle, and I herd them to the available infirmaries. When those fill up, we use the personal Reconstructors in the high-ranking Gold's rooms.

Caspian helps, and finally, when the trickle of bodies slow, I gather my courage to inform my mother about Max.

It isn't hard to find her. I just backtrack the path of the wounded until I'm walking through the battlefield. The stench of blood and gunpowder hits me hard, awakening nerve endings I never knew existed and putting my body on edge.

Bodies litter the ground—Rebels and Centurions. In the delicate moonlight, it's nearly impossible to tell them apart. Our soldiers walk around the grassy hills. Every few seconds a thunderous boom splits the air.

They're executing the survivors.

I scan each soldier's face, searching for Nicolai's masked face and mangled, cloaked form. But I know he would never stay after his failed double-cross, especially after alerting the Archduchess our small crew was inside the castle.

The bastard thought he could make the Archduchess do his dirty work and get rid of me once and for all.

What I wouldn't give to tear him apart piece by piece right now.

My revenge fantasy falls away the second I see my mother. She's standing tall on a ridge, her cape billowing in the light breeze.

As I imagine the words, "The Archduchess took Max," leaving my mouth, a sick feeling nearly doubles me over.

She spots me before I can think of a way to tell her, and beckons me over. Even in this light, I can make out the feverish shine in her eyes. A mixture of excitement and horror and fatigue.

Two torches burn brightly around her, their orange glow casting deep shadows over her eye sockets and giving her a ghoulish look.

Dropping to one knee, she wipes her blade on the thick

grass at her boots, leaving a dark smear of blood. "Did you find it?"

I shake my head as the air thins around me.

"Excuse me? I need words, Maia."

"No." My throat is closing up. My lungs shrinking. "We—*I* failed."

My mother once said that, at some point in their life, every leader experiences a failure so disastrous that it leaves an aching wound on their soul. I know this is mine. I have to claim it, have to let it sink inside me, no matter the cost.

She rises and stares at me for a long moment. Then she motions for the two soldiers at her side to disperse.

I watch them go, unable to look at her. Afraid she'll read the guilt over losing Max in my eyes. As if, somehow, not saying it aloud means it never happened.

"Tell me, Maia." Her words are soft, and if I didn't know better, I would think there was kindness in them.

But I can feel the weight of all her condescension just beneath the surface. Waiting for me to confirm my failure.

"We—I left Max and the others to help Teagan and Lash near the door. They were pinned down. They would have died."

"And?"

"And when I found the others again, it was too late."

One side of her jaw twitches. "Where is Max, Maia?"

Fighting the urge to look at my feet, I raise my head and lock eyes with my mother. The feeling is similar to having a knife twisted just below my sternum. "Taken. By the Archduchess."

An emotion flickers across her face. It takes me a moment to decipher it—pain. Then it sinks down into her apathetic mask as if she never felt it, and derision replaces the hurt.

"You let her take him? Knowing what kind of monster she is? He would be better off if you'd *killed* him."

Her voice is soft, but there's acid in it. A quiet sort of disgust.

"I . . ." My voice falters. It's as if a beast lurks just below my sternum and snatches my words. "Even if I had been there, we were betrayed by Nicolai."

"I asked you to watch out for Max," she continues, as if she didn't hear what I just said. "I ordered you to keep him safe, Maia. *Safe.* Blood should always come before friends."

"Riser stayed with him. Even if I'd been there—"

"Stop making excuses. You're better than that."

I can't breathe. My heart feels like it will crack right open and then crumble into shards.

Finding my voice, I force out, "I can make this right somehow. I'll find a way to get him back."

Her teeth flash in a bitter smile. "Oh? You'll find a way to rescue him? How, exactly? Will you just fly up there to Hyperion and ask for him back? He's in the most secure place in the universe, Maia, surrounded by space and armed guards and technology you've never even encountered before. But you'll . . . get him back?"

Each word that flings from her lips is a barb that tangles inside me; each second she looks at me like that, like I'm nothing, *worse* than nothing, is torture.

"From this point forward, our resources must be focused on finding the Mercurian, not some doomed rescue mission." She glances at the battlefield. Somehow she still appears triumphant, a general to be feared. Even though she's lost a son . . . and now a daughter. "Leave me."

I turn to do just that and then pivot to face her. "What does it feel like?"

"Excuse me?"

"What does it feel like to be so damn heartless that both your children despise you?" She opens her mouth but I keep going, my anger and hurt growing hotter and hotter. "You know, you might accept that Max is gone—you're practiced at losing your children, after all—but I can't. I won't. So screw you and the stupid horse you rode in on. You can ride it right back out of my life for all I care."

I flee before she can gather herself to respond. First walking then running then flat-out sprinting. Until the only thing I can feel is the burn of my lungs and the pounding of my heart and everything else fades away to a bearable hum.

Gods, that felt good. I should have told my mother off a long time ago.

By the time I slow down, dawn creeps in on silvery wings. Sweat soaks my forehead and plasters my hair to my skull. I'm on a ridge two hundred yards from the castle wall, overlooking the water's edge of the lake.

The battle must have been heavy here because blood darkens the grass in long stretches. A few bodies lay scattered on the rocks above, obviously dead by their positions. Crows already gather, and I shoo them away.

A flash of red catches my eye. A Swifter, buried in the high grass along the ridge, just beside a carriage-sized boulder. Even from here, half submerged in the grass, I can tell it's a nice one. The paint smooth and polished, bright as blood.

My focus catches on the short blonde hair splashing out from the vehicle, shreds of silken gold. As I approach, I make out a high-forehead, a pert nose, round cheekbones . . .

Holy Fienian hell. I know her.

"Delphine?" I whisper.

Her eyelashes flutter then snap open. Her shoulders flex as she tries to move, but her Swifter pins her arms and torso to the ground.

Baring her teeth, she snarls, "Get it over with, Rebel scum!"

My attention has attracted others, and two more Rebels top the ridge. A girl and a boy. They wield stolen Centurion pistols. The girl has big-bones and flat, ruddy cheekbones, her hair tied off in thick orange braids. A hard smile twists her face.

She aligns the pistol with Delphine's heart. "It's your kill, but can I do it? I don't have that many yet."

Shivering at the murderous excitement in the girl's voice, I look down at Delphine. Part of me wants to kill her myself. Wants to slake the rage fomenting just below my cavernous pit of anguish.

Don't forget how cruel she was to you. Remember the hazing? The apple?

I should hate her. I *do* hate her. But I can't kill her, not in cold blood. Especially because that would make me exactly like her.

"No." I shove her pistol away from Delphine. "I'm taking her prisoner."

The girl frowns, reassessing me like I could be the enemy. "Lady Graystone said to kill all the survivors."

"Not this one." Despite feeling like I might fall over, I find the strength to glare at the girl.

"Lady Graystone is going to be furious when I tell her what happened."

A tired grin somehow finds my face. "Good. I'm Maia, by the way. If you need a name to tell her. Maia Graystone."

The two Rebels exchange wary glances. "You're her daughter?"

I shrug. "Not by choice."

The girl stares at me like I'm crazy. Then she curses as they stalk away, searching the hills for more survivors to murder.

The thought makes me sick.

Delphine sneers up at me. "Look at you. This is war, idiot. What'd you expect?"

Ignoring her barbs, I bend down. "Are you hurt?"

"Hurt?" She's so angry spittle flies from her lips. "Are you really that stupid? Kill me. There's no reason to keep me alive. You lost. The Emperor's safe in Hyperion, and this little war is over."

It's then I realize that's what she wants. An easy, quick death. "Sorry, Delphine, but there's a prison cell with your name on it."

She screams in rage, that scream turning to wails of pain as I shove the Swifter off her body and drag her up. *She's definitely broken some bones*, I think as I take in the twisted angle of her arm, the way she bends over and guards her ribs.

Actually, she's wheezing now too, her face tinted blue. *Well, crap.*

"You lucked out," I mutter, shoving her toward the castle. "You're going to the infirmary."

She snorts, hugging her ribs as if the act is painful. "Are you kidding me? How weak are you? You can't kill me, and now you want to . . . to heal me?"

"You might call that being weak, I just call it being human. Now *move.*"

SEVENTEEN

The infirmary is packed with the dead and dying. I handcuff a petulant Delphine to a bed before rushing to the Reconstructor side. The Rebel from earlier looks up from a casket lid and meets my eyes. I flinch, terrified that her gaze will hint somehow Riser is gone.

Instead, her lips curl into a little smile and she jerks her chin to a bed in the back, near a window. "It was close—he nearly died. Most people would have. He must be really tough."

"Or stubborn," I breathe, staring down at him.

His eyes are closed, his raven-black lashes two slashes across ivory flesh that could be carved from marble. A sheet covers his body up to mid-chest, revealing a faint red scar where his wound was. Beneath the sheet, his body trembles.

Bramble hops up onto the Reconstructor lid and then curls up on Riser's chest. I grab him, the sleek metal shell of his body warming up. He's trying to help Riser.

"No, Bramble," I say, trying to pull him away, but he scampers out of my reach and settles into Riser's neck.

His antennae flash *no* back at me.

Gods, he's like a two-year-old Max.

I don't have the strength to argue with Bramble, so I turn back to the girl. "He's cold."

"That's normal after a severe Reconstruction like this." Her gaze flits to Bramble. "Once he wakes up, he'll be nauseous and feel abnormally cold. He'll probably spike a fever for a few days as well."

"But . . . he's alright?" I persist. I want her to say it. Need her to say it.

"Any other patient, I'd wager the chances aren't great. His wound was too deep. He's had too many reconstructions done already, which increases the odds of complications. But he's a fighter. Give him a few days. If anyone can pull through this, it's this guy."

She jumps up and with a nod to the other caskets, leaves me alone with Riser.

Maybe isn't good enough, but that's all the confirmation I'll get. I settle on a chair beside him, lay my hand on his chest. It's cold and hard, prickled with gooseflesh and bruises. *What did they do to you?*

He stirs beneath my touch, moans. Bramble chirps in alarm. He doesn't say it, but I feel the sting of the truth anyway.

My fault. All my fault.

"What happened, Riser?" I lay my head on his shoulder. "How did it all go so wrong?"

I could have been there. Could have stopped it.

His lips open, slightly, like he's trying to talk. To tell me something. But I brush his dark hair back from his forehead, part of it pasted by dried blood, and then stand. "Don't you dare leave me, Pit Boy. That's a command."

Bramble lifts up, torn between Riser and me. "Stay with him, Bramble. Keep him safe."

Bramble sags back into the pillow beside his head, content

to stay with Riser. I can see him vibrating, trying to create as much warmth for Riser as he can.

Grayish light pierces the windowpane and illuminates Riser's face, pulling out the deep, rich blues from his hair, matted and splayed across the pillow. I stare at his lips, full and chapped and still partially open. At the scorpion tattoo darkening his neck.

I drink him in . . . just in case. Like I would do to Max if he were here right now. Storing him in the parts of my brain no one could ever reach.

Then I force myself to leave him. As much as I want to help somehow, he has to fight this battle alone.

You're strong. You'll come back to me.

I'm halfway across the infirmary before I remember I left a livid Delphine shackled to a bed. *I'd better find her before someone strangles her . . . or vice versa.*

She's sitting on the floor, her good arm—the one I hand-cuffed—hanging high above her. Medical supplies dot the floor around her boots where she's obviously kicked things over. Two injured Rebels are approaching her with makeshift weapons—part of an IV pole, a syringe.

She holds a tray in her broken arm, teeth bared and eyes wild. But she's wheezing harder than before, working for every breath. And I can't tell if she's seconds away from either murdering someone or passing out.

"Get back, you savages!" she screeches.

Oh, hell.

I'm about to intervene when, from my periphery, I see Lash approach. Annoyed at the distraction, he gives Delphine a stern look that warns of a tongue-lashing . . . and then goes rigid. His body actually *recoils* from her. He already looks ill, dark circles rimming his eyes, his skin feverish and flushed—but the second he sees Delphine, he's jolted from his waking slumber into a strange sort of panic.

"Delph?" he rasps, taking a tiny step in her direction even as his entire body seems to flinch.

Her injured arm is raised, about to fling the tray at the approaching patients, and she whips to face Lash. I watch, mesmerized, as her face goes from desperate savagery to . . . first shock. Similar to Lash's.

Then *joy.* "Brig?" The tray drops with a clang, and the two Rebels halt, looking from Delphine to us. "Briggan? Is it really you?"

After everything that happened, my brain is firing in slow motion, and it takes a moment to figure out how they know each other. How Lash would know any Gold in the Royalist court.

He was once a Silver. And he once loved a girl above his station . . .

"Fienian hell, Lash." I grab his arm. "*This* is her. The girl who you fell in love with, who had you whipped until you couldn't walk? It's freaking *Countess* Delphine Bloodwood?"

A muscle in his temple twitches. Then his face hardens and I can physically see him shutting down any emotions. "Are we treating Royalists now?"

"We're treating everyone injured."

"That's not what I've heard," an older Rebel boy says. He sneers over at Delphine, the look in his eyes hinting she won't last long here.

"Well you're hearing it now. Lash, treat her and then I'll take her to the prison."

The boy looks me up and down. "And how would you even know there's a prison here? I heard the Emperor executes everyone on sight."

I'm too tired for this. Pinching the bridge of my nose, I approach until we're within touching distance. "Because my blood probably still stains the floor of one of the cells where I was held. Now, anyone who touches this prisoner answers to me. And, considering my mood, you don't want that."

The boy retreats a step but otherwise holds his ground. "She's the general's daughter. Do you know what he did to my older brother when he refused to become a Centurion? Cut off his dominant hand so he could never work, never write his name."

"Well," I snap, "If we're trading horror stories, she forced me to put a gun to my head and pull the trigger, had someone shoot an arrow at an apple I held between my teeth, sent me into a maze of horrors, and then later tried to murder me for sport."

The boy runs a finger over the blade at his waist. "And how exactly is that supposed to make me not want to murder her?"

I look around, unable to control my fury. "All of us have stories like this. But if you kill her, a wounded prisoner shackled and helpless"—I might be pushing it with the help-less bit—"then you're just like them."

I can tell by his narrowed eyes the boy doesn't get my logic, but he stomps away, and the onlookers slowly find other things to do.

I fix a pleading look on Lash. "I know what she did to you, and I'm sorry. Just . . . set her bones or whatever you do and then I'll take her, and you never have to see her again. Okay?"

Delphine slumps against the metal bed's leg. She's looking like she could actually crash soon, her face now a sickly gray, her mouth gaping wide, fighting for every labored breath.

"I didn't . . . do anything." She insists. "Tried to stop . . ."

Lash looks unmoved as he grabs something off a tray—a syringe—and stomps over to her. Before she can look up, he jabs the needle into her arm and slams the plunger down.

"Wait . . ." Her words fade as she melts to the floor, her

arm hanging above her the only thing keeping her from falling all the way over.

"There." Lash cuts his eyes at me, making his distaste for my orders clear. "If you insist that I fix her, then you can help me get her on the bed."

"Okay . . . Brig."

He shoots me a murderous look from beneath lowered brows. "Graystone, in the last fifteen hours, I've been shot at, hit in the ass with a bullet—about the least manly place it could go—and watched patients bleed out in front of me. I haven't eaten or drank or even pissed since the battle started. This is not the time to bring up stupid nicknames."

"You're right. You deserve a medal." I flash a tired smile. "For the record, I haven't peed either and I really need to. Now, c'mon, let's lift her."

Ignoring the furious looks from the patients around us, Lash and I somehow manage to get Delphine onto the bed. When she's stripped of her armor and shirt, Lash presses a stethoscope onto her chest.

He listens to both lungs and frowns.

"Hey," I say. "Finish up with her and then go get some food and rest. Doctor's orders. And don't let them hurt her . . . okay?"

He nods, his face solemn. "She's my patient now. The only thing killing her is that collapsed lung, unless I can do something about it."

Thank you, I mouth, before slipping out.

The morning sun blasts the windows of the corridors as I walk, warming the halls and illuminating the carnage just outside. I try not to look as I go about the day. I find food stores and set up orderly lines of distribution for the hungry —basically everyone. I secure the armory with soldiers I trust, ensuring Nicolai's Rebels don't have access to more weapons.

I assign people to oversee the distribution of rooms and other resources.

I push myself to keep going, keep going, when my body feels one step short of collapsing, all of it in an effort to distract myself from the truth: We're no closer to finding the Mercurian than we were yesterday, Max is gone—probably forever—and we're one day closer to total annihilation.

Somehow still standing, I wander into a high-ranking Gold's room, shocked and pleased to discover non-protocol amenities like a heated shower and whirlpool tub. Thank the freaking gods. It's just enough to pump life back into my veins.

After fiddling with the shower until I figure out how to work it, I stand beneath the stream, my mind gone, enjoying this one simple pleasure more than I've ever enjoyed anything in my life.

Afterward, I can't bear to put my dirty clothes back on, instead falling into bed naked and wet. I need sleep. I need to forget the last few hours for a spell. To wipe the heartache from my body so I can function.

But now that I can't busy my mind with tasks, the horror of what happened hits me like a wave. Every time I close my eyes I see Max in the Archduchess's grip. See him trying to say something. Struggling. Begging.

If only I could read his lips. If only I could understand what he's saying . . .

As if suddenly his face falls into focus, I can read his lips perfectly.

You left me. You left me. You left me.

Then there's no noise, just the ramp closing as I watch his face disappear.

Task—I need a task, something to quiet my memories. I jolt from bed. Rummage in the closet of whoever used to live here.

A tunic and too-big pants later, I slip on my muddy boots and leave the room. There's so much to do, and yet I feel like I'm wading through invisible mud. Moving too slow. Losing focus.

There's no way I can get anything done until I clear my head. I leave the castle for the gardens. As soon as the sun hits my cheeks, the scent of evergreens and roses filling my nose, the invisible noose around my neck loosens enough that I can breathe again.

And I start planning my next move.

EIGHTEEN

I don't know how long I stare into the koi pond. I made it here somehow, drawn by my memories of last night. If only I had refused to leave when I heard Teagan's distress call. If only I had killed those guards sooner.

There are a thousand different scenarios in my head that could have saved Max. I should have left sooner. Or never left at all. Or sent Caspian with Teagan and Lash in the first place.

My fault.

I look into the water, but the fish are either all hiding or dead. The charge must have hurt them somehow. Only one pure orange koi shows itself, and it skims the surface before diving down low to hide too.

A face appears in the water's reflection, rippled and warped between the lily pads. But I still recognize the golden hair, the odd leap of my heart.

"Caspian." I sound tired, even to my own ears.

"Hey." He glances at the spot where the Centurions died. "Care if I join you?"

"Sure. Fair warning, I'm not much for talking right now."

"That makes two of us." He slides beside me, takes off his

boots, and lets his feet slip into the water. "I'm sorry . . . about Max."

His name feels like the barbed end of an arrow being yanked out of my chest. "I—yeah."

"The Archduchess, she won't hurt him yet. They'll use him for propaganda first. Not that that's any consolation."

"It's not." I rub my eyes, trying to massage away the burn of not sleeping. "And she will eventually."

Leaning back, he releases a long sigh. "I don't know how it got so bad. I can't remember what it was like, before."

"Before what?"

"My mother died. I can't remember if my father was normal then, or if he's always been so cruel."

His mother—killed in a terrorist bombing by Ezra Croft. Sometimes I forget Caspian has his own set of jacked up traumas. Dead mother, murdered siblings. His own twin sister killed by his father.

We're two damaged peas in a pod. Another reason we get along so well.

I lift my shoulders in a tight shrug. "I don't think it matters. The amount of people he's hurt could fill a lifetime."

"No, you're right."

The anguish in his tone startles me back to reality. Caspian has lost everything, just like me. "Caspian, you're not responsible for your father's actions."

"You sure about that?" A dark smile graces his face as he stares at the water. "Look, I just wanted to say that what happened here, my hesitating—it won't happen again."

I glance at his face. His jaw is clenched, his eyes unblinking as they stare at something beyond the water. Blood splatters his flaxen hair, little flecks that could be his or someone else's.

"I know," I say. I get to my feet, expecting him to follow

me back to the castle, but he stays, still staring at something I can't see.

———

LASH FINDS me near the kitchens. He's limping so hard I'm surprised he doesn't fall down before he reaches me. "Riser."

My heart punches into my throat. "Riser? Riser what?"

"He's awake."

Grabbing Lash's shoulder, I prop him up as we hurry to the infirmary. As soon as the doors appear, I sprint through the crowded room.

Riser sits up in bed, batting away the Rebel girl as she tries to examine him while Bramble screeches at her. Despite Riser being weak, he and my traitorous sensor-child somehow manage to fight the poor girl off.

She turns her annoyed gaze on me, her cheeks pink with frustration.

"Tell them I need to examine him," she says. "Tell them he could have a heart arrhythmia or other major complications that we can't rule out without an exam. Tell them!"

Riser rips off the sheet and tries to swing his leg over the side of the bed. Bramble cheers him on with a barrage of chirps. Riser must be too weak still because his leg catches on the side. He grunts and tries again.

"Riser!" I grab his arm and force him to sit still. His eyes are wild as his gaze lands on me, and for a moment, I fear he doesn't recognize me. His nostrils are flared, teeth bared.

Slowly, the panic fades from his eyes, his pupils constricting to a normal size.

"Riser, you're safe," I say, my voice low and soothing. "But I need you healthy, which means you have to do whatever she says."

Bramble beeps at me and I turn on him. "And you. You're

not helping!" Screwing my face into a stern look, I point to my shoulder. "Get up here."

The stubborn sensor flashes a succession of no's, but I grit my teeth and say, "Right now."

Once Bramble slinks up my arm onto my shoulder, the girl flashes me a thankful look before approaching Riser.

She holds her hands up in a submissive position. "See? I don't have anything that can hurt you, I just need to do a proper exam to check your heart and lungs."

Riser's chest sways up and down, but he nods, slowly.

"Riser." I take his hand, startled by the coldness of his flesh. "You're okay."

"What happened?" His voice is hoarse, sandpapery. "Where's Rivet? Max?"

I jerk my head to a bed on the other side of the room. "Rivet's over there. Lash is working on her, but . . ."

The truth is, I don't know. I haven't had the nerve to ask about her recently.

A vein throbs in his temple as he deciphers what I left unsaid, and he faces me. His eyes are pleading. "Max? Did she . . . is he . . ."

"Not dead"—cautious relief flickers over his face—"but . . . she took him." My voice breaks on the last two words.

As my words sink in, he tries to get up. Alarms on the Reconstructor begin to blare. The girl and I both force him back into the sheets, and then he stops moving and I realize, to my horror, that his eyes have rolled back in his head. His body jerking spasmodically like he's possessed.

"He's seizing," the girl growls. "Help me hold him!"

In shock, I hesitate.

"Now!"

Her words spur me into action, and I grab Riser's shoulder, helping her flip him on his side. She rams a pillow between the side of the bed and his head to protect it. His body jerks and kicks, his muscles clenched and popping from his flesh like eels.

Slowly, his movements become less violent. His muscles smooth; his breathing slows.

She leans back, watching him to make sure he doesn't seize again. "There. He's on his side, his head protected. That's all we can do."

"That's it?" I demand. "There has to be something else, a . . . a medicine or procedure to stop it, right?"

She shakes her head, her dull brown hair falling into her eyes. "His body is responding to the stress of everything." She swipes the hair out of her face. "I think it's best you don't come back until he's . . . better."

"Why?" But even as she says it, I know why. I made him seize.

Why did I tell him the truth? I should have waited. He wasn't ready.

"I'll keep you updated on his condition. Just, give him time to heal."

I feel sick as I leave Riser's bed and make my way back to Delphine. Lash is sitting in a chair beside her, his head resting on his chin. Eyes closed. Snoring.

Delphine, however, is wide awake. And she's pissed. Even more so when her gaze lands on me. "What the hell, Maia? Get me out of here."

I raise an eyebrow. "You want to go to the prison cells?"

"I'd rather go anywhere than here. It stinks, it's noisy and gross and I have to pee."

I glare at her for a moment. Really all I want is to go find something to eat, maybe talk to Caspian about trying to search for the Mercurian, if only to stay busy.

"Lash, is she healthy enough to leave?" I ask. When he doesn't respond, I kick his chair. "Lash!"

Delphine raises her eyebrows at the name, watching him

curiously as his eyes snap open and he nearly falls out of his seat.

"What? I'm awake!" His focus settles on me, the whites of his eyes tinged red.

"Is this patient okay to transfer now?"

He frowns at Delphine, biting the corner of his lip. "Yeah. Just bring her back if she has trouble breathing again. Or . . . don't."

Delphine doesn't fight as I unshackle her wrist from the bed, manacle her hands behind her back, and lead her out. She doesn't look at the pistol in my hand—picked up from a Centurion who didn't need it anymore—but I know she sees it.

Silence fills the air between us, both of us thankful for a bit of quiet.

When we near the tower, my body begins to react. My muscles tense, my gut clenches, and it suddenly becomes hard to draw in breath. I force her up the stairs, walking behind her just in case she tries something.

It's hard to not think about how, just over a week ago, this was me. Shackled and imprisoned inside these dark, dank cells. This horrible place.

At least Delphine won't be tortured, I think.

At the top, the door to the cells creaks open and I place Delphine inside the first room on the right. Light pours in from the tiny windows above each cell, the place brighter than I remember. Less terrifying.

I find an old key ring, rummaging around until I find the key I think fits. Once the lock clicks shut, I release a sigh. "I'll have someone bring you water and food."

"What about the other thing?" she asks. Gone is her usual condescending tone, and when I don't seem to understand, she elaborates, "I have to pee."

"There's a hole in the floor near the corner," I offer, trying not to smile. "If you're lucky, it won't be full."

I expect Delphine to complain, but she hobbles over and begins to unzip her pants. I turn away, ready to leave this place and the headache it's giving me. But something—a feeling, a gut instinct—makes me check the other cells.

Just in case the Emperor left anyone alive, as improbable as that is.

It's a wild, silly hope. The Emperor isn't in the business of keeping people alive, especially known Rebels.

Still . . .

The second to last cell seems different than the others. The stench, for one thing. And the thin layer of dust coating the floor has been disturbed recently. I try the door but it's locked.

Fumbling for the keys, I jam four in before finding the right one.

For a moment I think the lock is broken and the key won't turn. But then it does with a soft *click*, and the door creaks open. Holding a hand over my nose and mouth, I enter. The stench of piss and worse burns my eyes. This cell is one of the few without a window, and I peer into the pooled shadows near the corner.

Something moves. A muffled groan stirs the air. "Please, please don't hurt me."

"Bramble," I whisper, afraid to scare the prisoner. "I need your light."

A white light erupts, vanquishing the darkness. I can't breathe, can't think as my vision works to readjust to the brightness.

The prisoner sits curled in the corner, trying to escape the light. His hands are up, protective, and he's whimpering. A wild nest of matted hair joins an equally tangled beard, silver hairs peppering the dark mess.

Eyes wild with fear stare unblinking at me. Bright against the bloodless, anemic flesh pulled tight over high cheekbones.

Oh, gods. A spark of hope ignites just below my sternum. It can't be . . . can it?

"Cage?"

The sound of his name breaks whatever trance he's in, and he finally blinks. "Who . . . no, no, it's a trick. A cruel trick."

"It's not a trick." My voice cracks. "Cage, it's me."

"Maia?"

The tentative hope in his voice nearly shatters me.

I fall to my knees, take his dirty hands in mine. "Cage, it's really me. The girl you once transformed into a butterfly, remember?"

I can literally see the realization that I'm real crash over him. That he's finally safe.

Finally free.

As he wraps me in a hug, his frail arms shaking with the effort, a tiny shard of me gets put back. A piece of me I thought I would never reclaim.

"Flame," I breathe. "We need to find Flame."

NINETEEN

He's too weak to move on his own, and even emaciated he's still too big for me alone, so I find a boy outside chopping wood and together, we half-carry half-support Cage down the stairs. Each step is painstaking. Each foot closer he takes to the sunlight and freedom a victory.

When I offer to get others to bring a stretcher, he stops me.

"I've waited countless hours to leave this place. I'm walking out of here, not being carried."

"Of course," I say.

When we open the door and the sunlight hits his face, he lets out a tiny noise. Not quite a wail, but close. Tears shimmer in his eyes. I flinch at the evidence of his condition in the light. Sores around his lips and nose speak of malnutrition, his body nearly crippled from wounds I can't see.

"Almost there," I say.

He lets out a raspy chuckle. "Liar."

It takes an hour to make it to the infirmary, broken up by periods of resting. I send another soldier off to procure broth and water. Then I tell someone to find Flame.

Except she finds us. We're just cresting the last set of stairs to the infirmary, Cage breathing so hard I think he might pass out. Actually, I think we might both pass out. I'm trying to convince him to rest, but he's being stubborn.

Flame stands near the wall, scolding a soldier on the way they carry their sword. She glances over at us like she's going to make a quip, grinning at me. Her gaze slides to Cage. To his ragged, bloody, burned clothes. His face.

For a breath, I think she won't recognize him. The boy she considers a brother, who got her through the streets, who fought with her against the Royalists and loves her unconditionally.

The sword falls to the stone with a clang and Flame—who never shows her emotions, never cries—begins to bawl. She slumps against the wall, legs shaking. Face crumpled with snot and tears.

Cage is the one to go to her, his long legs propelling him into her arms. The moment they embrace, Flame sags into him and he's the one holding her up, despite being injured and starved.

For all her bluster, I realize, Flame is just like me. I imagine how strong she had to be this whole time, despite thinking Cage was dead.

Just like I have to be now for Max, I realize. I can't give up hope.

Despite what my mother says, I need to find a way to save him. Knowing Cage survived when we all thought he was gone . . . it's reminded me that hope isn't silly. It isn't naïve or weak.

Sometimes, hope is the only thing left. The only thing that keeps the all-consuming darkness at bay. To give up now on Max would be blowing out the last tiny spark of resistance remaining in my heart.

Like hell I'm going to abandon my little brother. Like *hell*.

Red, puffy eyes find mine. Flame mouths, *thank you*, and

then she and Cage hobble into the infirmary where a half-asleep Lash meets them.

A few moments later, the entire room erupts in cheers. The glorious sound fills my chest, ripping away the fist of defeat that's been clenching my heart.

After so many deaths, so many disappointments, we'll desperately grasp at any victory we can to preserve hope.

SHADOW FALL HITS as we take our lunch.

Lash, Teagan, and I eat outside, on a stone table near a cluster of live oak trees. Torches, activated by the promise of Shadow Fall, flicker to life around us. Lanterns hang from tree boughs, torches illuminating from the hedges and pink hydrangea bushes.

Flame joins us once Cage falls asleep. Lash says he's malnourished and has several broken bones that need resetting, but that he's remarkably healthy considering.

"Great," Lash moans as Pandora's shadow falls over us, coloring the trees and rose bushes silver-gray. "It's like today wants to punish me. I go outside and the sun disappears."

"Stop whining and eat," I order.

He frowns at the biscuits I shove in front of him before shoving one into his mouth whole.

"Don't forget to chew, you savage," Flame growls, batting away Bramble as he tries to swipe a crumb from her plate. "And maybe try sitting like a normal person."

Lash, who's propped on the bench on his knees, makes a dramatic face. "I was shot in my beautiful, one-of-a-kind ass. Why does no one realize how painful that is?"

Teagan rolls her eyes and pulls out her flask. All of us stare at the metallic thing like it's the last piece of joy on Earth.

She hands it to me first, grinning. "For finding Cage. Cheers to small miracles."

The flask reminds me of Max and Rivet, both begging for a pull. I push the memory aside, take a sip, and pass it. "To Lash and his beautiful, bullet-ridden ass."

Flame goes next, then Lash.

Afterward, all of us are quiet, lost in our own torturous thoughts.

"So," Teagan begins, keeping her voice steady despite the hope glimmering in her eyes. "The Mercurian? Are we any closer?"

I shake my head. "I'm meeting Caspian in a few hours to search."

"And Nicolai?" Flame asks. Her brow furrows at the Puppet Master's name. "Any sign of him?"

Again, I shake my head. "He must have escaped after our reserve forces overwhelmed his."

"And Riser?" Flame prods.

Lash and I share a look. He must know what happened earlier. I reach for the flask and swallow a three-second gulp before saying, "He's recovering."

We eat the rest of our meal in silence, surrounded by the dancing flames and birdsong. When the food is gone—an alarming portion pilfered by Bramble and stored in his cache —we all stand.

"Well, this was fun but—" Lash begins, but Flame shushes him. That's when I hear it too. Crackling. Near the treetops.

I glance up in time to see the rift screen solidify. A moment later, a face appears above us. My fatigued brain takes in the wild mop of golden curls, the big blue eyes . . .

Max.

Seeing his face feels like someone hit me just below the sternum. I gasp, gripping the side of the table. The image is crystal clear. If not for the large size of him, the occasional pixelated screen, I would think he's real.

"What is your name?" a female voice asks, and recognition strips any remaining air from my lungs. The Archduchess.

"Max Graystone," Max says.

He's looking directly into the camera, trying his best to appear proud and unafraid. But his lips tremble, and his hands . . . they ball in his lap.

"And who is your sister?" she prods.

"Maia." His eyes stare from the screen and pierce my heart.

It's as if he can see me. As if he's begging me for help.

"And what would you like to tell your sister, Max?"

A muscle flickers beneath his jaw. He hesitates.

Don't fight them, Max. Do what she says.

But, my brave, stupid brother suddenly stands and yells, "Don't do it! They—"

I squeeze my thigh as the screen cuts away to the Archduchess. She's livid, an angry crimson flush spreading across her cheeks. In the background, I hear a crack and a cry of pain.

They're hurting him. Oh, gods. They're hurting him.

"He's a child!" I scream.

I'll murder them all. Gods, I'll destroy them for this.

"Baroness Lillian Graystone," the Archduchess continues, oblivious to my rage. "The Emperor has a message for you."

I wonder where my mom is, if she's seeing this.

The screen flashes to the Emperor. He sits on a high-backed throne inside an opulent chamber. A silver and gold chandelier hangs above him, and courtiers stand rigid at his back.

"Lillian," the Emperor begins. "You betrayed us. You betrayed *me*. I gave you power, I gave you wealth and more, and you spit in the face of our cause. Your actions have illuminated your poisonous, traitorous tendencies, for which the penalty is death."

Cheers and murmurs of approval rise up around him, and he holds up his hand to quiet his court. "In your absence, there is only one thing to be done. Your son, Maximus Graystone, son of a traitorous father and a lying, duplicitous mother, is sentenced to a public hanging in two days' time."

Cold blood rushes into my extremities, and I go numb. Completely, utterly unable to feel my body. Two days?

Lash reaches for me but I pull away, still staring at the screen.

"Look away, Maia," he commands softly.

But I can't. I refuse. Even though I know there's a chance . . . a chance they will execute him live.

Don't do this. Please.

He's so far away, so helpless. The camera pans back to Max, and I see the tears in his eyes he's too brave to spill. The blood darkening his golden hair at the temple where they struck him.

"Darling," Teagan says, brushing her hand over mine. "You should—"

"I'm not looking away." I glance at my friends, their horrified faces. "He deserves as much."

Teagan's mouth tightens, but she nods. "He's a tough kid, just like his sister. You should be proud."

The Archduchess approaches Max, and it takes all my strength not to scream again as she runs the end of her hatpin against his throat.

"So, young," she purrs. "And yet, he's already been poisoned by the Rebel scum to be a killer. How many civilians have you murdered, Rebel?"

Max stares into the camera, his eyes searching, as if trying to find me. He refuses to look at her.

"So brave," I whisper, pretending he can hear me. "You're so brave."

The Archduchess smiles like she can see me from space. "There is, however, a way for you to save your male heir, Lillian."

My breath catches, and I lean forward. Hardly daring to hope.

"The Emperor misses his only surviving son and heir, Caspian. You have two days to make a trade. Bring us your daughter and Prince Caspian for your son, Max. Make that trade, and your line has a chance of continuing on. Failure to do so and your son dies publicly."

Then the screen shimmers above the trees and disappears.

TWENTY

I know my mother saw the video the moment I find her in the armory. I can tell by the way her flesh is two shades lighter, as if all the blood has left her body. I can tell by the pain she tries to hide, buried deep beneath an angry frown.

As soon as she spots me, the façade starts to crumble. Her hands tremble over the pistol she cleans, and she looks away from me, wiping at her eyes before looking back. "What is it?"

My throat clenches. "Did you see?"

"Of course I saw. The entire Island did." She waves me off as if I'm asking to discuss the weather.

"We need to talk about it."

"Do we?" She rubs angrily at the muzzle of the revolver, working a cloth over its dull body. "Why?"

"Mom . . ."

She wrenches her gaze from the gun. "What? Would you like to trade yourself for your brother? Is that it?"

My mouth opens, but what can I say? If I knew for sure they would make the trade, I would do it. As stupid, foolish, and naïve as that decision is. "I don't know, maybe."

"Don't be a fool, Maia!" she snaps. "Max is gone."

Gone? How can she think that way? Anger purls through me, a dark rage so strong I can taste it, like metal and blood. "Since when do you give up so easily?"

She slams her hands down on the counter, making me jump. "Give up? The Emperor wants us to act irrationally. But trading you for Max isn't a fair trade."

"Why?" A secret part of me wants her to say because she loves me. Because she values me as much as my brother.

"Because there's still a chance we can find the Mercurian, and you are the only person who can unlock it. Without you, there is absolutely no chance we can stop Pandora. The Emperor knows that by the time we make the trade, it may be too late to activate the Mercurian. He's counting on this as a distraction to ensure Pandora destroys us."

"Wow, you make the decision sound so rational and cold."

"Because it is," she snaps. "How do you think I've survived in the Emperor's court for so long?"

"Well, you might have but Dad didn't."

She blinks at me in rage, her chest heaving. "That was his decision. Not mine."

"I don't believe you. You'd do anything to ensure your grip on power. Kill your husband. Let your kids be orphaned and imprisoned. It's a wonder you have any family left!"

I storm out before she can see the tears pricking my eyes, a sign of weakness. Part of me is relieved she didn't suggest trading me, but I know that's only because it isn't tactically to her advantage.

If it helped our cause in any way, she would. Without hesitation.

I have to find a way to save Max without trading myself and ruining our chances to stop Pandora. There has to be a way.

THE LAST LINGERING shadows evanesce as Caspian meets me outside near the Emperor's beloved fountain. I blink against the reawakened sun, remembering the night of the bombing when the fountain was blown to bits. It was here, in this pond, where we lit funeral pyres for our friends before the whole world seemed to explode.

"You okay?" Caspian asks. He's standing tall beneath the sun's glare, eyes golden half-slits. My heart gives a little jump at how beautiful he is, even tarnished by grief.

I shrug. "You saw?"

He nods, raking his hand through his hair. "I'm sorry. My father . . . I don't even recognize him anymore."

"He wants you back."

"He wants the heir to his throne back." A dark smile tugs his lips. "Without a viable heir, the throne is weakened."

"He sounds just like my mother."

Caspian chuckles. "I remember her from court. As curious as I was, I could never get a good read on her."

"You found my mother curious? Why?"

"Not your mother, Maia. You. I wanted to know more about *you* and thought perhaps I could learn more about you through her."

"You didn't think I was a traitor?"

One corner of his lip lifts. "By then I'd learned not to trust everything they told me. All I knew for sure was you were different, in a good way. And that I couldn't stop thinking about you. *Ever.*"

Heat tinges my cheeks, and I jerk my head toward the forest. "Should we check the Simulator first? In case it's working?"

I know it's a longshot, but if my father's message is still embedded in the Sim . . .

"Yeah." He shoves his hands into his pockets as we walk, Bramble's tiny feet crunching leaves as he follows us. The Simulator sits half a mile away, on the other side of the woods. It's hard not to think about the last time I came here, when everything first went wrong.

It's also hard not to remember how hard Caspian fought to protect me, outnumbered and against his own soldiers. Even when he must have known I wasn't who I said I was. That I had deceived him.

I shake the thought from my head as we leave the woods and approach the stairs leading to the hidden underground chamber. The Simulator isn't in the direction that Max was headed before I left him, but there's a small possibility it could either harness the Mercurian or have information to lead me there.

I breathe in the musty forest air, thankful for a change from the smoky ruins of the castle grounds, still permeated with the stench of death. The lake shimmers blue-green on our left. Sand grates beneath our boots. A few frogs leap into the murky water as our shadows touch them, causing soft *plunks*.

At the bottom of the stairs, Caspian reaches to punch in a code on the keypad, but I brush past him and push the heavy iron door. It creaks open.

My shoulder blades tighten. *Not a good sign.*

The Simulator chamber is dark, and we need two lumens to light the room. As the orbs float across the walls, reflecting their light off the metal panels, my hope dwindles. Charred areas show up black and gray, the air tinny with the remnants of smoke.

"Someone got to it already." I kick the door, startling Bramble, who scuttles into the shadows.

Even though we made it clear to all the Rebels that nothing was to be destroyed on the Island, a lot of them ignored that order. Not that I expected much restraint from Fienians, but still.

With a frustrated grunt, Caspian tries the panel on the wall, punching in numbers and directions that go unheeded.

Finally, he gives in to the truth, slamming his palms against the wall. "Dammit! Why would they destroy the one thing that might save them?"

I suck in my bottom lip. *How to explain?* "You can't oppress a group of people for centuries, Caspian, and then expect them to behave rationally. They're *angry.*"

He swallows, guilt darkening his face.

"I didn't mean you personally, I just meant . . ." I pause, watching him trace a line on the dusty floor with his boot. "Caspian, from here on out, you're going to be faced with the horrible things your dad did. But that has nothing to do with you. Feeling shame for his actions will only make the healing harder."

His champagne eyes lift from beneath lowered brows. "This is exactly what I'm talking about when I said you were different. The way you see things . . ."

His statement makes me uncomfortable, and I change the subject. "Anyway, this was worth a try. Besides, if this was the Mercurian, it would have reacted the last time when I was inside, right?"

I say this, but I'm not really sure. Not about any of it. But I need a reason to believe the Mercurian, wherever it is, is undamaged.

Caspian rubs his forehead, nodding. "Probably. I just . . . this was the most obvious place it would be. It's underground, protected, and your father constructed it."

"Well, knowing my father, that means this is definitely not it." I laugh. "But it still sucks because there was a message inside the Sim. I heard part of it the last time we were here."

He grins. "You mean, when you passed out?"

"Yeah." Blushing at the memory, I cross to the middle of the floor. "I woke up to you hovering over me. You were so kind. I think you gave me your cloak."

A chuckle. "I'm a gentleman like that."

The sun is ebbing into the treetops as we climb the stairs. I shiver, the air cooler than before. Something slips over my shoulders—Caspian's charcoal jacket.

"See," he says. "Gentleman."

"I'd expect nothing less from a prince." I ignore the way Bramble tugs at the jacket, trying to pull it from my shoulders.

Caspian glances at the woods and back at me. "Want to go back yet?"

No, I realize. *I don't.*

The Archduchess's message still haunts me, as does Max's face as he tried to be brave. "Can we stay for a few more minutes?"

"Sure."

There's a cement platform just above the site, perhaps marking it, and we settle onto the slab.

Caspian rubs his knuckles on his thighs. "Thanks."

"For what?"

"Not treating me like the enemy. Trusting me, despite what happened yesterday."

I pull my knees into my chest and trace circles over the tops. "This has to be hard for you."

"Yeah. I just . . ." He glances over as if assessing if I can be trusted, a newfound vulnerability tugging his lips to the side. "I've always known my part, you know? Always known where I belonged. I was the heir to the throne, the perfect Royalist. I was beloved, not really for any merits of my own, but it still felt . . . good. Looking back now all I see is this cocky, stupid, naïve kid."

"You belong here."

"Thanks, but we both know that isn't true. The Rebels despise me, and I don't blame them."

"My father once said hate is a learned condition, and that only by forgiving others can we release the thorn of hatred from our hearts and minds."

I'm not sure why my father's words suddenly seem relevant here, and they nearly choke me, but deep down, I know they're true.

"Even if the citizens think they hate you," I add, "even if they blame you for your father's sins, the only way we all get out of this continuous cycle of violence is by forgiving and trying to move forward."

He kicks a pebble. "That sounds lovely, but, truth is, I don't know who I am or where I belong anymore. My entire life is a lie, and I have only myself to blame. So the Rebels can despise me, but not more than I already despise myself."

"Caspian . . . I—I'm so sorry."

He shrugs, trying to minimize his pain even as his face darkens. "It's like I'm trapped inside a . . . I don't know. A web of moving shadows. Like I'm stuck and no matter what I do, I can't find the light, can't find a way out."

My shoulder brushes his. "You know I'm here for you, and you can always talk to me."

"Thanks. The same goes for you—if you want to talk about anything."

"That could take all night." But the joke falls flat.

He clears his throat. "Maia . . . about my father's message."

I shiver again, this time not because of the cold. "Yeah?"

"I think you should forget about the deal."

"What, you don't want to go back?"

"Part of me does. But now that I know the truth about my father, now that I know there's a way to stop our world's destruction, I can't. Not without hating myself or worse, murdering him. My own father. Can you imagine?"

"I can, actually," I say. "I've never told anyone this but . . . in the pit, I used to dream that when the Centurions busted into our house, they killed my mother instead of my father. And I would wake up so happy, so full of vindication that she finally paid for her crimes."

"Wow, that's . . . " He shoves his hand through his hair.

I release a long breath and stretch out my legs. "Let's talk about something else. Hey, remember the last time we were here?"

A grin tugs his lips. "Yeah, we rode together on my stallion."

"His name was . . . Poseidon? Right?"

"Yep. He was a beautiful pain in the ass." Caspian's Adam's apple slides down his throat as he swallows. "You sat in front of me and I remember"—he hesitates, glancing over at me—"I remember you were warm and soft against my chest, your hair this bewitching color, like the sunrise."

"Oh, gods." I cringe. "I'm pretty sure I was sweaty and disgusting."

"No. You smelled like . . . I don't know, honeysuckles and something else, something familiar. I wanted to lean in and figure out what it was, but I didn't want you to think I was a creep." He turns to look at me, his lips parted. "When you were in my arms, you were a stranger and yet I had this feeling that I knew you. That . . . it would be the easiest thing in the world to love you."

My throat suddenly feels tight. "Caspian . . ."

"You feel it too, right?" He leans closer until the warmth of his breath heats my lips. It's near dark, the trees swaying lightly in the breeze. "Like a bond between us?"

"I do but—"

"Because that's the only thing right now keeping me

together. Knowing there's a chance . . . you can still love me, despite what I've done."

I startle as his lips brush over mine. Before I can gather my thoughts, he slides his arm around my waist, holding me in place as he kisses me. My mouth parts to say something but he takes this as an invitation, his tongue slipping between my lips.

His kiss is soft, but firm. Claiming.

Fighting against the soft tug at my core, the safe, warm feeling of belonging, I tense inside his arms. An inner voice shouts, *wrong. This is all wrong.*

An image of Riser flashes inside my head, and a wave of cold extinguishes any desire I might have felt. I pull away, lips throbbing, a whirlwind of confusing emotions hitting all at once.

Guilt. Embarrassment. Confusion.

But one thing's clear: seeing Riser's face while making out with Caspian isn't normal, and it's not the actions of someone in love.

Oh, gods. Riser. He's still injured. And I . . . I . . .

My thoughts dissipate as a screeching noise erupts beside us. Bramble spins in circles on the platform. His sensors flash like alarms, casting red lights over the rocks.

"What's happening to him?" Caspian's words tumble out fast and throaty, his neck flushed red. Adjusting his collar, he adds, "Is he malfunctioning?"

I would say yes, except his circles are too perfect. And I could swear every few seconds one of his sensors points my direction . . . the act almost accusatory.

Faker.

Caspian reaches out to touch him. "Let me help you little guy—"

The instant Caspian's fingers make contact with his back,

Caspian yells and jerks his hand away. "I think he—he shocked me."

Bramble chirps, the sound almost defiant, and then scuttles off the platform into the woods.

I jump to my feet. "Bramble!"

It takes me a few minutes to find him. He's perched on a boulder that reaches my hip, his antennae pointed in the opposite direction, toward a subtle path in the woods.

"Are you proud of yourself?" I scold, hands on my hips.

Bramble ignores me. He's darting back and forth on the rock, antennae still pointed toward the path, making a series of chirps I recognize.

Oh, no. It's the exact same happy song he performs when he's around Riser.

"Bramble, was Riser here, in the forest?" I gasp. "Did he see what happened?"

Bramble's green light flashes *yes*, over and over. But I don't need Bramble to confirm what the tight ball in my gut is already telling me—Riser was here, and he witnessed everything.

TWENTY-ONE

"So, let me get this straight," Teagan drawls. "You kissed Prince Laevus and you think Riser saw you?"

We're in the bathroom of the Gold room she claimed, with a balcony and huge, claw-footed tub in the bathroom. The porcelain beauty steams with soapy water. Lash's head juts from the suds, his eyes half-open slits of pleasure.

"I *know* he saw." I glare at Bramble, curled up in the corner of the windowsill. He's been refusing to look at me since we got here.

"Did you somehow mistake princes?" Lash purrs, enjoying this more than he should.

"Stop it right now, Lash, or I'll tell Teagan your real name."

"Now that's just cruel."

The tub is huge, but Lash fills it to the brim, his knees rising from the water like bony mountains. Water darkens his hair to the color of old blood, the shoulder-length locks combed back, the tips floating in the water.

As I watch, he dips his hands into the soap bubbles and

makes little foam pyramids on the tops of his knees, then blows them down.

"And . . . you didn't mean to kiss him?" Lash continues.

"No, of course not." Bramble chirps at me and I let my head fall back, torn between ordering Bramble to electrocute Lash in the bathtub or stealing his clothes and making him walk the halls naked. Both feel like logical options right now. "I mean, I don't know. Maybe a part of me wanted to try it— just to make sure."

"Make sure?" Teagan arches an eyebrow. "He's not a piece of chocolate you can sample."

"I *know*." I smash the pads of my thumbs into my eyelids. "Look, it was an accident."

Lash chuckles. "Unless you tripped and your lips fell into his, it wasn't an accident."

I groan, resting my head in my hands. "What kind of person am I? I kissed his brother while he was in the hospital. I'm a monster."

"No," Teagan amends. "You're a girl who's been through more traumas in the last day than most experience in a lifetime."

"That's not an excuse. I don't know how I'm going to face him."

"Well, unless you figure something out fast, love," Lash says, "you won't have to worry about that much longer."

Teagan and I cut our eyes at him, his dark joke hanging in the air like steam.

"What?" He splashes bubbles at us. "Can we not talk about the fact we're almost out of time? That bitch of a planet is only four days away, and pretending otherwise is silly. So, unless Maia found the Mercurian earlier while she and lover-prince were searching and no one informed me, we're screwed."

Even though I've already told Teagan the disappointing

news, she still looks to me, perhaps hoping I'll tell her that we're close to finding it after all.

"No, you're right," I say. "After the Sim, when I couldn't find Riser, Caspian and I searched the castle and found nothing."

"So, that's it?" Teagan frowns. "We're out of options?"

"I mean, unless you have a way of flying to Hyperion, somehow boarding unnoticed, rescuing Max and then getting us both safely back to . . ."

Holy. Fienian. Hell. My words fall away as something hits me. Not an idea, exactly. The promise of one.

Teagan narrows her eyes. "What?"

"Suppose we *do* go to Hyperion," I say, carefully.

An idea nibbles the edges of my skull, but it's loose, incorporeal. I don't want to get anyone's hopes up yet.

"How, exactly, would we do that and not die?" she prods.

Drumming my fingertips over my lips, I work to gather my thoughts. "What if we somehow made them think we belonged there?"

The water ripples out, making a splashing noise against the tub as Lash lifts up until his chest and part of his abdomen shows. "I've heard rumors that Hyperion is entirely Sim based."

"Meaning . . ." Teagan says.

"Meaning," I finish, trying not to get overly excited even as adrenaline jolts my body,

"when we return Caspian, we could change our faces in the Sim to look like, I don't know, missing Royalists maybe?"

Teagan frowns. "You could do that?"

"Not me, but perhaps—"

"Flame," Teagan interrupts.

Lash leaps to his feet and Teagan and I both yell, turning around before we see any of his man bits.

"Don't look, you heathens," he scolds. "Unless you want

to be jealous for the rest of your existence that this fine piece of meat is off limits."

"Lash!" we both growl as his bare feet slap against the stone. He pads over and I hear him grab *hopefully* a towel off the rack.

Bramble chitters with excitement as Teagan and I follow a now covered Lash to the bedroom. I try not to stare at the mangled, pitted flesh of his back, the warped muscles that disappear into the towel wrapped around his waist as we form a plan to meet in thirty with the others.

Despite my fatigue, I feel like skipping. We have a plan. It's tentative, flimsy, and pretty insane. But it's something.

On the way out, Teagan and I both spy Lash's shirt and pants on the bed, and she gives me a conspiratorial nod. I grab his clothes and slip out the door, grinning as he yells, "That's just plain mean, Graystone!"

"It's only cruel to those who have to see your naked ass!" Teagan teases before bursting into laughter. I join her, reveling in the fleeting moment of happiness after so much death and destruction.

"An atrocious lie, Aster," Lash retorts. "Even shot up, my ass is still a gift from the gods."

A few minutes later, cheers drift down the hall behind us as Lash undoubtedly strolls, half-clothed, through the castle. Enjoying every bit of his nude cameo.

I know this is no time for jokes, but I grin anyway. According to one of my mother's famous essays, part of being a good leader is knowing when to rally your soldiers with humor.

And I can't think of anything funnier right now than Lash streaking through the halls like some beautiful god of old.

My sliver of joy slowly fades, taking my smile with it as the reality of our plan takes hold. My mother also once said a plan was only good if the scenarios that led to failure could be mitigated to exactly one.

Yet, no matter what we do, the ways in which this plan can fail are like the stars in the sky. Too numerous to even bother counting.

Except it has to go exactly right—the entire world is counting on us.

TWENTY-TWO

T he war room inside Laevus Castle is cavernous, a high-
ceilinged monstrosity in desperate need of windows to
lighten the dark room. I cringe at the head of a tusked boar
just above the door. Game of every kind, probably hunted
from the surrounding woods, line the rafters, and giant
leather maps decorate the walls.

Two fireplaces yawn on either side, gold phoenixes
cresting the mantles. If most war rooms are meant to look
opposing, this one was made to impress with its sheer
opulence and wealth.

My mother's ivory cape slithers across the floor, the hem
darkened with soil and what I assume is blood. She waves a
hand and the torches on the chandeliers and walls erupt,
casting the room in tangerine light.

An oval table spans the length of two carriages in the
middle of the room. The banners of all the houses hang
above it.

Strange, to be in this room where the Emperor once
plotted the deaths of so many. Stranger still how comfortable
my mother looks in it. Like she's been here a thousand times.

Lash strides in wearing a flashy doublet and loose tunic over shiny gold pants. He glares at me. "One word about my outfit and I'll murder you."

"Who's getting murdered?" Teagan says as she breezes in. Her gaze snags on Lash's outfit. "Wow, Lash. You're so . . . sparkly."

"Aster!" Lash raises his russet eyebrows in warning.

My mother gives us all a look, and we settle around the table. I take the head seat just as Flame and the others arrive. After what happened with Caspian, I haven't talked to Riser, and I switch between wanting to meet his eye and assess what he saw and wanting to avoid him altogether.

Riser makes the decision for me by ignoring everyone as he takes his seat on the other side, next to Flame. Sour by nature, it's weird to see Flame beaming, her face brightened by hope. Finding Cage did that.

I don't outright dare to hope for the same outcome for Max, instead keeping the possibility hidden, a tiny dancing spark of promise. A weapon. Ready to wield when the moment is right.

Adding insult to injury, Bramble scurries from my shoulder, scuttles across the table, and leaps into Riser's lap. Forcing my focus on the others, I watch Flame and Teagan whisper for a moment, their heads pressed conspiratorially together, before risking a glance at Caspian.

Just like Riser, he seems intent on hiding his emotions behind a tight, closed-off mask. His lips are tight, his brow furrowed so that his golden eyebrows nearly meet.

Sensing my focus, his gaze brushes mine, lingering for a too-long moment before looking away.

I stifle a groan. *Why did you let him kiss you, genius?*

My mother finally takes the last seat next to me at the table. Thanks to the Emperor's food stores, we have much better food than the last meeting—oranges, pears, buttery crackers that melt in my mouth, and thick slices of cured ham. Bramble has already started depositing the feast from the platters to Riser's plate, as if he senses Riser's dark mood and is trying to fix it with food.

Fienian hell, if only it were that easy.

Two Rebels attend to everything quickly before I wave them off, anxious to get started.

"We have a plan," I say, forgoing any pleasantries.

"We?" My mother rests her elbows on the table, speaking like someone used to everyone listening.

Teagan and I share a tense glance. Under my mother's sharp glare, my plan suddenly feels flimsy and juvenile.

Squaring my shoulders, I shove my chair back and stand. "We might have a way to get Max back."

"Might?" She lifts a bored eyebrow. "Or do?"

"Do. We do." My face burns as I feel Riser's gaze suddenly boring into me. "The Emperor demanded Caspian and I in return for Max. So, let's give him what he wants."

My mother blinks at me, the disappointment clear in the downturn of her lips. "We've already discussed the folly of that plan."

I grin. "But we haven't discussed what would happen if I went as someone *else*."

"Someone else?" She cants her head to the side a half-inch, suddenly interested. "Who?"

"Well, if Flame's up to the task"—she scowls at my hesitation over her skill—"Countess Delphine Bloodwood might just accompany Caspian. As a sign of our good faith. From what we've heard, Hyperion is one giant Sim. Metal walls are made to look like stone, ceilings are turned into clear blue skies, floors transformed into sweeping meadows. So why can't my face become Delphine's?"

Caspian goes from leaning casually back in his chair to sitting up straight. "That might work . . . with the right skills.

Hyperion's tech is advanced beyond anything you've ever seen, with over forty programmers running the entire operation. A tech with clumsy code would be noticed immediately."

Flame sneers at Caspian. "Boy, I'm the best tech in the entire nation."

"Boy?" Caspian retorts. "Don't you mean *Prince*?"

For a long, stretched-out second, we all look to see how Flame will react. Then Caspian's stern lips crack into a smile as he chuckles, and we all laugh, even Flame.

Everyone except my mother. As the humor dissipates, our focus draws back to her.

"The plan is flawed," my mother says, and I hold my breath waiting for her reason why. "Maia, you're needed here."

My jaw goes slack. That was the last thing I was expecting. "Why? No, I'm going. Who else can play Delphine?"

"Anyone, that's the point. Anyone can wear Delphine's face."

"I don't want it to be anyone, because I don't trust just anyone to get Max back. And we all know even after we give the Emperor Caspian and *Delphine*, he won't give Max up without hurting him somehow, or making a spectacle. I'm going to make sure he honors his bargain."

"That's a lovely, noble idea, Maia. But what happens to the Mercurian if you fail? With you here, there's still a chance."

"If something goes wrong up there, it won't matter if I'm here or not. We'll never find the Mercurian without Max."

"You're being emotional," she accuses.

"You're damn right, I am." I hold her stare as I pace around the table, refusing to back down. "Because I'm a human being, and I can't abandon someone I love just because it serves some cause. You can't make every decision using numbers and probabilities. Sometimes, you just have to follow your heart and do what's right."

"And what if I can't lose you too?" my mother barks, the anger in her voice surprising.

I don't mean to say it—but the words tumble from my lips like Hot Weapons. "You lost me years ago, so problem solved."

A long moment of silence stretches out, interrupted only by my pounding heartbeat, and for the first time ever, I truly understand that words can be the most effective weapons of all.

Unable to admit defeat, my mother glances around the room, searching for allies. "You can't seriously entertain sending my daughter to Hyperion."

Riser slowly stands. He doesn't look at me as he says, "I do. In fact, I'll only go if she leads us."

My mouth falls open as the others follow suit. Each person echoing Riser's statement.

My friends won't go without me.

My throat pinches with emotion. A part of me feels unworthy of such support. "There," I add, glaring at my mother. "Does that help move this argument along?"

My mother's lips part as if she's about to speak . . . but then, whatever words she was about to say never materialize.

I ball my hands into fists on the table. "Then it's settled."

After that, we focus on the details, and anxiety turns to excitement as we discuss the plan well through dinnertime, all of us too amped up to eat the food on the platters right in front of us.

It makes sense that if I'm to impersonate Delphine then she'll impersonate me. The larger problem comes with how to silence her—and Flame's suggestion to cut out her tongue isn't an option.

Not a humane one, at least.

"Chemical lobotomy?" Flame suggests next, grinning with cruel pride.

I don't even answer that one, and the group moves on, with Lash swearing to fix the problem by tomorrow.

Tomorrow. We'll be on Hyperion tomorrow.

It all feels too fast. Too surreal. Too . . . something.

I never once thought I would see the famed Hyperion. Even when I fought in the Trials. And now, in less than a day, we'll be inside the floating city—with no chance to escape if something goes wrong.

We finish fleshing out the few details, and no matter how much I try to ignore him, my focus drifts to Riser. He never speaks. Not once.

He does, however, watch everything with eagle eyes, nodding now and then or frowning at an idea he dislikes.

And he never meets my stare. Never responds to my suggestions or even reacts.

Why did I hurt him? Despite his cool façade, I know how many times he's been wounded, disappointed, betrayed. I never thought I would add to that list.

Maybe that's what love is—dropping your armor and letting someone in knowing they'll eventually injure you. That they can't help it. That we're porcupines, all of us carrying these quills of anger and pain, and whenever someone gets too close we can't help but stab them.

The talk goes late into the evening. There's also other things to discuss, such as fortifying the grounds in case Nicolai tries to retake the castle. His absence is alarming, like the calm before a storm.

When it's well past midnight, we finally have our plan. And despite the risks, for the first time since Max was taken, I let the spark of hope I've been harboring become a flame. We might have a chance. If I can pull this off, if everything goes exactly according to plan, if they believe I'm Delphine, Max might be home in time to still activate the Mercurian.

If. If. If.

I've never both loved and hated a word more.

TEAGAN AND I SHARE A BED. It's enormous, enough to fit three people. Something Lash was quick to point out right before we made him leave. Teagan sleeps like the dead. But I fidget and kick through a slew of nightmares until Bramble finally gets annoyed and moves from my pillow to the end of the bed.

When dawn trickles through the massive bay window, I slog to my feet and dress. I glance over at Bramble, lying on his back, metal legs twitching as he rests in the yawning morning light.

Today's the day.

I find Flame in the dining hall looking as tired as I feel. She was up all night working on the code that will transform my face into Delphine's inside Hyperion. Lash, Riser, Teagan, and her will all have new faces as well. Flame explains that she used the faces of Royalists who died on the battlefield.

"Won't the Emperor wonder why we're feeling so generous?" I ask, peeling a bruised banana.

Flame takes a sip of the dark coffee steaming from a tin cup. "No, he'll assume your mother really wants Max back because he's the last remaining heir to her line."

"Oh." I take a bite of my banana.

"I'm not saying that's how she thinks, that's just how the Emperor thinks."

"Right."

Lash appears with a handful of muffins stacked along his

forearms. "You can say it, ladies," he announces as he slips in beside me at the table.

I discard my half-eaten banana and steal a blueberry muffin from him. "Say what?"

"That I'm a genius."

Flame scoffs. "Why the Fienian hell would we say that?"

"Because," Lash says, taking a bite of a burnt muffin. His words are muffled. "I found a way to silence Delphine."

I raise my eyebrows in impatience.

"Paralyze her vocal cords." He gestures as if he's injecting his neck with something. "Works for, oh, at least thirty-six hours to keep her quiet."

"Can we test the first batch on you?" Flame mutters.

Lash clicks his tongue. "No appreciation."

"You did well, Lash," I say, patting his head and cooing. "Good boy."

Flame rolls her eyes just as Teagan shows up. She snatches some coffee and joins us. "Why are we petting Lash like a dog?"

"Because he solved our Delphine problem, and it didn't even involve cutting off body parts," I say as I stand. "See you guys at the craft?"

All of the starcrafts suffered damage in the battle, and mechanics worked all night to make sure one could fly by this morning.

My friends wave me off as I rush to find my mother before we leave. I can't imagine she has any words of encouragement beyond *don't screw this up like you do everything else,* but I still want to see her.

To give her the option, I suppose, of proving me wrong.

I'm almost to the room she's camped in when I hear her talking to someone. I freeze just outside the door as an older male's voice responds.

"I never suspected your betrayal, Lillian."

The Emperor—I would know his voice anywhere. Heart racing, I flatten against the wall and angle my head to hear better.

"Oh, you had to know I'd make a power play eventually," my mother says, casually, as if she's discussing a move on a chessboard.

"Hmm. Is that what this is? I thought you might be supporting the Rebel's cause. That maybe, all these years that I confided in you, supported you, you were plotting against me."

My mother's high-pitched laugh erupts. "Always paranoid, Marcus. Perhaps I simply saw an opportunity and took it. You're not the only one who lusts after power."

She's so convincing I actually believe her.

A pause. "Have you decided to accept my offer?"

"I have. I'm even sweetening the deal for you. There are some high-ranking Gold children I'm sending back with Caspian."

"And why, Lillian, would you do that?" Suspicion drips from his every word.

"Because I want to make sure Max comes back in one piece." My mother's tone has gone steely. "Unharmed, Marcus. He's the last of my line and he's—"

"He's one of *them*," the Emperor interrupts.

"Perhaps, but he's so young. So pliable. There's still a chance to mold him into the Royalist ideals, to shape his mind to our principals."

Unlike me, I don't dare mutter. That ship sailed years ago. Whatever I am, there is no molding me into something better. Something more to her standards.

More silence. Holding my breath, I peek around the door frame. My mother sits to the right in front of a rift screen. The Emperor's face fills the screen, and I flinch.

How did my mother deal with such a monster all these years?

Takes one to know one.

"And you're willing to give up your daughter?" the Emperor questions.

"Will you take the deal without her?"

A shadow passes over the Emperor's face. "You know that can't happen. Not after she murdered hundreds on the Island. She's a terrorist, and letting her escape justice would set a terrible example."

"Then promise me you won't kill her."

The Emperor peers at my mother, and I'm surprised to still see affection there, despite her betrayal. "If she publicly confesses, she may live out her days in prison on Hyperion. Although, I promise you, death would be kinder."

I'm not sure why my mother presses the point when it will be Delphine instead of me. Perhaps because the Emperor would expect nothing less.

"Done." My mother's shoulders sag.

The Emperor grins. "It must sting. Trading one child for another."

"You'd do the same if Ophelia was still alive. Trade her for Caspian, even if she was always your favorite child."

The Emperor doesn't even flinch at the mention of the daughter he murdered—but I do, especially knowing that she was his favorite and he still killed her without hesitation. "You always did have a soft spot for Maximus. But, as I recall, Maia never lived up to your standards."

Bastard.

My breath catches as I wait for my mother to refute this, my heart hammering against my skull so loud I can hardly hear her reply.

"Children are like that, are they not?" Her voice is soft, and I strain to catch it all. "For all the time and resources you put into molding them into your image, some become the opposite just to spite you."

"If your daughter is a disappointment to you, you only have yourself to blame. Should have had her reconstructed in the womb like I implored and none of this would have befallen her."

Disappointment? I sag against the wall, fighting to keep the declaration from poisoning my newfound hope. Any words of reconciliation I imagined between us are forgotten.

I know she is playing his game, but I also know, deep down, that she's always felt this way about me. Hearing her admit aloud my absolute failure to be anything worthy of love feels like ripping a scab off a wound that's been festering for years.

Taking a deep breath, I force myself to march down the hall. Shoulders back. Head held high.

I can't control how she views me. Nor can I be who she wants me to be. All I can do is prove her wrong.

I may not be like her—cold, calculating, able to use others as pawns to achieve my goals—but I'm determined as hell and filled with enough righteous fury to take down the Emperor himself.

TWENTY-THREE

The roof still smells like a war zone. The air pungent with old blood and spilled oil. Sunlight glints off shards of glass piled in corners, dark smoke stains ringing areas where crafts used to rest. Most of the completely ruined ones have already been semi-dismantled for anything useful —wires, tech, metal.

Their broken hulls rest, charred and blackened, like the bizarre skeletons of mythical beasts.

The others surround a starcraft near the middle. Squeezing past soldiers working on the other crafts, I pick my way through the wreckage toward them. Bramble shadows me, darting around the debris scattering the roof.

As I join the others, the sun bursting over the treetops and warming my cheeks, Lash pulls me aside. "I checked on Rivet before I came up here."

"And?" But tendrils of dread slip around my heart and squeeze as I take in the veiled agony in his expression. "No, Lash."

"I tried, love. I truly did."

An ache swells at the back of my throat. "Are you absolutely sure?"

He swallows. "She's not going to make it."

"Have you told the others?"

"No. They don't need to know until we return."

I nod, struggling to grapple with the grief of her loss. To package it somehow to make it manageable until I can afford to grieve.

"I only told you because, well, I know you can handle it. You're strong." He squeezes my shoulder before limping toward the craft. I watch him, surprised by his words.

Strong? I don't feel strong. I feel on the verge of collapse, a pane of glass fractured to the point that a strong wind could shatter it. I feel cobbled together like one of Max's school projects, a cheap, distorted version of what I should be.

Of what I *need* to be to pull this off.

A fraud—I'm a fraud and if my friends knew that . . . if they knew how weak and incapable I was—

Stop. Get your crap together.

My sudden vulnerability makes me search out Riser, only to find him already watching me.

In the glorious mid-morning light, the different colors of his eyes are highlighted. The gold rimming the pupil of his reconstructed green eye catches in the light, while the deep blues of his other eye match the lake in the distance.

"Maia." He nods his head and goes to turn away.

Below him, Bramble does his weird little dance, but Riser either doesn't see or doesn't react.

I grab his arm, noticing the way his flesh seems to shiver beneath my touch. "Wait. I—I'm glad you're okay. I was really worried."

"Thanks." There's no mistaking the curtness of his tone, and my chest tightens.

"Look, I don't know what you saw, but . . . it's not what you think."

A tendon in his neck trembles and pops, and he forces himself to once again meet my stare. "You said to give you your space, so that's what I'm doing. I thought it was because of your mom, but"—he flicks a glance at Caspian—"whatever the reason, I'm respecting your wishes."

The others are all pretending not to listen as they focus on anything but us. I want to explain everything, but this isn't the time to lose focus or let myself become distracted.

"I think we should . . . talk about this."

Ugh. Why is this so hard? I wish I could just spill my thoughts into his brain so he understood it was an accident. That a part of me needed to know—to make absolutely sure —Caspian and I weren't meant to be together.

Now I know, but it might be too late.

He flicks a cold glance at Caspian, the dark promise of violence glittering in his mismatched eyes. "I'm not sure if now is a good time, unless you want me to kill my brother before we board." The corners of his lips tighten. "Pretty sure that would put a wrinkle in our plan."

"Right." Panic trills through me, and not just because I can tell by the way he's gone still, like the way a panther does right before it pounces, that he's serious. But because I realize now how badly I've hurt him. That there are no quick words to make it go away.

Maybe there shouldn't be. Maybe when you hurt some-one, there should always be consequences. But right now I just want my friend back. My confidante. The boy I trusted beyond measure.

As if he can read my thoughts, he says, "Don't worry—I still have your back up there." There's an undercurrent of solemnity in his voice. "I pledged my loyalty to you and that doesn't change."

That doesn't, but so much else has.

"Thank you," I manage. "And I'm sorry. More than you know. When all of this is over, I'll prove that to you."

How could I not realize kissing Caspian would wound Riser more than almost anything else? He's lived in the Golden Prince's shadow for his entire life. Watched everything he deserved—love, respect, admiration—go to Caspian while he was left to rot.

And then when he found out I was matched to Caspian . . .

I release a breath, trying to tamp down the wild flood of emotions coursing through me. He's right about boarding. We're running out of time, and I need to focus. They need me to be a strong leader.

So I nod, biting my cheek to steady my voice. "Just . . . take it easy, with your Reconstruction and all."

Take it easy? What the Fienian hell, Maia.

Riser stares at me for a heartbeat longer before turning away, leaving me awkwardly still grasping his bicep like an idiot.

Let go of his arm, genius.

I do, finally, dropping my hand as I try to clear my mind of Riser and anything else not important to this mission.

Get. It. Together.

As I climb the ramp and enter the craft, a whisper of panic jolts through me. Cameras that upload the landscape outside and display it on the interior of the craft make it appear as if we're inside a clear bubble. Seats line the walls.

Last time I was inside one of these, bad things happened right after. And I very much doubt this time will be an exception.

A Rebel pilot nods to us all as we strap in. I sit next to Lash and lock my harness into place with a click. The seats are soft, supple leather, much nicer than the craft that brought me here weeks ago for the Trials. I assume that's because this is a starcraft that takes people into space, built for Golds.

Space. I'm not yet comfortable with the fact that in a few short hours we'll be thousands of miles into the sky among the stars. I also think, on Hyperion, space is the least of my worries, and before I can stop it, a barrage of nerves flings bad scenarios at me.

What if Flame's code doesn't work? If the Emperor somehow knows we're tricking him? My friends will be imprisoned, tortured, and executed in horrible ways. What if Max is already dead?

What if . . .

Sighing, I lean my head back—and freeze as Caspian falls into the seat on my left.

Caspian's golden eyes light up as he says, "Seat taken?"

What can I say? Yes? I can feel my chest prickle with heat as I shake my head.

Although Riser doesn't look my way, a smirk dances across his face. Adding salt to the wound, Bramble scampers up his leg, circles twice, and settles in his lap.

Traitor.

Flame enters next, shoving a pissed-off looking Delphine. After a day in the prison cell, her short blonde hair is greasy and her face gaunt. Dark smudges darken her cheeks and forehead. With every step, Delphine tries to resist, twisting against Flame's hold on her wrists manacled behind her.

And every foot, Flame shoves her forward.

Flame glares at us all. "Why did I get stuck with this one?"

"I will murder you," Delphine snarls. "All of you."

Flame's glare hones in on Lash. "I thought you were going to mute her. Does this sound like silence to you, boy?"

Delphine's face goes red with rage, but then Flame kicks the back of her legs at the knee joint and she falls forward.

Using the momentum, Flame wrangles the Royalist into a harness, just barely avoiding the girl's kicks.

Delphine suddenly stops struggling, her eyes wild and tongue lolling. "You're all going to die! Idiots. Ugh!"

"Lash!" Flame growls.

Lurching across the craft, Lash positions himself above Delphine. Her all-white eyes roll up to meet his.

Shrieks of laughter burst from her lips. "Look at you, Brig. So powerful now. I bet you love this. I bet you—"

He jams the needle into her neck, right in the middle of her throat. The needle is small and it's a quick jab. In and out. A small dot of blood appears where the needle went in.

"Why do you keep doing that?" she rages. Her voice doesn't sound any different, except maybe a bit sharper with anger, and all of us watch her anxiously. "Why are you all staring at me? Gods, you're all so stupid. You have no idea what you're doing. The Emperor will kill you, he'll kill all of . . . of . . ."

Her eyes go wide. Her lips opening and closing like a fish on land. But no sound comes out.

"Hallelujah," Teagan mutters. "The demon has been excised."

Realizing what happened, Delphine suddenly leaps forward. The harness wasn't clicked tight and she breaks free —only to have Flame ram into her and wrestle with the first buckle until it snaps together with a resounding *clack*. The other side takes a little more effort.

By the time they're done, both girls are sweaty and red-faced. Delphine looks like she might have a stroke.

Not that I'd be sad about it.

A screen flashes to life in the space between our seats and the pilot's. My mother's face appears, and I feel a tug of . . . something. An emotion both equal parts hopeful and disappointed.

Hopeful, because I want to pretend this message is for me, a proper goodbye.

And disappointed because I know that's a decent human gesture my mother isn't capable of.

"I'm sorry I couldn't be there to see you off," she begins, her voice impersonal and eyes cold. "But I wanted to say how important your mission is. Calculating in the flight time to get back with both Maia and Max, you have forty hours at most to pull this off."

Tension fills the craft, my shoulders tightening.

"After forty hours, the remaining citizens here will be funneled into the Emperor's shelters below as we await impact." I swear her eyes find mine. "Godspeed."

Then the screen dies and the ramp to the craft closes with a soft *thud*. Butterflies burst under my ribs as we shoot into the air, the pilot calling out a mixture of curses and apologies. Flame dives to her seat and straps in.

No one mentions my mother's speech.

Maybe that's because we're all trying hard not to panic as the craft lurches through the sky. Up up up so fast we're melted to our seats, flesh and bone smashed against metal and plastic.

One second the castle takes up the entire bottom of the craft. The next, it's hardly a dot against the green of the Island.

Another second and the Island disappears into a smudge of turquoise. A breath after that, there are no more details on the land. Only flowing swaths of green and blue, softened by the occasional quilt of clouds.

If I tilt my head a bit to the right, I can see Pandora blazing in the sky. Flames ring her body, and her usually dark, pitted mass appears lighter, flecked with browns and yellows. She used to feel like an evil eye watching us. Now she feels like a raging beast.

Suddenly the craft accelerates, the force making my head feel heavy. Sweat crops up on my cheeks as my belly churns, and I bite down a hot wave of vomit.

Lash holds his stomach, groaning. "Who thought being able to see outside was a good idea?"

Somehow the craft goes even faster, pinning me into my seat so that I couldn't move even if I wanted to. Vibrations wrack the hull, violent and jerky and terrifying.

With a quiet moan, Lash bends over and throws up.

No one says anything. We're all trying to avoid the same fate.

Thank the gods, the pilot has the sense to flip the video feed off. The outside images disappear and we all relax as our bodies slowly get used to the rocking. Once we're through the atmosphere, the ship smooths out and my nausea eases.

Caspian uses the lull to explain what to expect on Hyperion. "Don't be alarmed by what you see," he begins. "Hyperion was built using the most advanced Sim technology in existence. You might be expecting a spaceship, but it's a floating city of wonders."

"It can't be more ostentatious than the Island," Flame remarks. "I doubt we'll be that impressed."

Caspian grins. "Oh?" He glances around the ship. "Then I guess you've seen huge snowy mountains and oceans that span miles beside rooms made of crystal and gold that are illuminated within by a thousand tiny flames, or chambers that appear to be galaxies—all inside the same ship?"

Lash whistles, and Flame can't seem to find a reply.

"Then there are the interactive rooms like the skyroom, where you can float across the clouds to your dinner table, or the waterworld where you can swim beneath the sea."

"I thought your father hated technology?" I point out, my voice sharper than I planned.

Caspian shrugs. "That's the beauty of it all. Because it's all inside a Sim, you never see the technology, and it's impossible to decipher the fake from the real."

"Exactly what we're counting on, darling," Teagan says.

"I'm not trying to brag," Caspian adds. "But I need you to know what to expect so that, when you first arrive, you don't react to the world. All of the Golds and their attendants have either been to Hyperion before or been prepped on what to expect. And don't say anything you don't want splayed across a screen. The only time you'll have privacy is in your room."

"Will we look different to each other?" I ask. The idea that Riser could glance at me and see Delphine's face feels wrong.

Flame shakes her head. She's taken out all her piercings and stripped the color from her hair, and if not for the one side being shaved, she almost looks innocent. "I have it set up where we look the same to anyone in our party." She pulls something out of a pack—the slim body of an uploader. "All of you need to use this to upload a map of Hyperion, as well as names and faces of the Royalists on board. You'll also need"—she fishes around the bag—"this."

Everyone stares at the silver blister pack of six tiny buttons.

"Mini-bombs," she explains, practically purring as she strokes the Hot Weapons. "They might be small, but they pack a punch. Stick them on anything you want to destroy. I have one with the Emperor's name on it."

Caspian grimaces. "Weapons aren't allowed onboard, but since everyone's already been vetted, no one's routinely checked. If you have a small dagger, stash it somewhere. Anything else, like pistols, for example, are too big to hide."

Flame frowns and begrudgingly shoves the long, silver rifle-like weapon under her seat. Then she nods to Lash, and he hands over a leather pouch, whatever's inside clinking.

Flame unzips the pouch slowly, pulling a cylindrical glass

vial out. White powder fills the glass like snow.

"If you're captured," she says, giving the vial a soft shake. "Swallow this."

"It's a sedative," Lash adds, his voice taking on an ominous tone. "At that dose, it will stop your breathing in less than a minute. But make sure you take all of it or it'll just make you drowsy."

After that, we pass around the uploader, divvy up the stash of tiny Hot Weapons, and each take a sedative to hide somewhere on our person. Then the lights dim and I curl on my side, resting my head on Lash's shoulder as I try to grab a few hours of sleep.

Every so often, the craft jerks or rattles. Otherwise, the soft hum of the ride lulls me into a half-sleep.

I see Max standing on a wooden platform just like the one the Archduchess used. A noose hangs around his neck. "Wait!" I cry, running toward him, but he's on a hill. And I can't push past the crowd. Can't seem to get to him.

All at once, the door at his feet thuds open and he falls. There's a sickening crack as his neck snaps . . .

I jerk awake making gurgling, half-screaming noises . . .

Dim lights. Harness. Pressurized craft. We're still in the starcraft. *Nightmare—that was a nightmare. A really effed up one.*

The first person I see is Riser, his face twisted in concern as he watches me.

It'll be okay, he mouths.

I nod back, grateful for his words. Even if I'm not sure I believe them. Bramble is back in my lap, and he stirs, sensing my agitation.

Lash yawns. "No worries, love. I'm right here."

"Maybe it's your breath that woke her," Teagan teases, stretching out her long legs.

"Impossible. Every part of me smells divine."

Flame chuckles. "Lash, did I forget to mention you're

impersonating the hideous, pimple-faced attendant of some rich Gold. Do at least try to act the part."

Lash gives an aggrieved sigh, combing his fingers through his russet hair, pulled back into a very neat man-bun. "I'll *try* very hard to hold back my charm and the animal magnetism that oozes from my very pores."

"Gods save us," Teagan mutters.

The light mood evaporates as the main lights flicker to life, and the craft begins to slow.

The pilot says, "Five minutes until docking."

My pulse races, and when I wipe my hands on my pants, my palms leave sweat streaks. Now that we're close to where Max is being held, I allow myself to think about him.

Is he hungry? Have they given him water? Is he cold? Has the Archduchess hurt him? Does he hate me? Does he think I'm coming back for him again?

My entire body shudders at the thought of Max and that sociopathic woman in the same room.

If she touched him . . .

The craft suddenly jerks to a stop, the harness digging into my chest and shoulders. Then it goes quiet. I quickly shut Bramble into sleep mode before he can figure out my plan and escape. The mode only allows for him to awaken if disrupted, so he won't be helpless if discovered.

Once he's safely settled beneath the craft's seat, hidden from view, I meet Riser's worried stare.

He nods, once, but I can't be sure if his calming gesture is directed toward Bramble or the shit-storm we're about to willingly enter.

"Welcome to Hyperion," Caspian says. "The most exclusive, luxurious, and guarded piece of real estate in existence. We're about to discover if Flame's code passed inspection."

"It did," Flame insists, just as the ramp slams open.

And the unsmiling faces of five Centurions await.

TWENTY-FOUR

"Out!" the guards order, their gruff voices threading my body with panic. Riser and I make eye contact, and I shake my head. We don't know if they know yet.

The others file out. I'm the last. As I stand and grab Delphine by the wrists from behind, herding her toward the awaiting Centurions, I force my face into a haughty sneer.

"Take the prisoner," I snap, shoving her down the last three steps. "She stinks."

Delphine snaps her head back and glares murder at me with her eyes.

The guards stare from me to Delphine, and I feel like the lie is written all over my face. Moment of truth to see if Flame's code works. From my periphery, I spy both Riser and Flame reaching for their weapons—ready for any sign we've been compromised.

"Why are there so many of you?" the Centurion asks, his face a mixture of confusion and distrust.

This is where the next part of our plan comes in. My mother already casually informed the Emperor there would be more prisoners. Now we have to sell it.

With the help of Caspian, we found Royalists who either died or were imprisoned during the battle and then had Flame use their identities. Riser's face is Delphine's assistant, whose body, I discovered, was only seven feet away from where I spotted Delphine.

The girl died protecting her, not that Delphine showed any remorse.

Flame is impersonating a high-ranking Gold friend of Delphine's. Hopefully, her status will be high enough to access restricted areas and discover where they're keeping Max.

Lash is her attendant, much to his annoyance. But using servants to powerful Golds has its uses. Like the Golds they serve, attendants can move freely through every part of the ship. But unlike Golds, most servants don't have family on the ship who might recognize something is off.

The Centurion is still watching me, his face growing tenser every second I don't respond. So I say what I practiced last night.

"I demanded my assistant back"—I give an offhand wave toward Riser—"and Caspian negotiated a few more prisoners to come with us. You know how kindhearted the prince is."

A frown settles over the Centurion's face. We all wait, not daring to breathe, my pulse racing.

Finally the Centurion takes a step forward, the suspicion fading. He reaches out a hand to grab my arm, but hesitates a few inches away. "The Emperor wants to see you."

Confidence makes his voice carry—but behind his confidence is . . . fear. Of me.

No, of Delphine.

"Don't touch me, pig," I hiss, pushing past his hand. *Too much?* Apparently not, because the other Centurions smirk at their abused brethren, almost like they expected it.

We must be inside Hyperion, but it's hard to tell from the

non-descript hanger. White walls reach three stories high, starcrafts glittering from their racks. Each rests inside its own separate cubby, stacked one on top of the other.

As we follow the Centurions to a door, I'm able to access the uploaded layout enough to know we're headed toward the west wing of the ship, a giant circular orb ringed with seven outer layers.

Still, whatever I'm expecting as we all file through the hanger door into Hyperion, nothing prepares me for the world we enter. I can't seem to figure out where to look because I want to stare at everything.

The arched cathedral ceilings that span at least ten stories. The ivory walls so white, so pure I want to touch them just to see if they're soft like clouds. Golden pillars wrap the room, and chandeliers as large as the starcraft we came here in hover above like bejeweled clouds of light, each one a unique masterpiece of thin gold branches covered in birds the vibrant color of emeralds and rubies.

I can't hold in a gasp as I spy rivers the color of the sky cutting through the floors. Royalists float down the meandering stream on jewel-toned boats, their laughter filling the air.

Remembering Caspian's warning, I tear my gaze from the grandeur all around me and screw my face into a look of bored disdain. We cut across the huge chamber and into a winding hallway that resembles a stormy afternoon.

I catch Lash staring and pinch him as we walk. But all of us can't seem to look forward or adopt an attitude of boredom, our gazes bouncing around wildly. Thank the gods, the guards hardly pay attention.

A circular glass disc sits in the center of the last room we enter. It hovers five feet off the ground, floating steps of glass leading up to it. I barely hesitate as I follow the guards up, along with the others.

What is this thing?

When the disc starts ascending, I gasp, before realizing this is an elevator.

Caspian slips his hand into mine and squeezes. For a moment, I nearly pull away before remembering who I am. Delphine. His *betrothed*. I feel Riser's stare fall over me, over my hand curled tightly in Caspian's.

It takes all my willpower not to pull away.

Especially when I see our faces splashed across the walls of the room, magnified to one hundred times our size. Tiny bubble-like orbs bob around us, capturing every move we make from several different angles.

Even knowing we're being filmed, it's hard to make my mind realize the girl I'm watching is me and not someone else. Caspian's face appears the same, but the rest of us all wear different faces.

I blink, and Delphine's eyes flutter on the screen. I lift my free hand and touch my hair—Delphine lifts her hand on the screen and touches her short blonde hair, bobbed at her chin.

Surreal. I turn my head, too disturbed by the image of my enemy's face on mine to continue.

They must have video screens built into every wall in this Sim. Caspian squeezes, and I realize that every single gesture between us will be watched and scrutinized. He clenches my hand *again*, twice, and I realize he's wanting me to show more affection.

The elevator is nearly to the top of the ceiling. My mouth is bone-dry. Standing on my tiptoes, I brush my lips over the shell of his ear as a flush of heat creeps up my neck. "Like . . . this?"

He gives a tiny, near-imperceptible nod before smiling for the cameras.

The sound of grunting draws my attention to the back of the disc where four guards surround Delphine. Her gag cuts deep into her mouth, her eyes bugged out as she struggles against her binds. One of the guards barely misses her boot as it crashes down on his foot, rattling the floor.

Without hesitation, the guard drives his elbow into her belly and she doubles over, gagging and wheezing for breath.

That's hardly a fraction of what she deserves. And yet . . . yet, I feel a twinge of sadness for her.

The disc stops moving and I once again hesitate as floating pavers, clear as ice, appear. We're ten stories high. No guardrails or safety nets in sight.

Just a Sim. Just a Sim.

The words do nothing for the fear knotting my belly and pinching my spine, the sweat dripping from my palms. The logical part of me knows, in reality, those steps are actually part of a long walkway with walls on each side. But the cowardly part of me doesn't care, and it takes Caspian going first before I can leave the safety of the elevator.

We trek across the air into a new room. As soon as I pass the threshold, I'm walking on land, plush green grass springy beneath my feet. Behind me, the earth falls away to nothing. As if an island floats in mid-air.

A castle rises in the distance, and we all stare in awe at the structure. The walls are crystalline, like deep slabs of ice, rainbows flitting off the curves of the four towers and dancing across the turrets.

Caspian leans into me like he's about to kiss my cheek. "This is where the highest-ranking Golds live on Hyperion, you and I included. Your room is on the fifth floor."

As soon as he says it, my brain fills in the gaps with the uploaded map. I see the inside of the castle, a glittering world of crystal and water. But the uploaded construct doesn't do the true experience justice.

How the Emperor created such a world, how he managed to make it all feel so real—I can't wrap my mind around it.

Even as I enter and *feel* my boots cross the slick crystalline floor. Even as fountains shoot up bursts of water in glorious blues and greens and golds, and the spray cools my cheeks where it hits. Even as lumens the size of watermelons hover around us, casting the most beautiful arrays of light I've ever seen.

"Welcome to the Crystal City," Caspian says. "My father had the nerve to dedicate it to my sister, Ophelia."

As soon as he says it, I recognize her in everything. The silvery-white drapes and rugs the color of her hair, the tan furniture the color of her golden eyes, one shade darker than her brother's. Roses like the ones she wore in her hair the day she died climb the pillars, the banisters.

It's creepy and solidifies my suspicion that the Emperor is a psychopath. Only someone without a conscience would want to be reminded every day of the daughter they'd murdered.

This time, instead of an elevator, a set of spiral stairs take us into the sky. Twisting faster and faster as we all ascend. The feeling is like riding a carousel that keeps rising, and a bubble of nausea swells just under my sternum until I have to close my eyes.

Near the top, the stairs suddenly stop moving. A group waits for us. As I scan the faces, my heart nearly stops. The Archduchess stands erect, mouth set in a thin line, wearing a black corseted dress and top hat that casts a dark pall over her face.

Beside her waits the Emperor, garbed in all white. The general, Delphine's father, is on the other side, along with what I assume is the general's wife, Delphine's mother. She has Delphine's same too-big eyes that give off false innocence. Pale, almost pigmentless hair falls in waves to her waist. A part of me wonders if Delphine cut hers short just to be different from her mother somehow.

Upon seeing her parents, the real Delphine begins to gurgle and thrash.

She tries to run to them but the guard who elbowed her last time grabs her by the arm. "In such a hurry to be tortured, traitor?" Grinning maliciously, he throws her at them and she falls on her side. "There. You have your wish."

I almost stop breathing when I see the excited gleam in the Archduchess's pale eyes. The Emperor smiles at her, almost the way one would proudly look at their best hunting dog. "She's all yours, Victoria. Just remember, don't kill her . . . yet."

So he lied to my mother. Surprise, surprise.

Delphine's eyes turn all white as two guards lift her by her armpits and carry her away, her boots dragging along the floor. She bucks and writhes the entire time, much to the Archduchess's delight.

I say another quick prayer of thanks to the gods that Flame's code worked. Then Delphine's parents are wrapping me in their arms. Even the general, who I remember as a cold, cruel man, holds me tight. Tears glint in his eyes.

I suppose even monsters have hearts. Not that Lash, who's glaring at the general and the man who had him whipped until he was lame, would agree.

"We thought you were dead, darling," Delphine's mom whispers, squeezing me in a way I once imagined my mother doing when we were reunited.

The general finally seems to remember himself and pulls away, dabbing jerkily at his eyes. Metallic flutters zigzag in my periphery. The cameras. Could this all be for show?

More importantly, how would Delphine react to all this?

Would she hug her parents back and cry or be irritated by the attention?

My decision is an easy one. With an annoyed huff, I roll my eyes and shove my mother away. "Give me space, Mom.

I'm fine. See? Now, I need a shower after being around Rebel scum for so long."

Delphine's mother wrings her hands, and I wonder if I've overplayed Delphine's personality. But then the general nods and flicks a curt glance at his wife. "Rachael, of course she's tired. Can you imagine the hell she went through? Don't smother her."

I almost feel bad for her mother as she looks at me with longing before pulling away, and I wonder if she wishes Delphine was different the way my mother wishes I was different.

Everyone looks to me expectantly . . . *oh*. They're waiting for me to storm off to my room.

I scramble for the directions in my head, the uploaded map flashing across my inner vision. But it's all jumbled, my nerves making it hard to access.

So I stall. "What about the stupid Fienian boy, the one being traded for us?"

I try to make my voice sound casual, like I could care less. But I have no idea if my desperation comes through.

The Emperor, who's busy inspecting Caspian like a prize mare, glances over at me. There's surprise and . . . suspicion in his eyes. "What about him?"

"I just thought he'd be here."

"Really, Delphine." Everyone is watching our interaction now, and I can feel my heart punching my throat. "When did you start caring about such things?"

Crap. Think fast. "Oh," I sneer, "I just thought it would be fun to see his expression when he realizes his sister is being traded for him." I know I have to tread carefully digging further, but I can't help adding, "Perhaps when we march him out to send him back, we can have her present?"

Especially because, knowing the Emperor, this may all be a double-cross. As much as I don't want to entertain the idea, they may not plan to honor their side of the bargain at all.

From my periphery I see Caspian relax, my answer satisfactory.

The Emperor's lips tug into a grin. "I very much doubt the Archduchess will give up her toy now that she finally has her back. And, besides. The boy isn't being sent back for a few more days. By then, his sister won't be able to move much less stand."

Despite my joy at learning that Max is, in fact, alive, it takes all my willpower to calm the shiver rippling through my chest.

That could be me.

And what does he mean, a few more days? I want to pry further, but Caspian's dark look tells me not to.

"Now," the Emperor says, sliding a glance at Caspian, "you must go prepare yourself."

With anyone else, Delphine would undoubtedly demand why. But this is the Emperor after all, and even Delphine wouldn't be stupid enough to demand anything from him. So I raise a demure, questioning eyebrow.

"Why, surely you haven't forgotten your wedding to my son?"

Thank the gods for Caspian's reaction, because otherwise my surprise would give me away.

"Wedding?" Caspian hisses, and his tone *is* demanding. "Today?"

"Didn't you tell him we moved up the ceremony?" the Emperor asks me.

"I was . . . waiting until we were truly safe."

The Emperor clicks his tongue and grins. "Tonight will be the celebratory dinner and tomorrow, the ceremony."

In a daze, I march past the gathering. Hoping against hope that my thudding heartbeat isn't being broadcast all over the ship as I stumble in the direction I think my room is. It all makes sense now.

Of course the Emperor wants me to be there to watch the boy I was once matched to marry another.

It's the final blow to the Rebels. Their leader, *me*, bound and helpless as Caspian and Delphine marry on Hyperion for all the world to see.

A wry smile finds my face as I imagine the Emperor's expression when he realizes that it isn't me at all who's bound and gagged, but his son's would-be-bride.

TWENTY-FIVE

The moment the door clicks shut behind me, I fall against the wall, drop my head back against the cool marble, and release a breath. "I can't go back out there."

"Love," Lash begins, his lips tugging into a grin. "You have a wedding to attend. I think you kind of *have* to."

As Delphine's best friend, it's only natural that the girl Flame impersonates would lend Delphine her attendant. Since, obviously, one personal slave isn't enough.

Riser glides across the room like a shadow, moving from corner to corner as he inspects the room for . . . what? Cameras? Hidden booby traps?

Once he's sure the room's okay, his shoulders loosen and he prowls over to me, the skin around his eyes pinched. "Clear."

The flatness of his voice drives me mad. No emotion. No, *hey, so you're getting married, let's talk about it.*

I take a deep breath, driving the panic from my chest. "Now that this new . . . development has transpired, I think we need to speed up the timeline."

Before, we technically had almost two days to find Max

and escape. Not that we wanted to stretch it out, but the first day here all attention would naturally be on us, making it harder to sneak around without being noticed.

Lash chuckles, finding this all a bit too humorous. "What. Can't we squeeze a rescue in between the 'I do's?'"

I glare at him. "The ceremony is tomorrow evening. What do you think happens afterward?"

Riser's face darkens, but Lash just grins that stupid smile. "The good stuff?"

Gods above, I could murder him right now. "It's called a honeymoon," I growl. "You know, that thing people do in private? And I doubt very much Delphine would be roaming the halls looking for Max when she's supposed to be off somewhere with Caspian."

"She's right." The apathy in Riser's voice has turned into something darker, but I can't pinpoint the emotion. "We need to start looking for Max tonight." Our eyes meet, and for a moment I think he's going to say something more, but then he turns on his heel toward the door. "I'll find the others."

As soon as he's gone, I release a ragged sigh, the air suddenly breathable. "I feel like I'm trapped in a never-ending nightmare that just keeps getting worse."

"You and me both." Lash crosses to the bed and flops onto the silky, powder blue covers. Lapis tiles in every shade of blue inlay the floor leading to a sweeping balcony. I follow the diamond pattern to the double-doors, my eyes riveted to the swathe of brilliant turquoise, tinged red at the horizon.

"An ocean?" I say, hardly believing it. I crack open the door and a balmy breeze hits my face, salty and briny and real. Seagulls caw and waves crash and it's all too much.

Lash isn't listening to me, though. He's too busy taking in his ex-girlfriend's room. The crystal decanter of dark liquor and matching set of tumblers on a golden tray atop her dresser. The silver comb lying next to them, a tangle of pale hairs caught in its metal teeth.

But mainly his eyes scour the images lining the walls. Paintings, mostly of her, but a few of her family too. Her parents dominate a larger painting in an alcove partially curtained with gold drapes.

A smaller painting of her and Roman, her cruel twin, rests on her nightstand.

As my gaze drifts over the rough-hewn edge of Roman's jaw, his deep-set eyes and prominent brow, another tendril of panic worms its way into me. "Oh, gods, Roman will know it's not Delphine the minute we're in the same room together. We have to find reasons to keep him far away."

How did I not think of this before? I might be able to fool the Emperor and Delphine's parents, but her twin will spy the difference immediately.

"Fienian hell, you're right." Lash, stretched out on the bed with his hands behind his head, suddenly lifts to a sitting position. "Roman's a brute, but he possesses a sharp sort of cunning that's allowed him to survive court this long. If anyone can guess you're not Delphine it's him."

Lash knows Roman. I'm not sure why that surprises me. I should have guessed as much when he revealed Delphine was the girl whose father had him whipped. In fact, this whole thing must be incredibly hard for Lash.

"Hey," I say, settling onto the bed beside him. "You okay? You know, being here and all. In her room."

"Dandy." His gaze draws on Delphine's face next to Roman's. It's an old painting, created several years ago when Delphine's face still retained a layer of baby fat that softened the hard edges of her cheeks and jaw.

"If you don't mind me asking, how could you fall for someone like her?"

Lash lets out a sigh and folds his hands in his lap. He

looks stricken, as if just allowing himself to think about that time in his life has opened up a chasm of old wounds. "Believe it or not, she wasn't always the fire-breathing shrew she is now. Or, maybe she was but I didn't see it. I don't know."

"How did you meet?"

A fleeting smile momentarily disrupts the shadow over his face. "My father was her father's physician. He was seeing him for an old war wound the Reconstructors couldn't fix, and I was waiting in their family's arboretum. The moment I saw her . . . I think I fell for her right there beneath all those trees."

"How old was she?" I ask.

"Fifteen, but she acted twice that. She was so beautiful it was painful. Like a shard of glass glittering in the morning light. I knew falling for her would hurt—I just didn't understand it would nearly kill me."

"Would you do it again?" I ask. "Knowing how it ends?"

A dark smile twists his lips. "Probably. Those are still the best three months of my life."

For the first time since I've known Lash, the irreverence is gone, replaced with a deep sense of grief. The fiery spark in his eyes, the implacable humor, all but disappeared.

I touch his arm and he flinches, startled from some raw memory. "I'm sorry, Lash."

His eyes brighten, a flicker of light. But the normal retorts I'd expect from him don't come.

Instead, he takes my hand in his and squeezes gently. "Maia, if I never tell you again what you mean to me, know that you're my world and I couldn't have asked the gods for a better friend or leader."

A wave of emotion tightens my chest, and I struggle for the words to reply. In the end, my throat is too pinched to say much, so I wrap him in a hug.

"Love, is this you telling me you want to—"

"Shut up, *Brig*," I interrupt, squeezing him until his ribs crack. "Don't ruin it."

"You're the worst." Except his voice says the opposite, and when he pulls back to look at me, his espresso-tinged eyes are dark with emotion. "Now, as much as I love holding you in my arms, don't we have a dinner to get you ready for? I forget, love, which prince are you marrying?"

"Don't even tease about that." I cringe at the thought of tonight. "As for getting ready, I don't think I need makeup, since they can't see my face anyway. But I'll have to change into a dress . . ."

A coy grin brightens his face.

"Not in front of you, perv," I amend, thumping his shoulder.

The golden door handle suddenly jiggles, hard. Our attention shifts to the sound. When the door doesn't open, violent raps thunder across the thick wood. "Del," a booming voice says. "It's me. Open up."

Roman.

TWENTY-SIX

Something heavy slams into the door, making it jump on its hinges.

"I think he's trying to break it down," Lash whispers.

"Shit." I slide to my feet, eyeing the door handle as it shakes so loud I think the lock will shatter. I look to Lash. "Go! Tell him something. I don't know. I'm . . . naked."

Lash scrambles to the door, slowing as he nears. He waits for a brief lull in the assault and calls out, "Del is getting dressed."

"Since when has that mattered?" The voice is belligerent, marred by arrogance and anger.

Muffled by the thick wood, I can't tell if there's suspicion lacing his voice or I'm just being paranoid. Either way, panic snakes up my spine.

"Sorry," Lash says again. "She'll come find you when she's ready."

The banging stops. The ensuing silence is somehow more worrisome. I imagine Roman's beady, deep-set eyes watching the door as he decides whether to kick it down or leave.

"You'd better tell her I stopped by, pissant," he orders, his tone promising retribution if Lash forgets.

I can't actually hear Roman's boots hitting the floor as he leaves, but I can *feel* the weight in the room lift. As if Roman carries his own force of gravity.

Lash sags against the door, his coppery hair splaying out against the white paneled wood like spilled wine. "You're going to have to face him, you know. Eventually."

He's right. A shudder wracks my body and steals my breath. I know once that happens, we'll be found out. We *could* incapacitate Roman somehow . . . but that wouldn't buy us much time, and he'd certainly be missed at his own sister's engagement dinner. I wouldn't be opposed to killing the brute—but that still left the problem of his absence.

Panicked, I scour my mind for a weakness, something I can use to hide my secret longer. Just for tonight. Just long enough to find Max. Something to dull his mind so that he doesn't notice I'm not Delphine.

My memories of Roman whir into a stream of images of Roman hazing us. Roman laughing as we came out of the maze, burned and traumatized and beaten. Roman trying to kill me on his Swifter with a blade the size of my head.

I blink and the culling ceremony surfaces like a bubble of air rising from a pond. The evening he hurt Ophelia in front of all of us, squeezing her cheeks and tearing the flowers from her hair. He was belligerent on power and wine . . .

"Wine," I blurt.

"Probably not the best time to get hammered."

"No, let's get *him* drunk," I clarify, my gaze falling on the crystal decanter sitting on the dresser near the alcove. A bay window rests above the decanter, glorious fake sunlight hitting the hundreds of facets cut into the crystal and refracting over the wall in wild, fiery prisms.

Lash follows my gaze. "Now?"

"As soon as possible." I cross the floor. The crystal lid, shaped like a phoenix head, tinkles as I lift it. Then I pull out the white powder and pour half of it into the amber colored liquor.

"Whoa, Graystone. Are you trying to kill him?"

I shrug as I approach him. "I only added half. You said less would make him drowsy."

Lash frowns as he watches the powder dissolve, hissing and bubbling. "But added into alcohol, which is another type of sedative . . . I can't promise he won't die."

"Well, it's a chance I'm willing to take." I thrust the bottle at him. "Here, take this to Roman and tell him I want to celebrate, that I'm already half-drunk and want him to catch up."

"That's not very convincing."

"Believe me," I say, shoving the decanter into his unwilling arms. "Roman won't need much convincing."

After Lash leaves to find Roman, I rifle through Delphine's closet for an appropriate dress. Dazzling gowns of gold and green and pink spread out before me, all colors that undoubtedly look amazing on Delphine. I run my fingers down them all, momentarily caught up in their sheer opulence before deciding on a svelte champagne number encrusted with thousands of diamonds.

Once I shimmy into the dress—which is heavier than it looks—and manage to zip it, I appraise myself in the dressing mirror to the right of the closet. The moment I see my face, I startle.

I was expecting the old face. Even if I can't remember, exactly, what that girl looked like. This one, though, feels foreign. A stranger I passed once in a crowd long ago. Just familiar enough to recognize; just different enough to not trust.

I run two fingers over the high, round cheekbones of my face, the freckles nearly imperceptible from here. I trace a finger down my straight nose, more symmetrical than my old one but not exactly small. Still, it fits my face, as does my high forehead and bowed lips.

My hair spills down my back, glossy and unnaturally red in this light. I decide not to do anything with it, since everyone will see Delphine's short blonde hair anyway.

A part of me wonders if things had been different and my match to Caspian was never broken, would I have worn something similar? What would I have done with my hair? Would I be nervous? Giddy?

Would I have assumed I loved him because I thought I was supposed to?

Brushing the thoughts aside, I slip on a pair of four-inch heels that feel strangely like flats—they probably are and the Sim makes them appear otherwise.

This time, I make sure I have the layout of where I'm going inside my head before I leave the room. As I focus, I see the Crystal Palace unfold, room after room of wonder and impossibility. I know without looking that if I walk straight thirty feet down the corridor I'll hit a chamber where you can dance on clouds.

Fifteen feet to my right are rooms even more opulent than mine, including Caspian's. I know that his room has four antechambers and a wraparound balcony overlooking the same fake ocean. That he has a bed double the size of Delphine's and a pool inside his bathroom instead of a tub.

I also know that Caspian isn't inside his room, but upstairs in his father's chamber.

Along with the uploaded layout of Hyperion, Flame embedded a locator code inside the programming that changed our appearances. This added tweak allows us to see where everyone is inside the uploaded layout.

All I have to do is close my eyes and think someone's name and a dot appears in the internal map.

It's handy, but also weird, like I'm spying on my friends. Not that it stops me from finding Riser next. A dot pulses along a long stretch of what I think at first are corridors. No, not corridors. They're too high, too narrow. And they show up in my mind as faint red lines crisscrossing the map.

They're air ducts deep inside the Crystal Palace.

He must be using them as a way to travel through the restricted areas. My heart races at the thought of him taking such risks. Of what would happen if he's caught.

Please be careful, I think, wishing Flame had added a code to let us talk to each other too. Maybe the distance would allow me to say all the things I can't up close to Riser. But that's impossible, and I just have to trust that he's savvy enough to make it back to me—and that I'll be brave enough to tell him how I feel when he returns.

With a final sigh, I cross the hallway to the left, which will take me to the elevator that leads to the dining hall where my celebratory dinner is being held. Knowing my every move is being recorded by cameras, I force my head high, schooling my expression into one of disdain instead of anxiety.

As I glide down the hall, my dress swishing softly over the polished marble floor, I say a quick prayer for all of us.

For Max to hold on a few hours longer.

For Riser not to get caught.

For Lash to get Roman drunk without killing him.

And for me to execute the most audacious plan ever.

If we pull this off, I'm going to owe the gods a crap-ton of favors.

TWENTY-SEVEN

An attendant finds me before I hit the end of the hallway. He's dressed in a silver and gold waistcoat, phoenix carved buttons lining either side of his cravat. "Lady Delphine," he murmurs, guiding me through an endless array of chambers and corridors illuminated by soft floor lights.

My stomach tightens as we approach a ten-foot wide canal. Gondolas bob on the surface of the deep blue water, attendants waiting to guide guests down an archway draped with yellow and purple orchids. The attendant helps me onto the wooden boat, which tilts slightly under my weight, and then he releases the rope anchoring it to the side.

As our boat rushes down the canal, passing apartments above, I catch sight of a dark figure hopping into a gondola with the grace of a cat. A dark swath of hair covers one eye, and as we bend around a curve and out of sight, our eyes meet.

For that flicker of a second, it's like a tether connects us. I wonder if my look conveys my happiness that Riser is safe—for now. Can he see how sorry I am?

Then high marble walls veined in gold replace his image, laden with strips of orchids and honeysuckle. And we're whisked deeper into the castle that isn't a castle, down a river that probably isn't a river, and a boat that probably isn't a real boat.

How could all these people agree to live here, knowing everything is an illusion? A Sim?

Another archway dripping flowers appears. I know whatever place they've chosen to host Caspian and Delphine's dinner will be elaborate, but I'm still not expecting what awaits me on the other side of the arch. A lake shimmers out, all turquoise and vibrant, ripples unfurling from the end of our boat and gliding across the water. As my gaze skims the sea-blue sky quilted with clouds, I feel a sense of disembodiment.

This can't be real. We're inside a spaceship. And yet . . . yet . . .

The sun kisses my face and the water cools my fingers as I dip them low.

A floating pavilion awaits, the orchids draped in long fingers of purple like banners scenting the air with a cloying-sweet fragrance. The bottom of the boat shudders as it hits the sandy bottom of the shore, and then pavers of lapis rise from the crystalline surface.

I want to hesitate. To take it all in for a breath longer. Instead, I cross over the pavers and onto the shore, the hem of my dress weighted with water.

The pavilion is roughly the size of a small building, large enough to fit countless Golds. They wear purple accented in gold, orchids pinned to their breasts' and smiles plastered across their faces.

Anger stirs inside me as I imagine the terror down below. As Pandora's dark shadow kisses our planet, the Golds dance and party.

It makes me sick.

Caspian looks regal inside a dark purple suit that high-lights his golden hair and eyes. Despite my discomfort, I smile when I see him. He waves me over, and I remember to slip on my Delphine persona. Grimacing and basically being a horrible person.

A waiter approaches with sparkly champagne flutes. I grab one of the delicate-stemmed glasses, offsetting the tray and then laughing when it crashes to the ground. The waiter, a Bronze man with thinning brown hair and terrified eyes, holds a hand up to his face—as if to ward off blows.

His abject fear makes me sick.

"You're lucky your clumsiness didn't ruin my dress," I snap, each hateful word like poison on my tongue. The poor man bows his head and averts his eyes as he plucks pieces of broken flutes around us.

Caspian takes my hand. His eyes have a strange shine to them that makes them look like perfectly smooth pieces of amber. He pulls me to a spot near the head of a long table in the middle of the pavilion.

"You look . . ." He swallows, presses his lips together. "I know this isn't real but, if it was, I would be the luckiest man in the world."

Something clumps beneath my sternum. Not dread, exactly, but an emotion I can't quite grasp. "Any luck finding my . . . missing bracelet?"

I can't afford to say Max's name, in case someone is listening.

Caspian shakes his head. "Sorry."

I try to hide the wave of disappointment that washes over me. If only I could go look for him without being noticed.

Biting back my impatience, I nod and scour the guests for the others. "Maybe they found something."

As if on cue, Riser leaps gracefully from the end of a gondola, landing softly on the sandy shore.

I try to look away. After all, he's only my attendant, a meek girl who probably wouldn't last a week with the real Delphine. But I'm drawn to the familiarity of his face, the sharp angles of his cheekbones and abrupt contrast of his pale skin against his raven-black hair.

Caspian clears his throat and I look away. A bell rings, and the disorderly clumps of people all form neat lines as they swarm the table to sit.

Placing two fingers just under my elbow, Caspian guides me to a chair near the Emperor, who occupies the head seat. My breath catches as his gaze falls over me. Shrewd and assessing. The weighted stare of a man who can end my life with a single gesture.

I ignore him as Delphine would, too caught up in her own world to care. Her parents sit directly across from me, but I ignore them too, as I imagine the real Delphine normally does. I make a show of motioning for more champagne— even if I'll have to surreptitiously pour it out.

An empty seat waits on my left.

The Emperor's gaze skips from me to the vacant chair, a frown twitching his lips. "Where is Roman tonight?"

I cast a lazy look at the Emperor, forcing my expression not to betray my hatred for him. "You know Roman. He'll be here."

The Emperor's eyes suddenly lift to focus behind me, where Riser must have taken his place as my attendant. The breath catches in my throat. For a second, his stare lingers. Can he somehow feel his son is behind me?

I know that's ludicrous, but still . . .

Delphine's father, the general, stands suddenly. He's in full military dress, his gray hair smartly combed to the side and his eyes sharp with excitement. I watch him make a speech about Caspian's and my happiness. Watch Caspian and I nod and smile like I'm viewing a movie with other people.

And then they all look to us as Caspian leans toward me, his eyes still gleaming with brightness, his cheeks flushed, and kisses me. His lips are warm and taste of champagne. His breath comes out ragged and hot.

The kiss is clumsy, awkward. Probably because I wasn't expecting it and because Riser is behind me.

A roar of clapping follows. The sound echoes over the water and fills my ears. The champagne keeps coming. It becomes harder and harder to pour it out. Harder and harder to refuse the drinks that never end.

I'm lightheaded, overcome with the attention and the alcohol and the unmitigated terror of being surrounded by so many enemies while my every move is watched from above.

An angry, slurred voice draws my focus to the shore, just as Roman falls out of a red gondola into the water. My heart punches into my throat. He's still a good way out, and Lash jumps in to help him to shore. All the while, Roman cusses and yells.

When he stumbles to shore, his cheeks are a violent shade of scarlet, his eyes glassy and unfocused. He trudges to the table as his parents and the Emperor watch, wearing disapproving expressions.

"Perhaps you should go lie down," the general says, disgust permeating his tone.

"And perhaps I should stay and have another drink. I'm quite thirsty, Father." Roman jerks his massive head at Lash. "Where's my drink, piss ant?"

Lash flashes me a look before scurrying over to a table filled with golden goblets.

I glance back at Roman, my chest tight and shoulders

clenched. What would Delphine do in this situation? Egg Roman on? Be embarrassed and try to make him leave?

Before I can react, Roman's sloppy gaze finds me, and his face goes remarkably still.

"There you are!" he bellows. His heavy body slams into the empty chair with a horrible thud, his elbow knocking over the champagne flute of the man to his left. His fingers clench painfully around my arm, forcing me to wince. "Why are you ignoring me, sister?"

"Let go, idiot." I somehow make my voice exactly like Delphine's. Pride and annoyance clipping her high tone.

And yet, Roman just stares and stares at me as if somehow, in his drunken state, he could penetrate the code that made him see his sister. "Who are you?"

Cringing, I reach for a champagne flute, hoping no one else heard him. "Cheers to my brother, who never fails to entertain us."

His fat fingers are still wrapped around my upper arm, and now they begin to squeeze. Harder and harder. My flesh aches beneath his grip, my bone bruised and hot.

Roman digs his nails into my flesh. "Who are you?"

"Let go of me," I order. The faces of the others are watching, but it's the Emperor and his sudden attention that makes my pulse leap into a wild tailspin.

"You're not . . . Delphine."

A flicker in my periphery. I just have time to turn to my left to see Lash holding a wine goblet tilted in my direction. Somehow, he manages to make it look like Roman knocks the drink he's giving him over. The dark liquid hits my chest and stomach before splattering the gold table cloth.

My reaction is immediate. I jump to my feet, the chair flying out behind me, and scream, "You idiot!"

Roman is blinking at the giant, spreading stain on my dress. Confusion watering down his drunken suspicion.

"Of course you would ruin everything, Roman!" I glare between him and my parents, imagining Delphine doing the same. "Can't you do something about him? You let him get away with everything!"

Motioning to Lash and Riser, I storm toward one of the boats, making sure to make frustrated noises as my heels puncture the sand. When I get to the shore, I wait with arms crossed as Riser steadies the boat and Lash lifts the hem of my ruined dress.

The boat wobbles and lurches with the weight of all three of us, but I've never felt such relief in my life. Riser and Lash row silently. And every foot of distance between the pavilion and our boat loosens another knot inside my stomach.

When the boat is far enough away that I feel safe, I sag into the seat and heave a long sigh. Only Roman could survive enough sedative to knock out a horse and somehow manage to become a *more* obnoxious version of himself.

If anyone's going to ruin this plan of ours, it's Roman.

TWENTY-EIGHT

As soon as we hit the dock where the gondolas stay, we all jump out. Riser looks around before saying, "Our *friends* might have found that thing you're looking for, Delphine."

My heart jumps in my chest. "Did they . . . is it in one piece?"

"All we know is they discovered an area not on the map. Some of the Bronze servants said they sometimes take food down there, but that the food is meager, biscuits and water, and they're stopped by guards at the bottom of the stairs."

"Like a prison."

He nods.

"That has to be where they're keeping *it*."

He and Lash exchange glances. "It's likely. But before we do anything we need to confirm it's there. Our best chance is retrieving it during the . . . ceremony tomorrow, when the entire population will be distracted."

His voice catches on the word *ceremony*.

"There's no way to do it tonight?" But even as I say it, I know rushing in tonight is a bad idea.

He shakes his head. "We need to confirm the intel first. Need to see how many guards there are, what type of place they're storing *it* in."

I rub angrily at my forehead. "Well *it* could be hungry . . . and cold. What if—what if they're hurting it?"

Riser reaches out as if to comfort me, then thinks better of it, his fingers curling inches from my shoulder. "You know I want it back as much as you do, but we have to be careful."

I nod even though I want to scream. "I can find a way to see if it's down there. Maybe Delphine will demand to see Maia in chains. That seems like something I'd do."

"Good." Riser watches me a second more. "Now go change into a new dress and then demand to see her. If that doesn't work, we'll just find another way."

Brimming with anxiety and hope, I quickly change into the emerald green dress with a slit down the side, then find my way back to the dinner just in time for dessert. Roman, thank the gods, is gone, hopefully passed out somewhere.

Pushing a fork around my chocolate lava cake, I give an annoyed sigh and announce how bored I am. By now, the Emperor and general are locked in a discussion about resources, and Delphine's mother has gotten thoroughly drunk. They hardly seem to notice me.

"How about a visit to the traitors?" I let a grin slowly settle over my face as if the idea is the only thing that will make me happy.

Delphine's mother waves her hand at me. "Why not dance instead, darling?"

"Because I don't want to dance, Mother." I glare at her. "This is my night, isn't it? And the best wedding present in the world is seeing the traitor who captured me and put me in chains punished."

The general flicks his gaze at us with a look like he's

trying to mediate between two armies. "What are you two arguing about now?"

Delphine's mother knocks back half her flute before answering. "She wants to see that Rebel girl."

"I *want* to see her punished."

The general looks to me. I can tell by the way his eyes shine that he's proud. "There's nothing more satisfying than seeing your enemy beaten. Go, but don't get any blood on your dress."

The Emperor's attention is suddenly on the conversation, and he nods to Caspian. "And take my son. He needs to see what happens to traitors." His gaze slides to his son, something close to disgust flickering in his eyes. "Someday the job of punishing those who challenge our reign will fall on you."

I feel sick to my stomach as Caspian slides from his chair to follow me. What sort of childhood must Caspian have endured? Was the Emperor always this way, or was it truly different before his mother died?

I don't have long to contemplate these mysteries before we're off, a Centurion guard leading the way to wherever they're keeping the prisoners. Back in the boat, we pass beneath the arches, but instead of stopping at the bend where we embarked from earlier, we continue. Wending our way deeper and deeper into the ship.

Apartments give way to meadows brimming with wildflowers, and mountainous landscapes dotted with cottages. Caspian whispers in my ear that some of the higher-ranking Golds live on mountaintops, while his own father lives inside a chamber that becomes a house in the clouds.

For the first time ever, I entertain a horrifying possibility. What if the Emperor never planned to save our planet at all? Why save something when you can just wait until the slate is wiped clean and then recreate the perfect world? One that functions as your own personal lavish playground using technology you've forbidden others to use?

With the predicted casualties, over half our population will be gone by the time the world is habitable again. Leaving the Emperor and his court to swoop down and take control— except, this time, there will be very little opposition to his rule.

And, if miraculously, the remaining Bronzes refuse enslavement, well . . . with the weapon my father created, the one meant to stop the asteroid, the Emperor would be unstoppable.

Dread swells my belly at the thought, and I blow out a calming breath. *One thing at a time.*

The river slows to a trickle, and we disembark. Steep stairs lead to a dingy, less developed portion of the ship. Concrete walls and metal glisten in the low light.

The Centurion nods to a door at the end of the chamber.

As soon as the door opens and the stairs appear, leading down into darkness, my breath hitches. Caspian takes my hand, pulling me down behind him. The stairwell is cramped, too tight to walk side-by-side. I follow Caspian's pale hair like a beacon as my pulse races.

And then the steps flatten out into a long, dank corridor. Lights flicker near the end where guards stand by another door. This door is all metal with a huge lock. My heart stutters into a wild symphony of beats as a gasp escapes my lips.

"He's there," I whisper, desperation edging my voice. "I know he is."

My brother is only a few steps away. It would take very little to free him. The realization dredges a sort of wild panic inside me. I eye the guards, the pistols firmly lodged in holsters at their waist. Crazy thoughts of overpowering them surge through me.

A shadow peels from the edges of the walls and a familiar

face greets me. Riser. He shakes his head, brushing a finger over my hand.

It's only a touch. It hardly lasts a second. But that simple gesture drags me from my dangerous ideas and plants me firmly back in reality.

If I break Max out now without a plan, we all die on this ship. We need to discover the locations of the cameras. How many guards rotate through here. How many exits.

Be smart. I release a hard breath and nod, forcing my heart to slow as the ideas of violence drain from my mind.

Instead, as the guards begin opening the door to whatever waits on the other side, I focus on drinking in as many details as possible.

One pair of keys. Four guards total on this side of the door. One entry and exit. Cameras everywhere.

We slip through the doorway into what looks like a huge chamber with white floors and white walls.

The first person I see is Delphine. She sits on the floor, arms hugging her knees. Her head lifts and recognition slowly spreads across her face. Followed by rage.

Jumping to her feet, she hurtles straight for us—

An invisible wall lights up, tendrils of neon green electricity surging across the empty space, and she crumples into a tiny ball. I watch her writhe for a horrible moment, thinking how that should be me . . .

And then a flicker in my periphery drags my focus to the middle of the room. A pang of familiarity hits me as I take in the soft planes of Max's face, half-man half-boy. His eyes, wide and bleary from lack of sunlight and sleep. His curls are matted to his head on one side as if he's been resting.

A deep purple bruise darkens his temple—

Look away. Look away.

"I want to see this prisoner," I order, my entire body tensing to keep from trembling as I point at Max.

Caspian and Riser both cast sharp glances at me. I'm going off script. But I have to find a way to let him know we're here. That we're trying. I need to give him hope, however small, to get him through one more night.

Two more guards are on this side of the cells, and they both shake their heads. "The Archduchess ordered no one but her to have contact with the prisoners."

The Archduchess. Where is she? The sudden realization that I haven't seen her hits me hard.

Channeling my inner bitch, I curl my lips into a rancid smile. "I am about to be empress, you idiots. Who do you think wields more power here? That deranged mongrel or *me*?"

They hesitate, both working to determine the answer to my question as if their lives depend on it—because they do. Finally the closest guard nods and hands over a metal circlet the size of a bracelet. "Put this on and you can enter the cell without being zapped."

I don't hesitate before slapping the circlet over my wrist. "Good," I snap, making sure the guard feels my annoyance over having to wait. "Now run along while I play a while."

The guard slips into the other room, taking the other one with him.

As soon as the door closes behind them, I go to Max, forcing myself to walk slowly when I want to run. He's still sitting, frowning at us with as much courage as he can muster.

His gaze keeps drifting from me to Caspian—probably wondering how Caspian got here.

A prickle of electricity hums in my bones as I cross the invisible fence that holds him prisoner, just enough to know it's there. Each step I take toward Max makes it harder for me to keep up my façade. All I want to do is take him in my arms, but I can't.

Even if they're in the other room, I have to assume our interaction is being monitored.

I can't afford to show Max any affection.

When I'm a foot away from him, Max cowers, shielding his face with his forearm as if I'm too bright. "What do you want?"

His voice—it's so brave, his fear barely detectable. My throat constricts.

"What's it like?" I drawl, my brain scrambling for a way to tell him I'm here without alerting anyone else.

Realizing that I'm not going to hurt him—at least, not yet —he drops his arm, revealing blue eyes tinged red and a busted lip. "What?"

"Being *so* close to your sister," I say, my voice losing its acid tone as my focus slides to Delphine in the next cell. "So close, yet you can't talk. She can't *comfort* you."

He squints at me, confused. Then his gaze follows mine to Delphine, who's moaning and still writhing on the ground.

Funny, I realize. *Max didn't react when Delphine was hurt.*

Knowing Max, if he truly thought that was me in pain, he would have acted out somehow. Which means . . .

He knows the prisoner next to him isn't me.

"I don't think she's able to comfort anyone right now," Max answers.

"Too bad." I lift one corner of my mouth, hoping he'll see the gesture. Any more would be pushing it for whoever's watching. "I bet she's a bossy big sister."

Max blinks. Once. Twice. Then something passes over him, the shadow darkening his face lightening.

"She is," he agrees. "It's annoying."

His face hasn't changed, but his eyes . . . tears wet the corners.

He *knows*.

Biting back a retort, I return to Delphine mode before

anyone can notice I'm not being horrible. "I'm getting married tomorrow. Perhaps I'll make you a guest. Be *ready* for your invitation, worm."

Max's eyes brighten, which I hope means he gets my message and isn't simply laughing at me.

Then, to finish this charade, he spits at my feet. "You're an idiot."

Takes one to know one, I almost reply.

But only a sister would say something so childish, so I pivot on my heel and stride away, laughing cruelly. "We'll see who's the idiot when your entire world burns, maggot."

Every step away from him feels like torture, and forcing myself to wrench off the cuff is nearly impossible. My heart hammers inside my skull as I toss the metal bracelet at the guard. I practically run as we retrace our route back through the door and up the stairs. Knowing that every second I don't flee increases the odds that I'll attack the guards instead.

Once we're close to Delphine's room, I fall against a wall. Unable to keep it together as the joy of seeing Max collides with the stress of leaving him.

"We left him," I breathe. "We left him."

Both Caspian and Riser rush to my side.

For a tense moment, they glare at each other, and I think there will be a fight. But then Riser must remember that, to anyone looking, I'm still Delphine, because he halts, just barely, his mismatched eyes meeting mine a breath before tearing away.

Caspian takes my hand as Riser slips into the shadows. I bite my lip to keep from calling out to him.

Now that we're so close, now that I've seen Max and know rescuing him is doable, we can't risk it.

Even if I want Riser in my arms right now, not Caspian. Even if I want to pour my heart out to Riser. To tell him I'm sorry. That I choose him.

Him, not his little brother.

Just one more night. Then this façade will be over and we can talk. Figure things out like a normal couple.

Couple.

But the word feels too normal for what we have, too optimistic, and my heart fears Riser is slipping away.

Caspian's hand is warm in mine as he leads me into my room and shuts the door. The lights are off. Delicate moonlight streams in from the windows. The door to the balcony is parted a few inches and the sound of rushing ocean fills the room.

"Gods above," I mutter, falling onto the bed. "I don't know what I was thinking talking to Max."

Caspian follows me, his hair pale gold in the moonlight. The bed sags under his weight as he lifts up on his elbow to look at me. "How did he seem?"

A proud smile lifts my cheeks. "Strong. Brave. My mom would be proud." I roll onto my back, surprised to see a skyscape of stars in the ceiling. It's an illusion, of course. I'm starting to think everything here is. But it's still beautiful and I find myself staring at it and wishing I could show Riser.

The bed shifts, and I look at Caspian in time to see him leaning over me. His fingers brush my cheek. "Gods, you're beautiful."

His declaration steals my response, and he must take my silence as something more because he leans forward. The warm brush of his lips over mine wakes me from my spell and I shoot up, shoving my hands into his chest.

"No," I breathe. "Caspian, I . . ."

"Sorry." He shoves a hand through his hair. "I thought—I don't know."

My heart flutters against my ribs and heat surges across my cheeks. "Caspian, you will always have a place in my heart. Always. But . . . I, I think I love Riser."

As soon as I say the words, I know they're true. I love Pit Boy—even if I've never told him as much. I think back to when he said the words to me right before I left to command the army. Fienian hell, I didn't say them back. But now, all I want to do is find him and tell him.

It's impossible to miss the way the light inside Caspian's eyes gutters.

His jaw tightens, and he rubs his forehead. "I know you and my brother have a history, but with time that could fade. You and I, Maia, we're matched. I may not believe all the things my father said, but I believe that." His voice softens to a whisper. "We're meant to be together."

"Caspian . . ." What can I say to that? I know that Caspian doesn't mean it. He's caught between his world and mine, lost. To him I'm an anchor.

"Just tell me there's a chance, Maia. That's all I need. Just to know that maybe, after this is over, you might care for me the way I do you. If I don't have that . . . I have nothing."

If I could tell him yes, I would. And part of me wants to because it's easier. A little lie to get us through this incredibly volatile plan. But I know now without a doubt that I'll never feel for Caspian the way I do Riser, and telling him otherwise would be a cruelty.

Maybe now, despite everything—or because of it—the truth is the only thing we have left. "What you talk about, Caspian, us feeling connected. I feel that, I do. I think our shared past plus being genetically compatible gives us a bond that few will ever have. But . . . I'm sorry, I love Riser in a way that I can never feel about you."

There, the hard truth. I stiffen, waiting for his anger, or perhaps more protests that I could love him. Instead, his face goes slack. Still. A shadow ripples over his expression, his eyes full of such sadness that I can't imagine he's ever smiled or laughed before.

I know I'm not the only reason for his emotions. That I was simply the thing he held onto to keep from drowning, and now that he doesn't have that . . .

"Thank you," he breathes in a voice frayed with emotion. "For respecting me enough to be honest with me. It's amazing how rare that quality is."

He slips to his feet and crosses the floor before I can think of what to say. At the door, he hesitates, glancing back at me one last time. But whatever words he wants to say die on his lips and he slips out, shutting the door soundlessly behind him.

I fall back on the bed, clutching my chest. If only I could have told him something different. If only I could have lied and said there was a chance . . . but I'm done lying. Caspian deserved the truth—however painful.

A light rap on the door startles me, and I snap to my feet, readying my mind to once again rebuff Caspian.

I swing open the door—

As soon as I spy Roman's face, I try to close it, but a boot wedges in the door and Roman's ugly face peers through. "Hello, *sister*."

TWENTY-NINE

R ed-hot pain shoots through my temple as the door slams into my head. The force sends me scrambling backward, but I right myself before I fall over. Roman's body takes up the entire door frame.

He slips inside and shuts the door quietly—so quietly.

"This is going to be fun," he whispers, and icy fingers of panic scrape down my spine.

Even though his voice is soft and slurred around the edges, the malice comes through. His breath rolls over me in a disgusting wave of brandy and stale saliva.

I back away, searching the room for a weapon. I can't use the mini-bombs strapped to my thigh, and the tiny dagger hidden on my other thigh will hardly faze Roman.

Something hard presses into the backs of my legs—the chest at the end of the bed. I lunge toward the dresser and grab the silver tray that held the decanter. The tray wobbles in my hands as I hold it up, ready to block Roman's advances.

"Oh, *sister*, you know how I love it when we fight." His beady eyes brighten as a brutal grin transforms his jaw. He steps closer, his boots stamping the floor tiles hard enough I wonder how they don't crack. "Now, who are you really?"

"Why don't you come closer and find out?" I snarl, circling to my left. If I can just reach the door—

The floor groans beneath Roman's weight as he lunges. I just barely have time to fling up the tray before he crashes into me. My arm aches as the edge of the metal tray hits bone. Roman growls and grabs for his brow above his left eye. Blood spews from the impact, his skin there split down to the bone.

"Bitch," he grunts.

Something hits me hard in the stomach, forcing the air from my lungs. Before I can recover he slams a fist into my cheek. Red blossoms inside my skull. I try to lift the tray to block his fists but he knocks it from my hand. Another flash of light pops across my skull as he lands a hard right hook to my cheek.

The blow almost forces me to my knees, but last second I remember my training. I leap back and dive from his hands, crashing into a chest. The furniture goes sprawling, as do I.

I jump to my feet to see Roman lumbering toward me.

Hatred flashes in his eyes. Blind, drunken hatred. "Where are you going?"

I reach out, grabbing blindly. Somehow manage to grab a crystal tumbler. I reach back, take aim, and throw the glass. It hits his face, glancing off his broad nose. Blood bursts from his face, and he stumbles.

Now!

Darting across the room, I aim for the door. My hand just brushes the handle—

Something grabs my hair and my head jerks back. Pain explodes in my neck as I fall backward. That beautiful ceiling of stars flashing across my vision. Then I'm on my back.

Roman towering over me, blocking out the fake stars. He's everywhere, a cancer of darkness I can't escape.

I roll to my side—

His boot collides with my ribs, the pain indescribable. I cry out, a sharp, pleading sound. Steel flashes across the tip of his boot.

Fienian hell, that explains the pain.

He kicks me again, over and over. I feel a rib crack, the noise surprisingly loud and hollow. Waves of pain crash over me.

I might vomit.

Curling my knees up to my chest, I throw up my hands to block the blow, knowing the steel rimming his toe will snap my fingers like twigs. But I don't care. I can't take another kick to my stomach.

Except nothing happens. Realizing I've closed my eyes, I open them. Roman is looking down at me, his eyes enormous. His lips gape like a wound, quivering and yawned wide, but no sound comes out. He's clawing at something around his neck, his thick fingers digging into an . . . arm.

I see Riser's face behind Roman's and then Roman is collapsing to the ground. His knees hit the stone, his eyes roll back in his head, and he falls sideways. Riser releases his chokehold on Roman and Roman hits the floor hard.

The second Roman is out of Riser's arms, he rushes to me. "Are you okay?"

I nod, trying to push up. The pain in my rib feels like fire exploding inside my chest. Unable to contain the anguish, I cry out.

"Slowly," he orders, slipping a hand beneath my arm. "I think the bastard broke your ribs."

I shiver at the anger lacing his words. He helps me to my knees and then checks me over, the rage tightening his eyes slowly giving way to tenderness. His fingers are gentle as they press on my face where Roman's fist connected.

"I'm okay," I manage, wincing. "What about him? Is he . . .?"

"Dead? No, but he deserves the blade." Something dark flashes inside his eyes as his gaze cuts to Roman. "Give me the word and I'll end him. He deserves it. For what he did to you, for what he's done to countless others."

Part of me longs to kill Roman. To end his violent life and avenge all those he's hurt, and all those he'll undoubtedly hurt in the future. Gods know a horrible, painful death wouldn't even come close to avenging all of Roman's victims.

And yet . . . the idea of Riser killing him while he's helpless doesn't sit well with me. It would be Roman's final blow, pushing Riser one step closer to his savage side.

"No." I splint my ribs as I move around Roman to assess the room. "But we can't let him go. We could incapacitate him somehow. Maybe . . . keep him bound and gagged in the bathtub."

"Won't he be missed?" Riser asks.

"Probably. But he was wasted tonight. If we're lucky, they'll think he's passed out somewhere."

Riser sighs, obviously disappointed I won't let him end Roman once and for all. "It will have to do."

Roman is too large for Riser and me to move alone, so Riser finds Lash and Teagan. Together, we bind Roman's thick wrists and ankles behind his back with strips of my silk sheets. Three wide strips go around his mouth, with an extra one balled up and shoved half-way down his throat.

There's a chance he could suffocate, but I'm beyond caring. I won't outright murder him while he's helpless, but if the universe wants to help shuffle Roman off this mortal coil, I won't be sad about it.

I try to help, but Lash forces me to sit on my bed while

Teagan checks me over. Grimacing under the pain in my side, I watch them heft Roman across the floor.

Eventually, the two manage to transfer a bound, gagged Roman into the porcelain beauty.

"What a brute," Teagan growls, glaring at Roman's inert form visible through the open doorway. "But I think you made the right decision not to kill him."

I chew my lip, watching as Lash whips together some sort of injectable sedative and gives Roman twice the usual amount.

"For the longest time, I just wanted to make everyone who hurt me pay," I admit. "But now I think I just want to make sure I'm not like them. That the world isn't like them. That's what my father wanted."

"He sounds like a wonderful man." Her eyes soften, lose focus. "My father used to say there are some people in this world who deserve to die."

"You don't think that's true?" I ask softly. She's never really talked much about her father.

She shakes her head. "I think if you tell yourself that enough, you can justify anything. But we all do terrible things to each other, and if we follow that logic, an endless cycle of violence and vengeance will eat away at our world until there's nothing left. Look at the Emperor. He's used his wife and baby's murders at the hands of Ezra Croft to justify his own monstrous acts for years."

The thought hits me hard, and I'm more than a little relieved when Lash and Riser leave the bathroom and Roman's chest is still moving.

Lash does a more thorough assessment on my aching body. "Thank the gods everyone will see Delphine's unblemished features," he says, "because all the ice in the world wouldn't bring down that bruising."

I groan, clutching my side. "And my ribs?"

"Hard to tell," he admits. "Probably fractured. But the area has low probability for puncturing your lung if the bone shifts, so . . . consider it a win?"

Once the room is tidied, my face cleaned and ribs bandaged, Lash and Teagan leave to catch a few hours of sleep before morning.

Without hesitation, I take Riser's hand in mine. "I have to talk to you."

"Funny," he says, staring down at me with an unreadable expression. "I was going to say the same thing."

THIRTY

After the onslaught of violence that just happened, I'm surprised by my need to tell Riser how I feel and explain the last few days. But, if anything, Roman's attack reminded me how dangerous this whole plan is.

If I don't tell Riser how I feel, there may not be a chance tomorrow. Or ever again.

Still, I do feel the need to get away from Delphine's room and the memory of a few minutes ago, so I lead Riser to the balcony. The air is balmy and wet, the briny sea breeze cleansing the whiff of blood from my nose.

We walk along the wrought iron balustrade fringed with wisteria, a few of the tiny purple petals blowing around our feet. Below, the sea crashes and foams in time with my pained breathing. A giant moon hovers just above the horizon, lending its silvery light.

"I can't believe this isn't real," I say, trailing a hand over the banister. It's cold and damp beneath my fingertips. "The ocean, the palace"—I squeeze a wisteria blossom between my thumb and forefinger—"this."

"I despise this place," Riser says. "I would rather live

inside the ugliness of the pit than be trapped here. At least in the pit the monsters didn't hide behind illusions."

I shudder at the memory, but it also reminds me of how far we've come. Together. "Riser," I begin, and it's impossible to disguise the nerves in my voice. "I'm sorry for kissing Caspian."

His throat bobs, but he stays silent. Letting me speak.

"I think I just needed to know if it was possible . . . between us. Maybe because my mother was pressuring me, or because I'm weak. Loving Caspian would be the easier choice."

He nods, a muscle in his neck cording. "And?"

"And I knew as soon as I kissed him that I felt nothing for him. I *feel* nothing. At least, nothing like I do with you. With Caspian it's like when I'm with Max."

"So," Riser breathes. "He's like a brother to you?"

I nod.

"I can't say I'm upset about that." A triumphant smile curves his lips. "And with me? Am I a brother to you?"

I shake my head, holding his stare. His eyes grow serious as he reaches for me, slipping his hands around my waist. He's careful with my injured side, his hands cupping my back and pulling me into him as he presses me into the wall. "And, do you still need a break to figure things out? Because if you do, I'll give it to you."

I grin. "Would you now?"

"I didn't say I'd be happy about it."

A small laugh escapes my lips. "I realize trying to be strong on my own doesn't work. I need you, all of you. Lash, Teagan, Caspian, even Flame. Besides, I already proved my strength in the pit, and a hundred times since. I don't need to send you away to prove it again to my mother or anyone else."

"So," he teases, his voice shivering with dark humor. "You were only weak when you kissed my brother?"

"Yes—"

His lips come down on mine, and the kiss is nothing like the one Caspian and I shared. There's a softness to it, but also a possessiveness. His body hard and claiming as his lips clash with mine. Our teeth scrape. I part my lips, his tongue warm as it brushes over mine. He presses deeper and I moan, fisting my hands through his hair, trying to pull him closer.

When he leans back, his eyes are molten with desire. He trails two fingers down my cheek, tracing the underside of my jaw. His expression is full of wonder as he regards me.

"Is it weird," I ask. "Seeing me now knowing what I used to look like?"

He doesn't hesitate before shaking his head. "You have the same look now as you did in the pit. Your eyes aflame with something no amount of reconstruction could extinguish. That's the part of you I love."

"And what are my eyes saying now?" I breathe, my gaze falling to his lips.

He exhales and, with a feline grin, lifts me into his arms. His lips brush the shell of my ear as he carries me into Delphine's room. "Is this okay? You aren't in pain?"

I quiet him with a kiss. The pain is there, a nagging throb, but so is my need for him. That ache is growing deeper, more insistent with every brush of his lips on mine.

The knowledge that this could be our only time together overrides any other feeling, including pain.

I want to be with him. Now. There is no later.

His arms tighten around me. And then he's lowering me onto Delphine's bed, gently, so gently.

Curling my finger, I beckon him to me. As he lowers himself over my body, I whisper, "I won't break."

He halts. A divot appears between his thick black

eyebrows. "I don't want to hurt you."

"Then don't."

My words sever the last tether of restraint containing him. He explores my body with his lips and hands. I'd forgotten how strong he is, even his fingers—all sinew and bone as they run along my back, my neck. Pressing gently over my bruised flesh . . .

And less gently in other places.

My hands slip beneath his shirt, trail along his sides to the corded muscles of his back. The knobs of his spine are hard and sharp like tiny daggers.

Laughing, he wrenches off his shirt. Buttons pop and snap against the wall.

On his knees, he hovers above me for a few breaths. Long enough for me to memorize the lines and curves of his body. The ridges of muscle, connected by bones and tendons. The scars that traverse his torso, silver and spider-silk thin.

I reach up and trace the largest one, a half-inch wide furrow that runs from his collarbone to his navel. And all the while he watches me with those mismatched eyes. It's strange, thinking of how he looked in the pit with his one eye and scars. I thought back then he was a monster—and maybe he was.

Maybe he still is.

But he's *my* monster . . .

Suddenly he bends down—

"What are you doing?" I whisper.

"Shh." His lips run along my jawbone first. They brush the bruise on my cheek.

I watch his muscles shiver and tremble as he moves, mesmerized by the art of him. The perfection in his imperfection. His scars and different colored eyes, the razor-sharp edges that will likely never soften. The chaotic energy radiating from his body that comes from years living in the pit.

I wait for him to kiss me again, but he doesn't move. Frozen above me. His face solemn and still.

"What are you doing?" I repeat.

"Looking at you."

I tremble as his fingers trail down my shoulders. Down my stomach. Lightly at first. The way you touch something to see how soft it is. But then his touch deepens into something more. He traces his fingers over my collarbone, my nose, my ribs, the way you'd run your finger over the edge of a sword.

Carefully. Reverently.

"Why do you do that?" I wonder aloud. "Trace my body?"

Without taking his eyes off my stomach, he replies, "When we were in the pit, there was no light. So I learned to map out the most important things by touch, to construct them in my mind."

I laugh. "So . . . you've mapped me out?"

"Not yet . . ." A devious grin finds his jaw. "Not all of you."

"Oh? For instance?"

"For instance, I know the way your jaw feels sharp, yet soft, your chin cleft in the middle." One hand strays to my hip bone, the heat of his flesh seeping through the thin fabric of my dress. "But I have yet to discover the curve of your hips. Are they soft or . . . bony?"

"Why don't you find out?" I tease.

My voice comes out a stranger's. Who the Fienian hell am I?

I find myself pressing into his hands. Wanting more. An ache opening up inside me with such ferocity that I can't focus on anything else.

My reaction seems to break a spell over him because he blows out a long breath. Then he retreats and stretches out beside me.

"Why'd you stop?" I whisper, disappointed.

He chuckles, the sound both teasing and frustrated. "Maia, I don't want our first time to be in Delphine's bed with her brother passed out in the bathroom and your impending wedding hours away. Not to mention . . . you're hurt."

"I don't care about that," I insist.

But he laughs again and settles me into him, his chest pressed warm and hard against my back, one arm slung over my stomach. "It matters to me. When the time comes, I want to be able to touch you without inflicting pain."

"But . . . what if . . ."

"Don't say it," he orders, reading my mind like normal. "We'll rescue Max and somehow make it back. Then we'll fix everything, and you and I can become two normal people— whatever that is."

Inexplicably, tears sting my throat. Faced with everything I might lose, I suddenly realize just how little chance we have of pulling this off.

For the first time ever, I can actually picture a future. Can actually feel the sweetness of what my life could be like in a different world. A better world.

"Whatever happens at the wedding," I say, turning to face him, "promise me that you'll stay safe."

He doesn't even hesitate before answering, "I promise that I'll keep you safe, because without you, there is no future, for me or anyone else."

"And without you, I have nothing." I squeeze his hand for emphasis.

He smiles, but his lips catch at the edges in a way that makes my heart clench. "You're the strongest person I know, Maia, and you don't need me to make this world a better place."

I tell myself his words mean nothing, but as I fall into a weary sleep, it feels like a chasm is splitting up between us and there's nothing I can do to keep him from floating away.

THIRTY-ONE

"You look . . ." Lash's voice trails off as he stares at me, and I do a stupid twirl, the organza layering the heavy ivory dress I wear rustling against the tile floor as the thick train tangles around my heels. Emeralds and rubies spark from the ensemble, the corset making my injured ribs throb like fire.

"Don't get all sappy on us now," Teagan says as she yanks on the ribbons at my back, pulling the corset even tighter.

"Ugh." I grip my side. "If my ribs weren't broken before, they are now."

"You're going on three days with almost no sleep. The pain will keep you alert. We're going to need clear minds to pull this off." Her gaze shifts to me, softens. "You do look lovely, darling. A real-life princess."

Countless mirrors hang above the marble counters and throw my image back to me. We're in the large dressing chamber adjoining the main onboard theater. The cloaks and costumes of the Silver actors brought along to perform in the theater hang from hooks on the wall.

In a way, it's perfect considering I'm about to act on the

biggest stage known to man. Only, if my acting is terrible, they won't boo. They'll string me up and watch the Archduchess disassemble me piece by piece.

"Thanks. You sure no one can see my face?" I mumble, kneading the lumps and darkening bruises mottling my cheeks and forehead.

"Only your friends," Lash insists, "and let me tell you, even beat up, you make a ravishing bride."

"Speaking of beat up—have you checked on our *friend*? The one taking the really long bath?"

Lash nods. "Sleeping like a babe."

"Too bad that sleep isn't more . . . permanent," Teagan adds.

Flashes of the violence Roman inflicted on me last night invade my mind. I massage a tender spot on my jaw before taking a deep breath to clear the memory.

Once my head is straight, I go over the plan. While I walk down the aisle to marry Caspian, Flame and Teague will break Max out. It shouldn't be hard. There are only four guards, one with a key. And everyone will be focused on the wedding. Flame has already taken care of the cameras.

The only wildcard is the Archduchess. It's clear the Emperor likes to keep her behind the scenes in Gold society— probably because she's an unrepentant psychopath with murderous tendencies, not to mention a Malignant. But I know she's here. I can practically feel her poisonous hatred for me seeping through the filtered air.

Perhaps that partially explains why, last minute, I ordered Riser to stay with me. He waits just outside our door. It makes sense that I would keep my attendant close for any necessary makeup fixes, and besides . . . I can't quell the kernel of unease I feel when I think about losing him.

After they break out Max, we'll have a small window of time before the escape is discovered.

There's a moment after the vows where we're allowed privacy in a separate room to take on each other's sigils in a marriage tradition many Royalists still favor. If all goes to plan, I'll get the signal from Riser as soon as we enter that room, and we'll sneak away before anyone notices.

By the time they do, we'll already be inside the starcraft, headed to safety.

It all feels deceptively easy—too easy.

The far door clicks open and Flame arrives holding the ornate tiara Delphine had specially made for today. She and Teagan share a brief look, both girls exchanging timid smiles.

Then Flame thrusts the crown at me and winks. "Made a few modifications like we discussed."

I blow out a breath and accept her offering. "It's . . . perfect."

"It's more than perfect. It's *killer*."

Holding back my laugh at her play on words, I examine the piece. The pear-shaped emeralds contrast sharply against my bright red hair. I try not to think how this accessory alone could feed an entire city for a week—especially since Flame managed to insert tiny Hot Weapons into the rim, giving me a powerful bargaining chip if everything goes to shit.

There's nothing like wearing emerald encrusted explosives on your head to make a girl feel special.

"There's something else," Flame says.

It's not until she slips the metal device inside my palm, and I recognize the sharp points that make up the pyramid, that I understand what she's handing me. Teagan frowns at the weapon, mirroring my unease.

"No." I shake my head, the explosive crown sliding along my brow. "I don't want this."

Scorpio-Fire. The name conjures gut-wrenching fear. I remember how it felt to be stung by the hundreds of tiny, mechanical scorpions. The terrible, unrelenting flames. Only people like the Redgraves would use such horrible weapons.

Recognizing my hesitation, Flame's tone softens. "It's a tool, that's all. You may need it."

She's right. Still, as I slip the device into one of the pockets hidden beneath the mound of organza, I pray I have no cause to use it.

"Good girl," Flame says.

I wait for her to leave, but she just watches me with that calculating gaze I find so unnerving.

Then she lifts on her tiptoes and . . .

Hugs me. The Fienian hugs me.

Not expecting affection from her, I stiffen, but she hardly seems to notice as she says, "Just so you know, I'm your soldier until the very end. What you've been through . . . and yet you still manage to hope for a better future . . ." She clears her throat. "If you had killed your *prisoner*, we would have never found the other *prisoner*." I can tell by her inflection she's talking about Delphine and Cage. "I always assumed your humanity made you weak, but I see now it's what makes you so strong."

I hug her back, her tiny body reminding me how young she is. How in any other world, she'd be a normal teenager, not an expert demolitionist with blood on her hands.

"Whatever happens," she continues quietly, "I hope you know that I will follow you anywhere."

A wave of emotion slams into me, stripping the words from my throat.

"*We'll* see you on the other side," she whispers before slipping from my arms and out the door.

"Ready, love?" Lash holds out his arm.

I nod, and he leads me to a smaller antechamber. Pale winter roses fill crystal vases on every counter, their heady perfume twisting my already tight stomach.

Riser waits for me near the door. As my attendant, he's expected to fix any last-minute wardrobe or hair malfunctions.

"What do you think?" I breathe, trying to joke away my nerves. "Do I look okay?"

Riser, who hasn't taken his gaze off me, exhales slowly. "I always imagined this moment . . . but I never—" He shakes his head, swallows. "I don't think it's possible there's ever been someone more beautiful than you are right now."

I'm a little taken aback. Riser seems more flustered than normal, his words not quite right. Then I remember he's watching me walk down the aisle to marry his half-brother. What did I expect?

Heat tinges my cheeks, and I murmur, "Thank you," before remembering my part. I throw back my head and add, "Besides, how could there be with the fortune my father dropped on this dress?"

The emotion drains from Riser's face as he dons his own attendant's mask, and then he's scuttling behind me to lift the garishly long train of my dress.

Breathe, I order myself as we begin the short procession down the hallway to the waiting crowd. *We're almost there.*

The moment I see what they've done to the theater where Delphine's wedding is held, my chest constricts, the air thinning so that I'm forced to work for every breath. A pale marble oval is centered in the middle of the chamber, floating in a sea of fat stars. Some shimmer, some give off a radiant glow so bright it could illuminate the entire room.

And some fall in dizzyingly-beautiful patterns that threaten to steal what's left of the oxygen in my lungs.

An aisle cuts through the middle of the oval, chairs packed full of impeccably dressed Royalists flanking either side. As Delphine's father, the general, holds out his arm to guide me, and I take my first step down the aisle, I notice the floor just below my feet is swimming with stars, almost like someone took the night sky and melted it.

The general flashes me a conspiratorial grin. "You're about to get everything you've ever deserved, Daughter."

Deserved? It takes all my willpower not to snort. Especially when Delphine's mother approaches, beaming. "Your father promised he would make you an empress, and now look at you. Remember that when you're in power."

Nausea roils my belly. I tear my gaze from Delphine's mother and place my hand on the general's arm, trying hard not to think of my own father's promises. How he once looked at me with the same pride and adoration. How, if he were here, he would twirl me around and tell me I was his everything.

How he was murdered by the very same people in the room who are watching me now, most smugly thinking they've tricked the entire world into letting them rule like gods.

Anger fills me, steeling my nerves. My hand is steady. My five-inch heels hardly make a sound against the floor.

At my back, I feel Riser's gaze—

Don't turn around.

But I do. And for a breath, I wonder how I would feel if he awaited me instead of Caspian. I'm definitely not ready to get married yet, but my stomach still flutters at the possibility, however small, that my future could hold something as normal as marriage.

After everything we've endured together, all the nightmares and horrors, something that beautiful feels like an illusion.

His lips tug upward. There's something in his eyes I can't quite name. An emotion that, in my adrenaline-infused state, eludes me.

Then I'm pushing forward, making sure to sway my hips

and walk slow enough that everyone takes in my expensive dress, the way the silk pools along the celestial walkway, the jewels dusting the organza shimmering like the stars at my feet.

Royalists stand as I pass, their awed murmurs mingling with the orchestral music wafting from hidden speakers. The Chosen are scattered throughout the audience, many whom I recognize, and when I meet their gazes I can't help but think about the Sleepers watching through their eyes. Do they hate Delphine and all she stands for, or have they bought into the Emperor's lie?

Sweat slicks my palms as I'm reminded how many lives depend on this ruse working, and I look ahead, my attention drifting to Caspian standing tall and proud next to his father.

A black ensemble accentuated with gold shows off Caspian's wide shoulders and narrow waist, and he wears a white rose on his lapel. His hair has been tousled to the side for the occasion, and I could swear it looks longer than yesterday.

In a word, he looks resplendent, and I nearly falter. In any other world, any other lifetime, I wouldn't think twice about marrying Caspian. And I know now, as I stand looking at the man a thousand tests matched me with, that if the girl who went into the pit were here now, she would love him still.

Just as he knows, looking back at me, that I'm no longer that girl.

Caspian and I lock gazes, and my anxiety bleeds away as I see the purpose in his clenched jaw and determined eyes.

This is all a huge distraction with one purpose: save Max and then the world.

If ever there was a reason to marry someone you don't love, this is it.

Lifting my chin, I leave the arm of the general and saunter toward my future husband. As I close the gap, Caspian's eyes drink me in, and he can't hide the fleeting look of longing that darkens his face.

The Emperor, for his part, is assessing me too. But there's no affection in his gaze, only the shrewd look of a businessman appraising an asset he's about to buy. A union between the two most powerful Royalist houses will shore up the Emperor's power, and there will be no one who can stop him.

Little do you know . . . I think, chancing a quick glance at the man who murdered my father and pitted my mother against me. The man who stole my childhood. My dreams.

He blinks lazily at me, and I blink lazily back, two cunning manipulators acknowledging one another and how they plan to use his son. Somehow I hate him now even more, if that's even possible.

Against my better judgment, I flash a slow, triumphant grin, and he manages a wary smile in return, probably assuming I'm gloating that I'm about to become the future empress. Hopefully in less than an hour, he'll remember this look and be riddled with rage.

An attendant takes my hand and places it over Caspian's. We stand facing one another, both of us hardly breathing, the eyes of the world watching as we repeat Royalist vows that feel like poison on my tongue.

I promise to serve you faithfully and dutifully.

I promise to honor the ideals of the empire.

I promise to hold no one but the Emperor above you in all things.

I talk slowly, my gaze darting to Riser more than I'd like. Our vows will be over soon. Any minute now, he's supposed to give me the signal that they've broken Max out.

Any minute now, we can stop this farce and escape this horrible, pretend world. My heart is racing, my head dizzy from trying to breathe through my broken ribs, the weight of my weaponized tiara getting heavier by the second.

And then something—a motion, a feeling—draws my focus to Riser and he gives me a quick nod.

Max is free.

He's free. The hope that surges through me is almost painful, the same way heat burns frozen fingers when they start to thaw. My chest flushes with nervous excitement, and I tilt my body away from the crowd so they can't see the angry splotches.

Caspian is looking at me expectantly—

Oh. The vows are done. It's time to receive our marriage marks.

The outline of a door appears against the starry background, and I follow Caspian through. On the other side is a plain room with a few scattered chairs. A woman holds a small oblong device with prongs on the end.

"Hold out your wrists," she says, her face near emotionless as she readies to tattoo our bodies and legitimize this sham of a marriage. Her brand marks her as Silver, and I wonder if she's the only one in her family to have been brought on board. Probably.

Caspian catches my gaze, and I nod, wincing as I do. We'll have to incapacitate her somehow, preferably *before* the marriage is finalized, but I don't relish hurting her.

The sound of the door swinging open draws my focus away from her. As soon as I see the Emperor's face, the hardness in his eyes, a chasm of fear opens in my belly.

"Caspian, Delphine, can you come back out here? There has been a . . . complication."

The furious edge in his voice confirms what my gut is telling me: something is wrong. Caspian reaches for the handle of his ceremonial sword, but his father shakes his head, his eyes never leaving mine.

Propelled by terror, I drag my gaze past the Emperor to the scene just beyond, and am consumed with horror.

The Archduchess stands in the middle of the aisle, amongst the beautiful river of stars, a pistol held in each hand.

Both weapons are pointed at the heads of Flame and Teagan and—

The second I spot Max on his knees, his eyes flicking over the crowd as he searches for me, I feel the world open up beneath me.

THIRTY-TWO

There's no running from this, no hiding. Despite my fear, I jerk my head up and let my mask fall so that the only emotion left is my burning rage. As I walk out to meet the crowd of Royalists, my face is defiant.

"Did you know," the Emperor begins conversationally, "that the Archduchess has a microplant inside her skull that allows her to monitor the prisoners? At the time, I thought it unnecessary, a whim so she could feed off the prisoners' agony even when she wasn't there. She does have a distasteful appetite for cruelty, as you're probably aware."

A fresh wave of revulsion crashes over me as I imagine the Archduchess getting off on Max's cries of pain and fear.

"But I see now, obliging her was smart, after all."

I flick my gaze over the room. Where is Riser and Lash? I don't see them with the others, so the Royalists haven't put together that they're with us yet.

But they will. It won't take long, if they haven't already.

"Of course, as soon as we discovered the traitors, I became curious about the prisoner, Maia. Especially since the Archduchess had yet to get her to utter a single word . . . and knowing Maia, she simply wasn't that brave."

Any hope I have left of getting Max out of this—of getting all of us home safely—evaporates as Delphine appears beside the Archduchess. Delphine's hair is wild, jutting out at odd angles, her face gaunt and haunted with the look of someone who's been tortured.

She's limping and breathing hard, and as soon as she sees me wearing her wedding dress, fury overtakes her expression.

But more damning than anything is that her face is no longer mine, but her true features. And beside her, wobbly but standing and very much alive, is Roman. His eyes are all-black, shimmering with murder as they rivet to me.

I'm going to kill you, he mouths.

"We discovered the code used to change Delphine's face to yours, Maia, and then a search of your room revealed an interesting surprise." The Emperor peers at me as if he can see through my illusion. "It won't take long to find and remove the code used on your face and the others."

My heartbeat hammers against my chest and rushes through my ears. The feeling of being almost disembodied comes over me, followed by an unnerving calm.

I rip the crown from my head, pulling out strands of my hair, and lunge for Caspian. My fingers close around the hilt of his ceremonial sword. The hiss of metal as the blade exits the leather sheath at his waist splits the air.

Before anyone can react, I'm positioned behind him, the blade held to his throat. I feel him tense, but otherwise he's remarkably calm. "I'm sorry," I murmur.

The Emperor slides his gaze to the sword at his son's neck, the crown in my hand, poised to throw, and then to me. He retreats backward slowly, his expression still so haughty, so sure he is in control.

The tiara in my hand trembles, throwing shards of emerald light against Caspian's neck and jaw.

"What, exactly, do you plan to do with that?" the Emperor asks quietly.

"It's rigged with explosives, so use your imagination," I hiss.

"You Fienians and your love of bombs." He tsks, his lips curled like he tastes something foul.

In my periphery I spot Centurions closing in.

"Let them go," I order, "or I kill your son."

I expect the Emperor to flinch, to show even a tiny shred of worry that Caspian's life hangs in the balance. Instead, his eyes remain calm, a little smile playing over his mouth.

"No, I don't think so. You're too weak. A scared little girl playing at being a Rebel." He regards Caspian, and finally, an emotion ripples over his countenance, but it's not the one I'm expecting. "Besides, you would be doing me a favor. My son has proved himself a traitor. Do you think I wouldn't find out that he's helping you? Although I do find it interesting that Caspian knew Victoria constantly monitored the prison. Why didn't he warn you, do you suppose?"

And just like that, the Emperor has taken away the final bargaining chip I have left. The air flees my lungs in a whoosh. The Centurions edge closer.

Caspian, for his part, is remarkably still. His breathing even. His gaze steady, unflinching. Did he betray us? I don't have time to work that angle out, nor can my heart bear the consequences if that's true.

Something moves in the distance, a quick motion that draws my attention behind the Archduchess. Riser.

No, no, *no*.

He should flee. There's no way he can take on the entire ship.

"She might be playing at being a Rebel," Riser says, his

voice carrying over the room. "But I'm not. And neither is he."

Confused gasps fill the room as Delphine's father, General Bloodwood, strolls toward the Emperor at the front of the aisle—a black device the size of a cigar held firmly in his outstretched hand.

"General Bloodwood, what is this?" the Emperor barks, but for the first time since this nightmare began, there's true fear in his voice.

The general smiles and then his face begins to change, pixelating, transforming until the mangled features become familiar and my brains rearranges the pieces into—

Oh, no. It can't be.

"Nicolai?" I gasp as the general's words from earlier—*you're about to get everything you've ever deserved*—take on new meaning.

Nicolai still grins, his ruined lips pulled taut as if they're pinned that way. "Ladies and lords, don't panic, but you should know beneath every seat in this room is a bomb large enough to atomize you in less than a second."

A few loud explosions rock the crowd. Nicolai shakes his head. "Did I forget to mention that standing sets the bombs off? My mistake. I can also press this handy little button and they all go boom at once."

Someone screams, but I don't know if it's in response to Nicolai's disfigured face or his declaration. His strange, electronic voice makes him seem even more monstrous somehow.

The Emperor stares and stares with a puzzled look, as if he just can't believe what he's seeing.

My mind is whirring as I try to put this new reality together. The starcraft training. He was planning this all along. It wasn't an invasion.

It's a suicide mission.

The Centurions who were creeping up on me have fanned

out to check the seats. After pushing their way down the rows, they all look to the Emperor, and even before I see their nods, I can tell by their waxen faces and hollow eyes that Nicolai is telling the truth.

"How did you get aboard this ship?" the Emperor demands.

"Oh, that." Nicolai lets his gaze shift to Riser. "Someone was kind enough to sneak me on, but not before gifting me a few curious details. Like the cache of smart bombs the general kept floating in a position not far from here?"

Riser . . . let Nicolai on Hyperion? Impossible.

I search his face, silently begging him to look at me, to disprove this betrayal somehow, but his focus never leaves the Emperor.

The Emperor blanches, finally having the sense to look shaken. He glances at Delphine's mother, whose guilty expression all but confirms the veracity of this new knowledge.

"What, did you think someone like the general wouldn't have a plan to wrest control away from you eventually? But, you're in luck. I killed him. You're welcome."

Delphine's mother gives a silent scream before falling into her chair. Delphine and Roman share nervous glances.

The Emperor shakes his head, over and over, as if unable to comprehend everything happening. "What do you want? Money? A place on Hyperion? Titles? I'm sure we can work something out."

Nicolai grins. "Oh, I've had most of those things. They're not as fulfilling as one expects. I would accept one thing from you, though."

Triumph sparks inside the Emperor's eyes. He thinks, like always, he can use his power and wealth to get out of this situation. "Go on."

"Give me back my sister, the one you had thrown in Rhine Prison to rot and die, and I'll take my bombs and leave."

A cold wave of shock ices my veins. His sister . . . Rhine Prison . . .

And suddenly everything clicks into place.

THIRTY-THREE

The Emperor comes to the same conclusion I do, and something changes in his expression, his demeanor. "You—you can't be . . . "

"Ezra Croft? The most prolific and notorious murdered Fienian Rebel leader?" Nicolai scrapes into a bow, every eye fixed on his thumb over the detonator in his hand. "In the flesh—or what's left of it."

"No." The Emperor points a shaking finger at him. "I—I killed you."

"You tried extremely hard, I'll give you that." His strange, warbling voice drips with a humor that doesn't reach his eyes. "But I promised that I would make you pay for my sister's death, and I'm a man of my word. So you see, I just couldn't give you the satisfaction of dying."

Every single person is frozen, paralyzed in an over-whelming whirlwind of terror and shock. Ezra Croft was the most feared man in history, his crimes horrific. And because the Emperor insisted on replaying the gruesome images of those crimes to the public almost daily, everyone in this room can picture exactly what will happen if Nicolai lifts his thumb a few millimeters.

Not to mention what the bombs will do to the Emperor's precious Hyperion. A blast of that size would be . . . devastating. It would destroy the entire ship.

Taking advantage of the sudden quiet, Riser approaches Nicolai. "I fulfilled my part of the bargain, now I'm taking Maia and the others and we're leaving."

Nicolai blinks. I can't help but realize that, as Ezra Croft, that makes Nicolai Riser's uncle. "I'm sorry, nephew, but I've changed things a little. Maia stays with me."

With everything that's happened, I've almost completely forgotten about Caspian, who's drifted from my embrace. He's watching everything, his body so very still. But as soon as Nicolai announced his plans for me, he changed. Began studying the scene and Nicolai in a way that tells me he's going to do something violent soon.

How did this all get away from me so quickly? I need to act, to do something, but what?

If it saved my friends, I would willingly give myself up for them. But what about the Mercurian?

Riser shakes his head. "Why keep her? She's nothing."

Nicolai actually has the audacity to look remorseful for this betrayal as he says, "You're right. She is nothing, but the thing inside her . . . I can't let her destroy Pandora."

"Why?"

"Don't you see? The only way to save our world is to destroy it. Only total annihilation will wipe out the Royalists' ideals. To kill a cancer you must excise every single corrupted piece of flesh along with the surrounding tissue."

Outrage bursts like a bomb inside my chest, and I rush down the steps, only halting when Nicolai waves the detonator at me. "You're a madman. You're talking about wiping out up to ninety percent of the population."

Nicolai shrugs. "That's up to mother nature, but yes, it's likely. But those that remain, they'll remember us. They'll remember our sacrifice. And they'll start anew."

Beside me, I feel Caspian's presence, his entire being laser focused on Nicolai. I catch Caspian lock eyes with Riser, and something passes between them. A plan I can't quite decipher. I ready myself for anything. Inching closer to Nicolai as I do.

"You're a monster," someone calls, and my stomach pits as I recognize Lash's refined voice.

He's providing a distraction, I realize, as Nicolai turned slightly to face Lash, who's limping past the Archduchess.

Roman's eyes narrow as he takes in Lash, perhaps remembering him as the Silver who dared to love his sister. A cruel grin carves his thick jaw.

I see the flicker of rage and intent a moment too late. The blade in Roman's hand glints as he lunges.

A scream barrels up my throat as the blade rams toward Lash's chest—

Delphine moves so quickly that I barely understand what she's doing. Not until she blocks the weapon with her body.

Roman jerks his hand down in an effort to stop the blow, but he was moving too fast and the knife sinks into her lower stomach.

Delphine stumbles. Gasps. A bright red spot blooms over her tunic. Roman lurches back as the realization of what he's done hits home.

"Del, why?" he says, looking at her as if she's a stranger.

She shakes her head, seemingly as confused as Roman, and then slumps into Lash's waiting arms.

We have to act now while Nicolai is distracted. Something flashes in my periphery. I follow the movement to Caspian, a small blade held firmly in his hand.

He strikes with the speed of a snake. Once. Twice. So fast

that I don't think Nicolai even knows he's been stabbed. Before the Puppet Master can put together what's happened, I close the distance between us and clamp my hands over the detonator, forcing his thumb to hold down pressure.

"What are you . . ." Nicolai's voice tapers off, and then he lets out a low chuckle. "Oh, I see. Clever."

His hand weakens beneath mine. His fingers release their hold of the detonator, and my thumb just manages to take the place of his before the little red button can fully depress and kill us all.

Thumb trembling, I raise my hand high in the air, sending the Centurions that were closing in scurrying back. Max rushes to my side, my cracked ribs practically groaning at the contact. But the pain is nothing compared to my relief, and I throw my free arm around him, just barely holding back the tears that threaten to fall.

"Are you hurt?" I demand before realizing that's a stupid question. Of course he's hurt.

He laughs, the sound pained. "Nothing I couldn't handle."

The bravado in his voice, tinged with the underlying fear he's trying to hide, cuts me to the core.

"I came back for you, Max. I came back this time."

A sob sounds in his throat, and he buries it down. "I knew you would. Now can we go home, please? I want to see Mom."

Home. The prospect suddenly seems so close, and yet . . .

I glance over my shoulder and spot Caspian lowering Nicolai to the ground. Blood drips from Nicolai's vest to the floor. His eyes are glazed, his lips parted. His hands curled inward like claws as if the effort of holding the detonator has made them useless.

For the first time since I've known him, his ruined face isn't twisted and taut with pain. He looks so small, almost a child—not the Rebel leader that terrorized a nation. Not the man who haunted my dreams, the Puppet Master who seemed to know everything.

Now he's simply a broken man taking his last few breaths.

I shift my focus to the others.

Roman is pressed into the crowd, his eyes hollow and fixed on Delphine, who's sitting against a chair, being tended to by Lash. Flame and Teagan are whispering with Riser. Their eyes go to me.

"We need to leave," I say, glancing around. The Archduchess is missing, and alarm bells ping inside my head as I try to form a plan. "I can hold down the button until we're far enough away and then . . ."

What? Release it?

Riser approaches, the others not far behind. He nods to me. "That's a sound plan, but it won't work."

"Why?"

Flame catches my gaze, her face somber in a way I don't quite understand. "The detonator has a low signal range. We wouldn't even make it to the hangar before the signal was lost . . . and with that particular type of setup, once activated, it's programmed to detonate if the signal flickers out."

I shake my head. "Well, then, we'll think of something."

"We don't have time for that."

That means . . .

"No." My hand clenches harder around the detonator. "We all go home."

"Someone has to stay, darling," Teagan adds, and the softness of her voice makes it all the more real.

"I can't—I can't lose any of you."

Flame reaches out her hand. "Give it here and I can check it for the failsafe." I don't budge, so she adds, "Sometimes there's a button that allows deactivation."

They're all watching me. In my periphery, I notice Nicolai has gone still.

"Maia," Max says. "Give it to her. We're running out of time."

I look out at the crowd of Royalists watching us, the weight of thousands of Sleepers watching to see what I'll do falling over me like an avalanche.

I nod and reach out to hand the detonator to Flame—

Before I can react, Riser slips his hand over mine.

I try to jerk away, but I can't tug too hard for fear of my thumb slipping off the button. "What are you doing?" I beg, strangely breathless.

"I'll never forget how beautiful you looked tonight, Maia," Riser says, his voice heavy with regret. "Never."

And then arms slip behind me and pull me back as Riser takes the detonator from my sweaty hand.

"No!" My yell warbles through the ship. Caspian and Flame have me in a vise grip and are dragging me away from the room of stars. Away from Riser. "Riser! Please, I can't do this without you!"

A sad smile flashes Riser's perfect teeth. "You've never needed me or anyone, Maia. You and you alone can save our world."

I twist to look back at Caspian. "Let me go. This won't work. As soon as we exit this room the Emperor will order the Centurions to rush Riser. He'd rather die than let us go."

"No, he won't. Because in his own sick, demented mind, he still thinks somehow with me alive, his name will live on in history." Over my head, Caspian shoots a hard stare at the Emperor. "Isn't that right, Father? Well, I promise you, history will remember you as a war criminal and a tyrant who nearly destroyed the planet."

Rage flares in the Emperor's eyes . . . but he doesn't order the Centurions to advance on Riser. And I know now that

Caspian's right. "You can say what you will about me, Son. But you will always be *my* creation. *My* legacy."

Caspian stares at his father, hurt and loathing contorting his face. "We may be bonded by blood, but I will never be your son. Never. Your legacy dies with you."

Caspian turns to me. "Maia, I'll carry you if I have to."

But I can't leave Riser alone to die. I can't. Not after all he's done for me. Not after everything we've been through. Not after I finally realized what he means to me.

I hold Riser's gaze. "Riser, *please*."

Riser looks at me, really looks at me, as if he's drinking me in for the last time. "I figured it out, how to redeem myself. It will be okay now, Maia, I promise. I'm not even scared."

Confusion twists my face. "You're not making any sense, Riser."

"Caspian," Riser orders, tearing his gaze from my face. And I know—I know it's the last time he'll look at me. "Protect her above all else. Promise me."

Caspian nods. "Until my dying breath."

"Thank you. Now, go. Please."

Caspian and Flame gently but forcefully begin to drag me away. Panic has me clawing at the air, trying to jerk from their grasp. Caspian is trying to calm me down, his voice whispering in my ear, but I can't hear him. Not through the frantic pounding of my heart, my ragged breaths.

Beside us, Lash supports Delphine, blood dripping to the floor. I vaguely make out the sound of Flame and him arguing, but they must agree to take her because the arguing stops.

Caspian's words trickle in and out of my ears. "What he wanted . . . stop fighting . . . please, listen . . ."

But it's jumbled and all mixed up and I want to scream. I want to kill Caspian for making me leave Riser. I want to murder Riser for thinking he had to sacrifice himself. I want to bring this entire ship down with my bare hands.

Lights flash inside the hangar, the sleek starcrafts all lined up in neat rows. As we approach the starcraft that brought us here, all the life drains out of me, and I slump into Caspian's arms. It feels like my chest will explode, just split right open.

I can't leave Riser.

Caspian helps me up the ramp and into the craft. The world spins. I feel something slide across my body and hear a click as Caspian buckles me in. Through the open door, I see Flame gliding from craft to craft, planting small bombs that will disable the machine's tech and render them inoperable.

"I got most of them," she calls as she slips inside, the ramp closing with a whoosh behind her. "Now let's go. We're already cutting the timeline close."

Caspian works on the dials and buttons on the dashboard as he programs the craft for our return flight, but I'm too angry to meet his gaze. Rage and grief swirl inside me, a black, poisonous cloud.

All I can think about is Riser alone. Surrounded by a father who never loved him, by enemies who would see him drawn and quartered, by a world that never accepted him.

He must be lonely, so lonely and afraid. Even if he's too stubborn to be fearful of death, he must grieve for the future he's given up. The future he and I planned not a full day ago.

Bending over, I throw a hand over my mouth. I'm going to throw up. I can't. I can't think about this. About him—

Gritting my teeth, I force myself to sit up just in time to spot Lash helping Delphine into a seat across from me. His hand presses a blood-drenched silk scarf into her wound, and a fresh surge of rage burns through me.

Screw forgiveness. She should be the one to die, not Riser.

She must feel my anger, or perhaps finally a sense of

morality has come over her, because she keeps her eyes trained on the floor, her face devoid of her usual disdain.

Or perhaps she's simply dying. By the blood dripping onto the metal seat, that's a possibility.

Max buckles in on my left. He fiddles with something in his lap and then a familiar chirping breaks through my bubble of agony . . .

"Bramble?"

The sensor rushes into my lap, his movements gentle, as if he can feel my heartache.

"I thought you could use Bramble right now," Max says, taking my hand in his. "It's okay, Maia. I'm safe. Bramble is safe. And Riser—"

"Riser is what?" I interrupt, causing Bramble to stir uneasily in my lap. "We left him there to die."

At my declaration, Bramble's chirps become frantic, his antennae whipping in the direction of Caspian.

As the craft shoots out the hangar door, hollowing out my stomach, I close my eyes, trying to picture Riser's face as I left. Trying to hold onto his image. To cling to it like it's the last breath in my lungs.

That last smile. Those perfect teeth . . .

Except . . .

My eyes snap open. Riser didn't have perfect teeth. He had a chip, small but noticeable.

Bramble is still beeping cheerfully and gesturing toward Caspian. Maybe it's traveling at hyper speed, or perhaps it's the circumstances, but the world seems to slow as I focus on Caspian in my periphery.

Done with the programming, he takes the seat on my right. His movements fluid and stealthy, just like . . .

No. I'm seeing what I want.

Closing my eyes, I bring up the tracker program with my mind. Even at this distance from the ship, it's still accessible. I search the name Riser, holding my breath, until the dot with his location pops up on my mental map—right next to me.

My eyelids pop open. How is this possible?

His fingers are warm and somehow familiar as they slip over mine. "I tried to tell you, tried to explain, but for our plan to work, the Emperor had to believe I was Caspian."

I exhale, afraid to take in what he's saying. What my heart is saying. Afraid it won't be true. Afraid I'll blink and this will all go away.

"Digger Girl," he says, imploring me with his voice. "I didn't leave you. How could you ever think I would?"

I know even before I look. But that doesn't stop the chaos of emotions from slamming into me as I turn and let my gaze rake over the features of—of—

"Riser?"

I drink in his real face with the chipped tooth and the mismatched eyes and the ghost of a scar peeking just above his undershirt. But it's only when Bramble scrambles into his lap that I know for sure it's him.

My sliver of hope becomes a tidal wave of relief. I throw my arms around him, relishing his warmth. "I thought—oh, gods, I thought you were gone," I whisper, burying my head in his neck. "But then—"

The realization hits like a bomb. If Riser was pretending to be Caspian, then . . .

No. Oh, no.

"Caspian. He switched places with you?"

Riser nods, his expression solemn.

"I don't understand."

"Let me explain." Riser squeezes my hand as his eyes implore me to forgive him. "But first, he asked for a chance to talk with you if anything went wrong. Flame, can you switch over all the comms so they have privacy? And activate the mic."

A low crackle sounds in my head, followed by Caspian's voice, still thrumming with that rich elegance despite everything.

"Hey, Maia," he begins. "I apologize for the hurt I know I just caused you."

"Caspian, I don't care about that. We're turning around—"

"No. Maia, please, let me get this off my chest."

Something in his voice makes me agree. "Okay, Caspian. Tell me what you want to say and then we'll . . . we'll figure this out."

"First, don't blame yourself. This isn't because you chose my brother over me. It's true, I love you—I think I'll love you until I die, which probably won't be very long from now." A ragged chuckle whispers into my head. "Sorry, that was cruel, but the time for hiding behind lies is gone." He releases a sigh. "Second, I want you to know, you've always been the one for me. The girl I dreamed of, the girl who made me want to be better—"

"Stop, Caspian." My voice breaks. The others can only hear my words, but it's enough to get the gist of the conversation, and everyone, even Delphine, looks overcome with sadness.

"Please," Caspian begs. "We're running out of time, and there's still so many things I want to say to you."

I blink, biting back my words, wondering how no one ever prepared me for the excruciating pain of knowing you're about to lose someone and not being able to stop it.

"Maia, even if you hadn't chosen Riser over me, I see now that I don't deserve you, and I'm ashamed when I think of how much suffering I overlooked, how many of my own people I watched this court oppress and slaughter." Pain weighs down his voice, and I pray the Emperor can hear him. "Deep down, Maia," he continues, "deep down, I knew it was wrong. We all did. I think that was the greatest crime of all."

"You tried." I tug at my seatbelt strap, willing him to hear me. To understand he's forgiven. "Once you understood everything that was happening."

"It wasn't enough. It will never be enough."

I close my eyes. "You don't have to do this. You can still try to make it to a starcraft—"

"No." The finality in his voice nearly breaks me. "My father will follow us. He'll do whatever it takes to continue his corrupt reign. Besides . . . I understand now what you said about forgiveness. That's why I gave Ezra, the man who killed my mother and sister, a chance to do what was right and absolve himself of those crimes."

I swallow as understanding clicks into place. "You knew there was a possibility he wouldn't let us go. You . . . you knew there was a high likelihood this would be the outcome."

"I don't want to die," Caspian clarifies, and I hear that truth in his tone, the grief over what could have been. "You have to know that. I want to live. I want to spend the rest of my life trying to prove I deserve you."

"Then do it. Live."

"It's my turn to do what's right, Maia. Surely you understand that?"

I shake my head, stubbornly refusing to accept that he has to die.

He clears his throat. "So . . . what should we talk about while I wait for your craft to reach the safety mark? Wait, I know. Tell me the story of Orion and the seven sisters. The one you were named after. I always loved that one."

I swallow, my throat aching, each word scraping out like a knife. "Orion, the giant huntsman, fell madly in love with the seven daughters of Atlas. When their father died, the sisters ended their lives, but Zeus took pity on them and turned them into stars. To this day, if you look at the sky, you'll see

Orion, still chasing them. Still madly in love with the thing he cannot have."

He sighs. "I remember when you wrote that poem. Roman and the others made fun of me, but then Ophelia took me aside. She said, 'Cas, I like this girl. She has heart.'" He pauses, then adds, "I should have guessed I was Orion in this story, loving someone who will forever be out of my reach."

My throat clenches, my jumbled response crumbling on my tongue.

"I finally understood you could never love me when you walked down the aisle. The way you looked back at me when you thought I was Riser—you've never looked at me that way, Maia." He sighs, but it's so soft I barely hear it. "I know that psychopath will take care of you. Tell him . . . tell him it was an honor to fight beside him, as equals. As . . . brothers. Tell them all that."

Emotion chokes back my words. "Come back and tell them yourself."

"Stubborn till the end. Gods, I'm going to miss that."

Another heart stopping pause. My fingers twist around the jewels embroidered into my wedding dress.

Not yet. Please, not yet.

"So, you've cleared the safety point, which means it's time for me to log off. Goodbye, Maia of the stars." Another pause and then I hear his voice, muffled and distant, as if he's talking to someone else. "This is for Ophelia."

The microplant comm goes dead. I dig my fist into my sternum, trapped in the agony of waiting for the inevitable while praying for just one more word from him. All the things I left unsaid pile up inside me, all the memories of our fleeting time together playing across my vision like a rift screen.

The first time I saw Caspian as a little kid watching his

mother and baby sister's murder. The sketch he drew of me. The first time I ran into him near the telescope.

Gods he was beautiful—beautiful but so confused about who he was, his purpose in this life.

And he loved me even then, although it took until just this moment to understand the depth of that love—

The explosion is muted, the sound barely a whisper. Hardly the cacophony I'd expect from the most coveted, expensive piece of real estate in the world being torn apart into nothing. A muffled rumble rocks the craft, and I open my eyes to a growing flame of orange in the distance where Hyperion once floated.

All those people—gone. Just gone.

The enormity of such destruction is too much to fathom. Perhaps someday I will mourn the souls who perished. Perhaps someday it won't matter that they were enemies, only human beings.

But in this moment, I only have the capacity to grieve one person.

Prince Caspian Laevus, Royalist turned rebel, my once-intended and almost-husband, my friend, ally, and one of the bravest people I've ever known, is dead.

THIRTY-FOUR

O n the way back down to Earth, I listen, numb, as Riser explains.

"Caspian came to me this morning before the ceremony," Riser says, eyes distant as he recalls what feels like days ago to me. "I thought at first when he suggested I have Flame add another code to switch his face with mine that it was some trick. But he implored me to trust him, brother to brother, and he made me promise that no matter what happened, I would go along with the ruse to protect you."

"Why didn't you tell me?" I ask, my voice strangely emotionless.

"There was no time." Riser drags a hand through his dark hair. "I've never seen him like that. He just kept saying that we both loved you, and it was our job to keep you safe no matter what."

Tears prickle the corners of my eyes, but I blink them back. A part of me is furious with Caspian. Our conversation right before he walked me to the ceremony, when I thought he was Riser, comes to mind.

The things he said.

He was saying goodbye.

"The Emperor said Caspian knew about the Archduchess's constant prison monitoring," I add, trying to work out his last thoughts and motives. "He must have known our plan to break Max from his cell was doomed no matter what we did."

"If I'd *known* that *his* plan included bringing Nicolai on board armed with a cache of explosives," Flame interjects, eyeing Riser pointedly, "I would have never agreed to the last-minute face swap."

"That's why he couldn't tell anyone," I add. "He must have figured out somehow Nicolai planned to board Hyperion, must have realized who Nicolai really was and that Riser was the only person Nicolai would trust. He knew Nicolai could betray him—but he was prepared for that too."

"Brave idiot," Riser growls, and I'm surprised by the emotion beneath his gruffness. "I hope our father realized it was Caspian before the explosion. I hope that bastard looked at his son's face—a son who was ten times the man he was—and wept."

At that, we all go quiet as we wait to enter a new hell. I haven't checked the time, but we have to be nearing the cutoff threshold to stop the asteroid. My chest tightens as I realize that when we return, there's a possibility we'll be mere minutes too late. If that's the case, we'll be forced directly into the underground bunker below the castle.

But even that failsafe doesn't have enough caskets for everyone to upload and survive.

Closing my eyes, I shove the thought aside and prepare to land.

Please, I pray to any of the old gods who might be listening, *let Caspian's sacrifice be worth something.*

I SPOT my mother's cloaked form before we land. She waits for us on the roof of the palace, her lean figure leaned into the wind, braided brown hair whipping behind her.

Night has long since fallen, the palace grounds layered in shadows. I don't dare look up at Pandora as I exit the craft, Bramble nestled into my shoulder and neck. Don't dare try to read my mother's face—or what it will tell me—until I've managed to compose myself.

But she's not focused on me anyway. She's frozen, trapped in the agony of waiting as her gaze scrapes over the door . . .

She's searching for Max.

And when she sees him, when she releases the breath she's been holding for gods know how long and the realization that he's safe hits, the mask my mother has worn since I can remember crumbles to reveal panic.

The clawing, drowning kind only a mother can feel for her children.

A strange noise leaves her throat and then, the woman who never runs, never shows a hint of emotion, sprints the few feet to where Max stands, wobbly and tired but alive. She pulls him to her, and for once I notice how thin her arms have gotten. How hollow her temples are. The lines etched into her forehead grooved so deep they could be claw marks.

She doesn't cry, not that I'm expecting her to. But her body shudders, and more than once, she inhales him the way I imagine a mother would an infant.

Perhaps it was the torture, but Max doesn't fight her attention. And when she leans in and whispers something, tears wet his eyes, and he answers her.

I fight off a wave of jealousy, the reminder that she's always loved him more. That no matter what I've done, no matter what I do, it will never be enough.

The last to exit the craft are Lash and Delphine. As they limp down the ramp, my mother jerks away from Max, takes in Delphine, the missing Caspian, and then dons her hard mask once more.

"There's no time to explain what happened above," she says. "We need to get Max inside the castle now. Once he leads us to the Mercurian, everyone but Maia and I must take refuge in the subterranean shelter below."

Riser positions himself in front of me, not even trying to hide his willingness to fight her, if necessary, to protect me. "The timeline passed."

It's less a question than a statement, and my heart clenches as I remember what happens once we go over the deadline.

Someone has to manually operate the device.

My mother hesitates before shaking her head. "We still have a few minutes. Almost all the civilians have already descended—"

"Then Maia needs to take shelter too," Riser interrupts, his steely countenance not in the least diminished by my mother's looming presence. Bramble, sensing the growing tension, stirs in alarm, his antennae switching between Riser and my mother.

"No." I step between them. "I've sacrificed everything to get to this moment. If there's a chance we can make it, I'm going."

Riser and I exchange glances and then he nods, accepting my order without a fight. Bramble settles back into my neck, chirping softly.

There's no more arguing. I command Teagan, Flame, and Lash to guide any remaining civilians to shelter. Riser will come with us and when Max's part is done and we find the Mercurian, Riser's job is to ensure Max makes it to safety.

As soon as we descend down the roof's stairwell and into the palace walls, Max's eyes light up, an unmistakable blue light piercing the darkness. A strange sort of quiet hangs heavy in the halls, the lights lining the walls flickering.

My mother peppers me with questions as we break into a jog, Riser guiding the near-blind Max. Agony spears my ribs with every step. I fill her in as best I can, grunting and wheezing through the pain and the adrenaline. All the while holding the stupid train of my dress up to keep from tripping.

Hardly breaking his stride, Riser takes a blade and cuts the heavy fabric from my thighs down, freeing me.

Any other time I would make a joke about how he's always wanted to do that—or something to that effect. But now everything feels so somber, the weight of the next few minutes crushing us all.

That, of course, doesn't stop my mother from asking about the wedding dress I'm wearing. I inform her of the unexpected ceremony. Nicolai's arrival and reveal. She doesn't even blink at learning he's Ezra Croft, which strengthens my suspicion that she knew all along.

There are so many mysteries shrouding my mother, so many questions about what she knows and her true motives, and I understand now as I rush down the halls beside this woman that I may never truly know her.

"And the prince?" my mother asks softly as we glide down yet another dark corridor.

"Dead," I answer, the coldness in my voice matching hers to hide my pain.

Her nostrils flare delicately. "The explosion?"

What must she have thought when she witnessed the fiery fate of Hyperion? Did she fear we had all died?

"That was him. He saved us, sacrificed himself and everything he's ever believed in to do it."

Her thin lips stretch into a grim smile. "I always knew that boy had goodness inside, no matter how hard Marcus tried to stamp it out of him."

A fresh torrent of grief swells my chest, and I focus on Max's light bouncing over the draperies and other adornments along the walls rather than feel the pain eating away at me.

But Riser notices, and he brushes a finger down my arm. A quick, calming gesture.

His mismatched eyes say: *I'm here until the end and I will never leave you. We can do this.*

The blue lights streaming from Max's eyes begin to pulse brighter and brighter.

"We're close," my mother murmurs.

It's then that I begin to recognize where we are. To my left, the door to the great hall where we were hazed by the Chosen is open, the room dark. My breath hitches, my heartbeat speeding up with every step I take, every memory that flashes in my mind.

"I know where we're going . . ." My words catch in my throat as we enter the long hallway where the royal family's portraits still hang. The images are larger than life, almost godlike as they watch us pass, their golden frames more ornate than I remember—

"Hall of the three-headed sphinx, caged in gold," I murmur.

My mother pauses. "What?"

"Dad whispered that to me in one of the Sims. It was a riddle. I didn't understand then, but I do now."

The paintings—three generations of the ruling Royalist family—framed inside their ornate golden cages. It seems so simple now.

But where would he hide the Mercurian?

For the briefest of seconds, I let my gaze linger on Caspian where he sits on his white throne, his crown askew, that irreverent half smile quirking his lips.

I can't help but think how, just as I was meant to be an

obedient Chosen girl before the pit changed me, Caspian was meant to be a great and thoughtful ruler before he was reshaped by war and tyranny into something else.

But he's wrong to think that something else was less than what he was meant to be.

Forged by so much blood and death, he became a Rebel hero who fought against everything he's ever known, his own family, in the name of justice, and his name will forever stand for freedom.

"I'll make sure of that," I whisper to him as I pass, endeavoring to ignore the rest of the paintings and the tyrants inside.

It doesn't fail me that, despite all of the Emperor's efforts, the only one from his house that remains is the one person whose portrait isn't featured—Riser.

Starlight pours from the windows of the domed observatory and casts the area in an ethereal glow. The blue beams Max is projecting sweep to fall on the tall telescope in the middle. The silver cylinder rises almost twenty feet high, and I wonder if it's still pointed at the Orion Nebula . . . where Caspian and I left it the last time we were here.

And then it hits me. "The telescope."

It's the Mercurian. The thing my father created and hid right under the Emperor's nose. Our salvation.

And he was trying to tell me even then, when my presence caused it to change its location to the sword inside the Orion Nebula.

Bramble gives off a series of rapid-fire beeps and scrambles down my arm. His metal legs click softly against the stone tiles as he rushes to examine the telescope.

I look to my mother and discover she's speechless, her face gripped with so much sadness that I take a step back.

"Of course," she murmurs, never taking her eyes off the telescope. "I should have guessed."

I grip the iron railing that leads to the platform holding the telescope before remembering Max. Glancing over my shoulder, I catch Riser's gaze. Hold. I can't define what passes between us, the emotion a mixture of everything we've been through, everything we've endured and overcome, the recent revelations of our feelings for one another, and something deeper, something I can't explain with words.

"Go," I say. "Get my brother to safety. Promise me that no matter what happens, you'll get him underground."

Riser smiles. "You have my word."

"Bramble," I call. "Go with them."

A defiant screech comes from the stubborn sensor, where he hesitates at the top of the stairs, near the telescope.

"Please," I say. "They need your protection, and I don't trust anyone else to do this. It's up to you, Bramble."

Riser grins at me. "It's true. We need you, little guy, for protection."

We're like two parents trying to trick our kid into doing what we want.

Emitting a string of frustrated beeps, Bramble scuttles down the stairs and into Riser's arms. As Riser, Bramble, and Max rush to leave, and I take the stairs two at a time, a fresh crop of worries enters my brain.

Will this work? What if I can't figure out how to activate the key? What if . . .

"You'll be fine," Riser calls out over his shoulder. "Now hurry and meet us so we can reminisce on how much we love underground spaces."

I smile despite my nerves.

Okay, you can do this. The hard part is out of the way.

Squaring my shoulders, I approach the weapon that's captivated the head of both the Royalists and the Fienians for years.

THIRTY-FIVE

M y mother joins me on the iron platform that elevates the telescope. Any traces of her grief have vanished beneath a veneer of absolute control. "You need to look into the telescope and then I'll activate the switch that reads the key."

"How do you know there's a switch?"

"Because I know your father." The pride in her voice is at odds with the condescending way I'm used to hearing her talk about him, but I push the oddity aside, slide onto my back, and peer beneath the telescope's slightly curved lens.

As my eyes adjust, and I take in that circle of pinkish-red hydrogen gas centered by the nursery of stars, my chest tightens.

The telescope is right where we left it the last time. Still pointing at the clue that should have marked it as the Mercurian from the beginning for me.

Above, my mother fiddles around at the base until I hear her breath catch, and then she releases a triumphant sigh. "Just where I thought it would be. Now, are you ready?"

"Yes."

The click of a depressed switch cuts through the air. I barely have time to ponder what happens next when blindingly-bright lasers spear from the frame of the lens. Soft heat moves over my left cheek as the lasers scan me, tracing methodical, choppy paths first over the left side and then—

"The key was hidden in plain sight the whole time," I breathe. "On my face."

"Your . . . freckles?"

"Yes." *The ones shaped like the constellations*, I don't say, the irony cutting deep as I also realize it's the one thing I used to hate about myself, and also the one thing Flame decided to leave during my Reconstruction.

"All this time," I continue as the lasers' warmth spread across the ridge of my cheekbone to my temple, "we assumed the key was hidden deep inside me."

I remember in prison when the Archduchess stared right at my unique freckles. All the times I had to cover them with foundation. I remember the sketch Caspian sent me when he was still a boy and I, a *naïve*, insecure girl.

The freckles he made into stars.

"This is so like your father," my mother says. "If I could talk to Philip right now, gods, I would throttle him."

I can't help but notice the way my mother's voice wobbles like she's crying. Except my mother doesn't cry. And she certainly doesn't mourn the loss of my father.

A sudden, horrifying thought comes to me. What if, just like the telescope and my freckles, my real mother has been hidden from me, waiting for me to find the true her?

The heat lifts from my cheeks. At the same time, a loud hum begins to emanate from the telescope, from the entire room, like the bowels of the earth stirring.

The most powerful weapon ever developed has just been activated.

Wiping my sweaty-damp palms against my bodice, I slide from beneath the weapon and jump to my feet. "So what now?"

A shadow falls over my mother's expression, there and gone, and I have the sudden realization there's something she isn't telling me. Something bad.

"Maia, I—" Her words cut off sharply as she jerks her gaze to the sky beyond the glass panes. "What is that?"

I follow her stare to the northern sky. At the same time, I hear the droning sigh of a starcraft speeding through the atmosphere at high speed. My eyes catch on the silver disc growing larger by the second.

Coming straight for us.

"Did any Royalists get out before the explosion?" my mother asks.

Before I can answer, her fingers claw into my arm as she drags me down the stairs with preternatural strength.

"Maia!"

"No—I don't know. Flame destroyed all the other starcrafts—"

But she didn't. There weren't enough bombs. My mind flashes to those last moments after Roman stabbed Delphine and we disarmed Nicolai. The chaos.

And afterward—

The Archduchess.

I don't remember seeing her after Caspian took possession of the detonator.

We hit the floor just as a shadow eclipses the starlight brightening the room, throwing us in eerie darkness. The glass window panes rattle above, harder, harder until I'm sure they'll shatter.

The whining sound has become a screech.

"The Mercurian!" I shout. If it's destroyed—

"Run!" my mother growls.

But it's too late.

I turn at the same time my mother does. A violent tremor rocks the building, shaking the floor beneath us. I careen sideways. If not for my mother's iron grip, I would have collapsed with the impact.

Throwing out my arms for balance, I watch in horrified slow motion as the silver edge of the craft rips through the faces of paintings—

The realization that I'm about to die hits with a strange sort of clarity.

Caught in the chaos of sound and explosions and panic, I don't feel my mother push me until I'm already tumbling through the air.

For a single heartbeat, my world becomes the scream of metal and the roar of fire.

The floor smacks the air from my lungs. The concussive force of the craft's impact rattles my bones so hard I think they'll crack.

My vision shudders. My head spins. The world tumbles away from me, and I can't seem to catch it.

White-hot pokers of pain stab my left side, thrusting me back to reality. My ribs. I run my tongue along my teeth, taste blood from a busted lip. Nothing else seems injured, but somewhere deep down I know my adrenaline is masking a lot.

A dull ringing floods my ears. Groaning, clutching my flank, I stumble to my feet. I prop my body against the wall as I struggle to piece together the last few moments and make sense of what's happening. To *breathe*.

A sense of urgency overtakes me. I was in the middle of . . . something.

Gouging the dust from my eyes, I scan my surroundings. As the darkness polluting my vision clears, I spy the open chasm of sky shimmering where the wall of paintings sat not seconds ago. Moonlight floods the hole, mortar dust and oily black smoke churning inside the silver prisms. Piles of rubble form mounds around the room.

My attention snaps to the thing occluding the hallway. Little fires flicker around it, but the structure itself seems mostly undamaged. I take in the ragged path the craft carved into the floor after it slammed into the palace.

Fienian hell, it slammed into the palace. Purposefully.

It all comes back in a wave of terror. The telescope. My freckles activated it, and then—

My mother.

A groan drags my focus to the rubble a few feet away. My mother is propped up on her elbows facing me, her legs splayed out at an odd angle and partially covered by chunks of stone and debris.

Never in my life has my mother not been completely composed, her outfit, her hair meticulously put together.

But now—seeing her this way, rich brown hair matted on one side and dark with blood, her cloak covered in dust and—

"Maia," she gasps, her pain-hewn voice spurring me to action.

I rush to her side, searching her body for wounds. Blood drips from her nose, and a large gash bleeds from her forehead. "How badly are you hurt?"

Her eyes shift to mine. If I had any doubts about the severity of her injuries, her dark expression drives them away. "I can't move my legs which means my back is probably broken. I also undoubtedly have a severe concussion, internal bleeding, and several broken bones."

A part of me reels from this news.

Her shrewd gaze slides to where I clutch my side. "You're

injured too. At the very least, you suffered a concussion and possibly a fracture, but you're going to have to fight through it. Do you understand?"

The matter-of-factness in her tone scares me. "I can do that —just tell me what to do. How do I operate the Mercurian?"

Pressing her palm into the wound on her forehead, she looks me directly in the eye and says, "First, you're going to have to fight, Maia, using every single lesson I've ever taught you about swordplay and battle."

As soon as the words leave her mouth, a soft whoosh sounds from the craft as the ramp parts and begins to lower. The craft must be more damaged than it appears because the ramp malfunctions before it fully lowers, leaving a three-foot gap for someone to exit.

"Take my sword," my mother orders calmly, her steady voice in direct contrast to the tightness around her mouth and eyes.

I peer at my mother's beloved blade, a gift from her grandfather. I would be lying if I said I didn't feel anything but revulsion at the sight of it. Growing up, the beautiful golden guard, shaped like two doves wrapped together, represented countless moments of self-loathing and defeat.

Every time its sharp end connected with me, every time the blade proved, once again, that I was too slow, too unskilled to stop it, it felt like another piece of my mother was taken away.

"Maia." My mother meets my hesitant stare. "Take it."

My palms are slick as I pull the rapier free from its leather sheath. The handle feels foreign in my hand, as if I've never held a blade before in my life.

"If my gut is correct," my mother continues, "you're about to face the most lethal swordswoman in the Emperor's court. She has no weaknesses, she doesn't tire, and she's physically the most dominant woman I've ever met."

The Archduchess. A spike of panic spears my gut, and I fixate on the ramp as my entire body goes cold. "Then how am I supposed to beat her?"

"Just like I've taught you," she answers, as if it's the simplest answer in the world.

I drag in a shaky breath. I've come so far from that girl that hid in the pit, and yet . . . I cannot beat the Archduchess. Not when it comes to swordplay.

Recognizing my fear, my mother pushes up on her elbows, ignoring the pain, and says, "Wipe the fear from your mind and remember who you are and what you fight for. Whether you know it or not, you've been preparing for this moment your entire life. You've faced bigger obstacles with less and won. Remember that."

For some reason, I recall the one and only time I managed to beat my mother in a duel. We'd been practicing for over an hour without any breaks. Sweat soaked every scrap of my clothing, and I could hardly hold my foil up.

I don't remember when, exactly, but something inside me snapped, and I looked her in the eyes, my anger and humiliation seeping from every pore, and seethed, "I hate you."

She'd blinked, her sword stilling, mouth partway open as if unsure how to respond. A flicker of hurt rippled across her countenance.

And in that moment, I used her surprise and pain to attack. The tip of my foil pressed into the soft flesh of her neck, just above her high collar. Her eyes widened slightly, and I knew I'd beaten her.

But that was once. Once in a lifetime of duels.

Cracking my neck, I position my body into a defensive stance, working to loosen my clenched muscles and clear my thoughts. Dark tendrils of smoke curl around the beveled steel of my mother's rapier.

I exhale. Once, twice. Clearing my mind as I ready myself for battle.

And then a dark form slips from the ramp opening and leaps gracefully to the floor, and I stare into the half-mad eyes of the Archduchess.

THIRTY-SIX

A fresh surge of terror rolls over me as my body reacts to the Archduchess. Her gliding, inhuman movements. The expert way she claims the space around her, her sword slicing through the air with an ease I'll never know. She's still in her outfit for the ceremony, but she's removed her skirt, her leather pants showing off her long legs and knee-high black boots.

"Did you really think I wouldn't follow you, maggot?" Her eyes have a terrifying nothingness to them.

"Why?" I snarl, foolishly trying to make sense of her intense hatred of me. "The Emperor is dead. There's no reason left to kill me. Why do you hate me so much?"

She blinks. Then her focus drifts to the telescope. "It must hurt, dying feet away from the thing your family sacrificed everything for."

Refusing to give in to her emotional game, I raise my sword. "Who says I'm going to die?"

She clicks her tongue. "Why are you prolonging the inevitable? Drop your weapon, and I will only draw out your suffering a little while."

Glaring at her, I clench the sword's cool golden handle. "Like hell."

"Do you really think you're a match for me, maggot? I've always been three steps ahead of you. How do you think I found you?"

Tracker, I realize. She must have implanted one inside Max, on the off chance he escaped.

"Well you missed," I point out.

"Did I?" the Archduchess taunts, her red lips peeling back in what I imagine is an attempt at smiling as her gaze slides to my mother. "Hello, Lillian. You look horribly . . . broken."

My mother peers at the Archduchess with her usual arrogance. "Victoria. I see you're still your father's attack dog."

Father? I swallow. Blink. Trying to catch up.

My mother's eyes meet mine. "Victoria was Marcus's firstborn, the daughter of a lowly Bronze servant. That was before he set his sights on Amandine, of course."

"Shut your mouth," the Archduchess snarls.

"I'm surprised you didn't have Riser murdered when he was in prison. Or did you not know you had a bastard brother? Oh, I see." If I didn't know my mother was injured, the smile she gives would make me think the opposite. "You thought you were special?"

My shock at learning the Archduchess is the Emperor's illegitimate daughter gives way to resolve as my mother's game becomes apparent.

To her, everything is a weapon. I learned that the hard way.

Now she's using this knowledge to get inside the Archduchess's head. To throw her off balance, make her act recklessly, driven by emotion.

My mother is trying to give me a chance.

"If you had been a legitimate heir from a Gold mother,

your father would never have allowed them to perform experimental Reconstruction on you," my mother continues.

The Archduchess is frozen in rage, her nostrils flared, eyes wild.

It's working.

"You were born a monster, Victoria, a Malignant, as your father eventually called your kind. The only reason he didn't cull you along with the rest of the Malignant children was because he knew you would make a perfect weapon, the loyal dog to do his bidding. Always begging for his praise. Lapping it up like—"

A rage-filled screech bursts from the Archduchess's sneering lips as she lunges at my mother—

Ready to act, I leap across a pile of stone and block her strike. The clang of steel on steel shreds the night, the impact reverberating through my wrist and arm. The strength of her blow alarms me, but I manage to knock her blade down and then counter with my own attack.

If I possessed the lethal skills of my mother, that mistake would have cost the Archduchess everything.

Instead, she glides just out of reach, moving effortlessly, her feet dancing over the floor and around the piles, her horrible blood-red lips sneering at me.

The Mercurian whirs at my back, my mother trapped and panting to my right. I have to protect both.

The Archduchess realizes this immediately and begins a terrifying game of cat and mouse.

She drives her sword toward my mother—

I rush to defend her, but the Archduchess whips toward the Mercurian with impossible speed. My bare feet slip over the dust coating the floor as I twist to counter the new attack, clumsily, grunting with exertion and pain.

Our blades barely meet before she's gliding to my right

again, her long reach eating up the distance between my mother and her. I leap and manage to stop her weapon from cutting into my mother's neck with only inches to spare.

We do this over and over, a slow, surreal dance serenaded by the humming purr of the Mercurian and my ragged breaths. My heart pounds louder and louder inside my head. Sweat seeps into my eyes.

My reaction time is slowing. My movements growing clumsier.

She's wearing me down. Cataloguing my weaknesses as she does. Taking in the way I cringe when I move too fast, my free hand flying to my injured ribs. The way I wobble slightly during the sporadic dizziness caused by either my concussion or lack of sleep.

Or perhaps she's simply stringing this out long enough to ensure the window for using the Mercurian and stopping Pandora passes.

I can't let that happen.

Summoning all my energy, I dart around a scattering of rubble toward her.

She defends my volley of clumsy attacks with an ease I find frightening, her breathing smooth and unhurried, her face placid.

"Look how weak she is," the Archduchess purrs as she slowly begins to advance on me. "How quivering and scared. She's always been a trembling little worm, so afraid of being squashed into dust like all the other worms. Whatever I am, at least my father knew he could count on me, while you, Lillian, will be forced to watch your daughter fail and then die."

"I'm not the girl you dredged up from the pit," I growl, forcing the fear from my expression.

"No? The terror in your eyes says otherwise." The Archduchess laughs, a mirthless noise, like a robot that's learned to mimic human emotions. "Just so you know, after I finish you off, I'm going to make your mother watch while I turn the Mercurian on the citizens you've undoubtedly tucked away below the palace."

Rage sears my chest, blinding in its intensity. I try to refocus, to calm my emotions and steady my mind—

She draws within striking distance, and I feint and lunge, a renewed sense of urgency clawing through my veins.

I'm all that's left. I have to find a way to stop her. I have to—

I don't see her move until her thin blade is already piercing my left flank. A cry rips from my lips. I hardly feel the pain, only a dull pressure, like I've been punched.

The Archduchess bares her teeth in a triumphant grin. Her horrifying eyes shift to my mother, unable to resist the temptation to feed off my mother's terror—

Now!

Ignoring the dull ache in my side, I rush the Archduchess, my weapon poised to pierce her gut.

But she moves with lightning speed, my momentum carrying me forward—

Pain shoots up my arm as her blade connects with mine in a horrifying clang. I watch as my sword jerks from my fingers. Watch it tumble end over end and disappear into the hole leading below.

There's a muffled echo as my weapon hits the floor below ours. Then silence.

Gasping against the fiery stab of pain in my side, I grab a fist sized piece of stone and hurl it at her face. She throws out her sword hand, blocking the impact with her forearm. Her other arm doesn't move.

I scramble for another bit of rubble, heave it at her again.

Again she blocks my throw with her sword arm, never breaking my gaze, her smile never faltering as she closes the distance between us. And, again, she never moves her left arm where it hangs limp at her side.

Backpedaling, I glance over at my mother. She's frozen, helpless, her face somehow managing to hide the terror I know she must feel.

The disappointment.

The wall smashes into my back. I have nowhere to run. No obvious weapons. The Archduchess slows her pace as she prowls toward me. Now that I'm no longer a threat, she's drawing this out. Making a gruesome display of her triumph for my mother to see.

When she's within a foot of me, she stops, sword held a little to the side. "I'm actually disappointed at how poorly you fought back. I've seen children with more skill. To think, Lillian Lockhart, one of the most brilliant statisticians in our court, has a daughter this pathetic." Her thin lips twist cruelly as she looks to my mother. "If only your husband had let us take her instead of dying to protect her, all of this heartache could have been avoided."

That realization hits me in the gut. I always thought they murdered him for his work. Biting back my tears, I meet my mother's stare, just for a breath. See the pain inside her hazel eyes, but also the fury.

"You're right," I agree, turning back to the Archduchess. "I've never been as brilliant as my mother. Never been as good with a sword. But I beat her once."

The Archduchess laughs, her strange pupils widening. "She let you win, maggot."

"Right again." After I pressed my sword tip into my mother's throat all those years ago, I paused to gloat—as she knew I would. "She let me draw closer, so proud of myself for finally getting the best of her. Let me think I'd won. But it wasn't to give me a false boost of confidence." I inch a step closer, readying myself. "It was to teach me a lesson."

Before the Archduchess can react, I slam my fist into her left upper arm, praying my observation—that she hadn't used that arm once, not even to block the rock I threw at her —is right.

A howl of pain rips from her throat. She tries to maneuver her sword to finish me off, but she let herself get too close and I manage to wrap my fingers around the sword hilt.

"Your arm," I snarl, striking her shoulder again.

Her face shudders with pain.

"You broke it during the crash."

An animalistic screech comes out of her as she rams her sword hand forward, trying to twist it from my grip. My hand trembles where it clenches the weapon, her strength overriding my own. I won't be able to hold her off for long, even wounded.

I hit her arm again and again, forcing her to scream with pain as she wrestles with the sword. I hit her until the pain ratchets her mouth into a gaping hole.

"The lesson my mother taught me?" I growl, digging my free hand into the hidden pocket of my corset. "Always know how many weapons your opponent has before you let your guard down."

The Scorpio-Fire box feels so small in my hand, so useless against a monster like the Archduchess. Using my thumb to compress the button that releases the poisonous metal beasts, I shove the device into the Archduchess's parted mouth and clamp her jaw shut.

Her eyes widen as realization takes hold. Releasing the sword, she clamps on to my arm, the one holding her mouth shut. Her throat convulses, the flesh beneath writhing and churning as the scorpions surge down inside her.

"I understand now," I say. "You hated me because my

father loved me enough to die, while yours couldn't stand the sight of you."

Somewhere in the deep recesses of her twisted mind, I can see the truth of my words take hold.

I drop my hand and step back. "This is going to hurt a lot."

Stumbling backward, the Archduchess claws at her neck, her mouth wrenched open. She's choking, trying to retch the foul creatures out, her face turning purple.

She falls to her knees. Our eyes meet.

"That's for Brogue," I say, stepping closer. "For my father." Another step draws me close enough that I can see the swelling of her flesh from all the stings. "And every single person you've ever hurt."

A rasp of pain trickles from her lips, and I think she's going to respond. But her face goes blank. Her eyes growing dim and unfocused. And then, the woman who haunts my dreams, who's only obsession for the last seven years was to find me and kill me, collapses.

Dead.

The Scorpio-Fire cage falls to the floor. Pressing a hand into my side to stem the bleeding, I kneel beside my mother. The chunks of rubble crushing her legs are heavy, but I manage to slide them enough to free her.

"Take me to the Mercurian," she whispers. "Hurry. We don't have much time left."

Bending down, I slip my hands under her armpits and try to lift, but without use of her legs, she's too heavy.

I try again. The pain in my side flares to life, but I keep struggling, keep working to move her.

When that doesn't work, I sink down and drag her, but we only make it a few feet before the room around me spins wildly and I have to sit before I pass out.

I'm about to start dragging her again when Riser appears from the top of the wrecked craft.

"Need help?"

Gods, please don't let this be a hallucination.

When I spy Bramble's metallic body darting toward me, I know it's real, and I sag beside my mother, overtaken with relief.

THIRTY-SEVEN

Riser takes in the full scene. Alarm widens his eyes, and he leaps from the craft and is by my side before I catch my breath to say a word. His dark gaze falls over my injuries, the Archduchess, and then my mother.

His mouth tightens. "Has the Mercurian been activated?"

My mother's hazel eyes are alarmingly unfocused as they find Riser. "No. You have to . . . carry me there."

I know how hard it is for my mom to ask for help, especially from someone like Riser, and a sinking dread falls over me.

Riser lifts her into his arms. I've never seen my mother look so small. So helpless.

"Is this okay?" he asks, gently.

She nods. "Stop being a gentleman and just get me to that fucking machine, Prince Thornbrook."

"Yes, ma'am."

I follow them up the stairs, Bramble weaving nervously around my feet. Riser sets her down on the platform and I help him slide her under the telescope.

"Now what?" I ask, on my knees. I'm ready to do

anything, whatever she asks to get this over with so I can get her to one of the Reconstructors in the shelter below.

"Now," my mother says calmly as she tears her gaze from the telescope to me, "you leave."

"What? No. We have time, just do what you have to do and Riser and I can carry—"

"Stop, Maia, just stop." She reaches out and takes my hand, her flesh startlingly cold. "Once we passed the first deadline, everything changed. The power needed to stop Pandora—it's too great. The moment I activate the Mercurian, the force from the blast will kill me."

"No." I pull my hand away. Was this her plan all along?

"I'm dying, Maia."

I barely hear her. "You don't get to do this. I haven't said the things I wanted to say. I haven't . . ."

Tears sting my eyes. I refuse to look at her. Refuse to see the truth in her expression.

"Maia," my mother says, and despite the condition she's in, her voice has never sounded more affectionate than now. "We don't have time. You have to leave me."

"I can't do this without you," I insist.

"You already have. Don't you see that?"

She fumbles with something near her collarbone—the dove cloak pin she's always wearing—and presses it into my hand. "Take this. There's something stored inside the pin. Watch it later, when you're safe."

Her eyes shift to Riser. "I'm sorry I ever doubted you, Prince. Sometimes it's easier to see the brokenness in people rather than the good. Keep her safe, please. And don't let her be too hard on Max."

Riser nods, pressing his hand to his heart. "I swear it."

My throat aches. I think of all the things left unsaid between us. All the transgressions still not forgiven. The arguments unresolved.

Careful not to jostle her injured body, I lean down, sweep my lips over my mother's cheek. It's cold, her breath fluttering against my ear in short, ragged bursts.

"I hope in the end . . . I was good enough," I breathe.

She clutches my hand again, squeezing hard, her pale face suddenly animated with determination. "Never, do you understand? Never was I disappointed in you, not for a single moment of your life." Her hand releases mine. She holds my stare for a breath, her eyes somehow conveying what words cannot, and then she turns her focus on the Mercurian. "There comes a point when a mother's job is done. Let me go, Maia."

I want to stay and argue with her. I want to order Riser to pick her up so that I can take her place. I want to prolong this moment until I'm emotionally ready to say goodbye.

Instead, I lean down and whisper in her ear.

Then I rise, take in my fading mother as she begins to type in coordinates, her jaw gritted against the pain, pushing herself beyond what any normal person could endure, and leave her to finally finish what my father started on that fateful day when he let himself die to give the world a chance.

The blood leaking from the wound on my flank covers my hands, making the climb over the slippery hull of the craft treacherous. Riser helps me over, Bramble clinging to his shoulder, and then we sprint down countless hallways and stairs. The adrenaline searing my veins is the only thing keeping me standing.

A vaulted door on the lowest level of the palace opens to an underground tunnel. More stairs, a seemingly endless amount, await us.

My world is reduced to the pounding of my heart, the increasingly difficult effort to drag enough air into my lungs. I can't say how many times Riser has to practically carry me. How many times I black out only to awaken in his arms.

When we enter the final door to the underground bunker, the Emperor's failsafe, I stumble inside. Hundreds of citizens are gathered in groups around the screens affixed to the cavernous walls. Despite the uncertainty, they comfort one another, handing out rations and helping the elderly and injured as they watch the live feeds of the castle grounds.

One of the screens features Pandora, the tyrant that's sewn chaos and destruction from the moment she made herself known. In the video's feed, she appears dark as night, the red corona surrounding her like hungry flames.

I scour the crowd for Max and the others, desperation constricting my vision.

"They're safe," Riser insists. "Now we need to get you to a Reconstructor."

"Wait. I have to see it."

He understands immediately, helping me as I push my failing body toward Pandora's image. We've barely entered the crowded area, scattered with fully stocked metal shelves brimming with supplies, before an eerie silence descends.

As I stare down the inanimate object that's hovered over us since I can remember, holding us hostage with fear and uncertainty, the blinding anger I've felt toward Pandora bleeds away.

True, she cast a shadow on our world, but we were the ones to forget that darkness can only exist in the presence of light.

Riser, still holding me up, takes my hand. "It's almost over," he promises me.

"And what if my mother fails?" I murmur. "What if we're too late?"

"Then we survive, together. We help as many people as we can. Most importantly, we never give up hope."

I shake my head, the word "hope" suddenly feeling like such a distant, unattainable thing.

His arm tightens gently around my waist. "The first time I met you, we were underground. You were a terrified girl hiding from the monsters that ruled the pit—and I was one of those monsters, hiding from the pain of my past. Hope brought us together, and hope—for a better world, for a better future—brought us to this very moment. Whatever happens in the next few seconds, whether the Mercurian fulfills its promise or not, we cling to that."

Max appears to my left along with my friends. He meets my stare, taking in my face, the raw grief lurking behind my eyes.

She's gone, I say with everything but my mouth.

But after what we've been through, we don't need words to communicate heartbreak, and a flicker of understanding shimmers inside his eyes before he tamps his emotions down with an efficiency a boy his age shouldn't possess.

We reach out and take one another's hands, all of us, people of every color and rank and age, as we watch the screen flicker, turn bright white, and then die. We don't let go. Not as the ground trembles beneath our feet. Not as the walls rumble, dust pattering softly to the floor, and the entire earth seems to groan.

Not even when the power fails and darkness consumes us. If anything, we squeeze tighter, holding onto each other for once.

Emergency lights embedded in the walls spark to life as the backup power takes over.

Beside me, I can feel Riser's attention turn in my direction. For some reason, the memory of when he left me in the pit to be sacrificed comes to mind.

How, secretly, in that semi-darkness, he loosened my binds so I could escape, despite what that act cost him.

"Maia," he murmurs, "you've done everything you can, now it's time to let go. If we don't get you to a Reconstructor, I could lose you. And I'm never letting that happen."

I nod, an image of my mother right before I left her, that bright ferocity burning from within, her eyes as they looked into mine, unafraid and full of love, flashes across my vision.

And I hold onto her face until my world goes dark.

THIRTY-EIGHT

SIX MONTHS LATER

The paper in my hand is wrinkled, the handwritten words smeared with sweat. I stare at the speech, written and erased and rewritten over months, and frown.

When I finished the speech, it felt good enough. But now, with the thrum of over a thousand people waiting on the lawn just outside the palace, my words feel empty. Unable to convey even a tiny portion of what's in my heart.

Riser draws up beside me, Bramble sunk into his shoulder. In the six months since we emerged from the underground bunker to a new world, he's grown out his hair. The sides are no longer cropped in the Rebel fashion, and other than a red streak—dyed recently by Flame, lest he forget his Rebel roots—he could pass for a Royalist.

Sometimes I have to remind myself there are no Rebels and Royalists anymore. No colors either—that was the first thing we abolished. There are no enemies, no opposing sides, only those of us grateful to have been given a second chance.

Riser glances over my words, his lips quirked. "I don't see any mention of a dashing, one-eyed psychopath in your speech."

I grin. "Saved that part for last."

"Hmm." He arches a dark eyebrow as he takes me in. "I see you didn't let Flame pierce your lip like she wanted?"

I laugh, remembering how annoyed she was when I resisted. "She thinks I'm not Fienian enough."

Cage and Flame were here earlier to help prepare me for the event. It felt a bit too much like old times as Cage swept a variety of brushes over my face, each one shimmering with pigments and powder. But instead of covering my cheeks, like before, he highlighted each one of my freckles with metallic gold.

Flame, for her part, talked me into a Rebel hairstyle, and now one side of my hair is wrangled into an elaborate array of braids that snake along my skull.

"I think," Riser murmurs, his gaze dropping to my lips, "you aren't Fienian or Royalist, you're just . . . you. And that's a good thing."

Slipping one arm behind my back, he draws me into a kiss. I lose myself in his gentleness, finding comfort in his protective embrace, the familiarity of his scent.

Bramble chirps in annoyance, like a kid watching his parents show affection, and we both chuckle as we pull away, breathless. Even after all these months above ground, our relationship still feels new.

In the aftermath of the war, we're like two completely different people falling in love all over again.

He tweaks my nose. "Stop worrying. They already love you. Fienian hell, I think they'd even make you empress, if you accepted."

In the months after we emerged, we managed to cobble together a government. A few people proposed that we elect an Emperor to rule as before, but the idea left a bitter taste in my mouth.

"No one should have that much power ever again," I say. "Even me."

We're still working to find the right path for this future world, and I imagine it will take countless years to fix the mess the Emperor left us.

But I don't have to worry about that today. Today is about remembering the fallen heroes of this war. The Emperor's fountain was destroyed, and a giant marble monument erected from the rubble. Interactive stars are embedded in the stone, making up the two constellations that ended up being the key: the Orion and the Pleiades.

Each star represents one of the Rebels who died. Spectators can press on a star and a hologram appears with the image and information about the person. It feels strange, condensing the brilliant, complex human beings I knew into five-minute snippets.

My father and mother are there. Ophelia and Caspian's stars rest side by side, two bright, pulsing spheres of light, just like in real life.

And Brogue . . . he gets a special spot in Orion's sword, near the tip. I tell myself he would have appreciated being part of a weapon.

It's not enough, not nearly. And my words today can hardly fill that gap.

But I'm going to *try*. Those who gave everything for the remaining survivors will eventually be forgotten, but not while I draw breath.

After my speech, I'll read their names aloud, one by one. I won't need to look at my paper for that part.

Every name, every face, every voice is engraved in my heart, a haunting calligraphy that will scar me forever.

"Hey," Riser says, picking up on my change in mood. "You can do this. I'll find you after your speech, okay?"

I nod and release a ragged breath. Outside, my friends are waiting in the crowd. Each one would willingly die for me—some nearly did.

I watch Riser leave, slipping out the door like smoke. He still moves with the unnerving stealth of a predator. Feet silent. Movements efficient and smooth. But some of the lethality has faded, as if, in this new world, we're all changing. Tentatively adjusting to the possibility of a better life.

The door has barely closed behind Riser when it parts and my brother rushes through. As our eyes meet and I take in his neatly combed blond curls and sharp red jacket, the Fienian Rebel scorpion crest pinned to his breast, my chest swells with pride.

"Ready?" he asks.

I nod and put my arm around him. Then I retrieve the dove cloak pin my mother handed me before she died. The one I haven't been able to watch until now.

As suspected, the pin pulls apart, revealing a hidden interceptor.

I press the small button and a life-sized hologram of my father fills the space in front of us. Max takes my hand. A low, near-imperceptible whir emanates from the device.

Both of us decided not to watch the message my mother left until today. For various reasons that all danced around the truth: I'm a coward.

The hologram solidifies. The wavering, lithe form is so lifelike that it takes all my willpower not to jump to my feet and hug my father. He looks so young, barely out of college, his soft brown hair full and longer than I remember, tucked awkwardly to the side as if he's too busy to mess with it. His face hasn't yet been marked with the lines of worry and fatigue I remember, his eyes not yet shadowed with the anxiety he tried to keep hidden from us.

Max stiffens beside me, his face mirroring my own conflicting emotions—a mixture of happiness and pain.

My father smiles that stupid, brilliant grin, as if he can actually see into the future to this very moment. He adjusts the glasses perched too far down on his long, slim nose, the unconscious habit opening a pang of longing inside my chest.

"This is the video testament of professor Philip Graystone," he begins. "As of today, I am declaring the Emperor an enemy of the people, and will be working against him to find a solution to the asteroid. There is a large chance I will die in vain, my efforts lost in the Royalist war machine."

He takes off his glasses and sighs, and I imagine all the worries running through his head. My father wasn't a violent man; he was kind, gentle, a rational, brilliant human being whose greatest wish was to raise his family.

Taking on the Emperor must have been the hardest decision of his life.

After a brief pause, he resumes looking straight ahead, as if he can see us. "To my children, who are both so very young. I hope someday this message finds you. I hope that when it does, your world will be once again filled with the hope and opportunity you deserve. Above all else, I pray that you remember how much your mother and I love you. You are the reason we're fighting back. The reason we're risking it all for a better world."

Static cuts across his image as he begins to fade.

The rational me knows I can't touch him, can't keep him here, but my fingers twitch to grab onto his non-existent flesh, to somehow pull him through space and time so I can hold him one more time. Feel the steady safety in his gentle embrace, the comforting smell of his well-worn corduroy jackets and aftershave.

Another image appears over the mini-interceptor. As I

take in my mother, a younger, happier version, my throat tightens.

"She seems barely older than us," Max whispers.

"This message is for my young children, Maia and Max," my mother begins, and I'm blown away by how soft her voice is, so unlike the confident demeanor I've always known.

Her brown hair is pulled into a messy bun, her skin bright and cheekbones full, hazel eyes brimming with a light I never saw.

In contrast to the woman I remember, the hardened, cold, analytical mother, this version seems like a stranger.

It comes to me all at once that this is the woman the Emperor robbed me of. The mother she would have been if things had been different.

"My name is Lillian Graystone," she continues, "and today, I have decided to infiltrate the Emperor's court as a spy for the Fienians. In doing so, I risk losing everything. My husband. My children. *Everything.* And yet I cannot stand by while such a grave injustice is being inflicted on our nation by a mad tyrant. If I do nothing, I would never be able to look my children in the eye."

I sag against Max. All this time, I'd assumed somehow she was playing both sides. Waiting to see which one was more advantageous.

And all along . . . all along she was working for the Rebels right under the nose of the Emperor.

She must have lived those years as a spy in such fear. Afraid of one single misstep. Of being discovered and executed, her family punished.

She twists her fingers together. I remember watching her do the same in that propaganda video. How did I never see through her unshakable façade to the real woman beneath?

"I will never regret this decision, but I worry for my children and what I'll need to do to prepare them. Sweet, funny

Max and headstrong, kind Maia." A hand flutters to her face. "She . . . she I worry about the most. Not because my daughter won't rise to the occasion. Quite the opposite. Already, I see that she possesses the noblest heart I've ever known and the rare qualities of a great leader. She is the key to fixing this world, and yet, I fear the Royalists will snuff out that goodness unless I equip her with an outer shell of strength."

She pauses, pressing her lips together as she stares off at something I can't see. "The person I must become, the person I must make her into . . . I fear my daughter will end up hating me."

I choke down the grief that bubbles in my chest. Max hugs me tighter.

My mother squares her shoulders and lifts her delicate chin, the one that's so much like my own. My heart clenches as I realize she's wrapping this up.

"My last words are for my children. Max, I will always love you. Always. And Maia." She swallows. "I see the way you look at me, even now. Please know, I'm hardest on you not because you're lacking . . . but because your inner brilliance has the potential to set the entire world on fire."

Before I have time to process my swell of emotions, the next image pops up—

My lips jerk into a smile as I recognize Brogue, his former pre-Reconstructed self, a handsome, athletic man with kind eyes and a roguish smile.

"Do I just look into the device and speak?" he asks someone off camera before turning to face us. "I'm Gabriel, Gold Cloak to Maia and Max Graystone, and I'm making a pact with Lillian and Philip Graystone to stop the Emperor, whatever the personal cost. I don't have much to say, and odds are, when I'm gone, no one will miss me. But, uh . . . Max, Maia . . ." He tips his head. "If you're all grown up now,

I hope you gave the Emperor hell. And if I'm not around to see it, don't be sad. We all have our part to play, but some of us only get a few lines. Never was much for speaking, anyway."

The interceptor powers down and goes silent, ending the last words from the three most important people in my life.

Max's eyes are dark with grief, but like me, there are no tears. Perhaps once you pass a certain point, your body can't cry.

"What did Mom say to you?" I ask, brushing one of his fat golden curls from his forehead. "When you returned from Hyperion and she whispered something in your ear."

His gaze grows unfocused, and he wipes at his nose. "She said that she loved me and that she was sorry."

"For abandoning us?"

He shakes his head, still staring at the spot where the holograms were. "For making it seem like she loved you more."

I blink at that, confusion stealing my response.

"You had to know how jealous I was, Maia. All those years she spent with you, training you, preparing you for this big role."

"I . . . I had no idea, Max. I thought—I thought she was so hard on me because I wasn't good enough."

Max shakes his head. Before he can say anything else, the door slams open and Lash pokes his head in the room. "Speech time, love. They're all waiting for you."

"Coming," I call as I begin shuffling my papers. Lash closes the door. When I look up, I see Max is staring at the front page. "Is . . . *her* name on there?"

I pause. Rivet. Max's grief lingers over the loss of his best friend. Sometimes he calls her name out in his sleep. Having to tell him she didn't make it was one of the hardest things I've done in my life.

Throat tight, I lean over and wrap him in a giant hug. "Of course."

"Do you think the hurt will ever go away?" he asks suddenly.

"I don't know," I lie, afraid to say what I feel.

That the pain from losing so many I cared about is now part of me. A living, breathing thing that whispers in my ear late at night when I can't sleep, or in moments when I'm too happy for its liking.

Out of everyone I've lost, its Caspian I dream of the most. Maybe because we were matched, or because he was so young, or simply because my mind is an asshole.

Max wipes his nose and then struggles from my grasp. "Almost time. You need to get out there, hot shot. The whole world is waiting."

I want to refuse. To hide behind these walls. But the girl who cowers is gone, so I follow Max out the door into the sunlight.

Teagan is already halfway across the lawn, looking handsome in a charcoal pantsuit and black and gold hat. When her gaze snags on me, she waves toward a large wooden podium in the distance, newly erected, just off the shore of the lake.

The timing of my speech is supposed to start at the same time Shadow Fall used to begin.

I ache to scour the clouds for Pandora. Six months still hasn't erased the unease I feel whenever my eyes wander upward.

But now is not the time to be afraid. Squaring my shoulders the way my mother did, I march to the podium, much to Teagan's relief, and find the microphone. A light wind ruffles my red hair, blood-orange colored beneath the sun's glare.

"I want to tell you a story," I say, looking out into the countless sea of faces, many of whom were once inside my head. "A story that started years ago, when a mother and father decided it was their duty to rise up against a tyrant."

My words go by in a blur. When it's time to say the names of those we honor, they claw up my throat, heavy on my lips.

Each one personal and painful and final.

Finished, I stuff my speech into my pocket, but something won't let me leave. Even as my body aches to flee, my palms sweaty, eyes darting from one face to another, I resist.

One by one, I find my friends in the crowd. Teagan, Lash, Flame, Cage, Riser, and Max. Bramble stirs in Riser's lap, unhappy that Riser won't let him run to me onstage. Even Delphine is here, sitting next to Lash, her eyes downcast.

We chose to forgive her past crimes and let her start anew. Not because she deserves it, but because our world needs second chances now more than ever.

My focus drifts to the clear blue sky, and say, "I used to hate Pandora, but I see now She wasn't the problem. *We* were. Beneath Her ominous shadow, we forgot the universal truth. Shadows cannot exist without light."

Tearing my gaze from the sky, I direct it at the people, survivors from all over the nation. "Now, just like those we memorialize today, we have a choice: cling to that darkness or stoke our flames and become a sky full of stars whose light will live on long after we've faded away."

The applause rattles the air, so loud it seems to shake the stage beneath my feet. Looking out into the sea of people, each one without color or label, not a single one better than the other, an overwhelming feeling sweeps through me.

Hope.

For the first time since we emerged from the bunker and realized that my mother succeeded and the asteroid's wrath missed us, tears wet the corners of my eyes.

Not long after, I flee the crowd and meet Riser near the

underground Sim, the one my father created. We relax on a grassy knoll just above it.

For a long time, neither of us speak. Riser holds me in his arms while Bramble scrambles around our feet, collecting twigs and other useless items. Birds call out from the trees, the occasional buzz of insects stirring the air.

Both of us silently watch the sun crawl across the sky until the pink haze of dusk appears.

"Thank you," he finally says. "For adding my mother to your speech."

She was the first name I spoke. Marquess Amandine Croft. Mistress to the Emperor, sister of the terrorist Rebel leader, and mother to the man I love.

"Tell me their sacrifice was worth it," I whisper. "Tell me humanity won't just mess up our world all over again."

Riser chuckles softly. "I can't. That's up to them. But . . . if someone like me can change, surely there's hope?"

Lifting my head from his shoulder, I stare into his mismatched eyes. One speaks of the horrors from the pit, the other of redemption. Looking into them feels a little like looking into the past and the future at the same time.

I brush my lips over his. "Speaking of changed, how do you feel about taking on one of the governorships we discussed?"

"Me?"

I laugh without breaking his gaze. "*You*. You are technically a prince, after all, and the face of the rebellion. And, somehow, people love you."

"Flame and Bramble don't count—"

"*I* love you."

He blinks, mirroring the shock I feel at my outburst, but it's true, and if this crapshow of a life has taught me anything, it's that we only get so many chances to say what we feel to those we love.

A slow smile overtakes his arrogant face. "I'd be honored. Especially if you say that again, Digger Girl."

"Fat chance, Pit Boy."

But I do, of course, and he says it back. We kiss, passing the magical hour of dusk in each other's arms. And when we both pull away and lock eyes, he says, "I don't know how you fell for someone like me, but I'll spend the rest of my life earning your love."

He draws me onto his lap. With his strong arms slung around my waist, we reminisce, telling stories about those we lost until the air chills and the sky swells with stars.

When it's time to leave the Island, I hesitate, despite all of the terrible things that happened here. All the memories that still haunt my dreams.

This will be the last time I ever visit Emerald Island, the playground of the greatest war criminal in our history. Eventually, after we've rebuilt the world, the Island will become a museum so that we never repeat this horrifying past.

I think of the people who might someday visit this palace of terror. I imagine them walking through these halls, their steps mirroring mine as they visit the dungeons and stroll the gardens.

Will they understand the sacrifices we made? The dangers we faced?

Like most unbelievable stories, eventually, ours will fade into a watered-down tale of good versus evil where the villains and heroes were set from the start.

People will forget.

The *world* will forget.

And another Emperor will arise to repeat the sins of the past.

When that time comes, I hope they hear the words I whispered to my mother before she sacrificed herself to save us, the same mantra we all cheered as we exited the bunker six months ago, unsure whether we would face life or a slow death sentence.

Shields up, daggers out, head high.

And I hope they fight with everything they have.

THE END

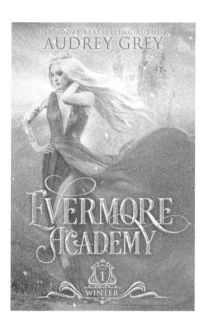

Welcome to EVERMORE ACADEMY where the magic is dark, the immortals are beautiful, and being human SUCKS.

After spending my entire life avoiding the creatures that murdered my parents, one stupid mistake binds me to them for four years.

My penance? Become a human shadow at the infamous Evermore Academy, finishing school for the Seelie and Unseelie Fae courts.

Day one, I make an enemy of the most powerful Fae in the academy. The Winter Prince is arrogant, cruel, and apparently also my Fae keeper. Meaning I'm in for months of torture.

But it only gets worse. Something dark and terrible looms over the academy. Humans are dying, ancient vendettas are resurfacing, and the courts are more bloodthirsty than ever.

What can one mortal girl do in a world full of gorgeous monsters?

Fight back with everything I have—and try not to fall in love in the process.

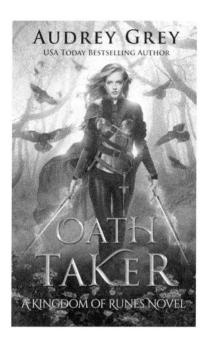

After the Prince of Penryth saved her from captivity, Haven Ashwood spends her days protecting the kind prince and her nights secretly fighting the monsters outside the castle walls.

When one of those monsters kidnaps Prince Bell, Haven must ally with Archeron Halfbane and his band of immortals to rescue her friend.

Her quest takes her deep into the domain of a warped and vicious queen where the rules are simple: break her curse or die.

Lost in a land of twisted magic and fabled creatures, Haven finds herself unprepared, not just for the feelings she develops for Archeron, but for the warring powers raging inside her.

Faced with forbidden love, heartbreaking betrayals, and impossible choices, only one thing remains certain.

Haven must shatter the curse or it will devour everything she loves.

ABOUT THE AUTHOR

Audrey Grey lives in the charming state of Oklahoma surrounded by animals, books, and little people. You can usually find Audrey hiding out in her office, downing copious amounts of caffeine while dreaming of tacos and holding entire conversations with her friends using gifs. Audrey considers her ability to travel to fantastical worlds a superpower and loves nothing more than bringing her readers with her.

Find her online at:

WWW.AUDREYGREY.COM

CPSIA information can be obtained
at www.ICGtesting.com
Printed in the USA
BVHW03191822062O
582090BV00001B/118

9 781734 947915